"Jordyn Redwood fans will not be disappointed with this third book in her Bloodline Trilogy. She's proven she's packed with talent, delivering yet another page-turning crime story that will have readers on edge. Not only does Jordyn bring her experience as an emergency room nurse into her writing, but she writes with such precise detail, it's hard not to wonder if she's also spent time in law enforcement. With a nail-biting plot, colorful characters, and an inspirational message threaded through, *Peril* is a must-read."

–Julie Cantrell, *New York Times* best-selling author of *Into the Free*

"In this perfect combination of drama and suspense, novelist Jordyn Redwood sets medical research on a crash course against all that makes us human. . . . A compelling read."

—Sue Harrison, best-selling author of *Mother Earth Father Sky*

"Gripping medical suspense from a writer who knows the profession."

—Richard L. Mabry, MD, award-winning author of *Stress Test* and the Prescription for Trouble series

"Jordyn Redwood does it again . . . with fast-paced action, deft humor, psychological twists, and characters wh̲ ̲ ̲ ̲ ̲ deep wounds. Don't miss this novel—

—S 'n *Distant Shores*

"Jordyn Redwood writes suspense that will not only keep you tu g, but will also touch your heart. I'm a fan!"

— Ginny L. Yttrup, Christy Award–winning author of *Words*

"Chilling, thought-provoking, brilliant—I lost count of how many times my jaw dropped. *Peril* is Redwood's finest work yet."

—Candace Calvert, best-selling author of *Trauma Plan* and *Rescue Team*

"A riveting, absorbing read. . . . The details are spot-on and the pace unrelenting."

—Laurie Kingery, RN and author of Brides of Simpson Creek series

"It's highly likely that Jordyn Redwood will pull you through her medical thriller faster than you intend to go. Give in and try to remember to breathe. *Peril* is worth it!"

—Shellie Rushing Tomlinson, Belle of All Things Southern and best-selling author of *Sue Ellen's Girl Ain't Fat, She Just Weighs Heavy!*

"Jordyn Redwood's firsthand medical knowledge and experience as an RN shines brilliantly in her fiction. If you enjoy medical suspense, don't miss reading *Peril*."

—Dianna T. Benson, author of *The Hidden Son*

"An astounding series finale. This meticulously researched, masterfully plotted medical thriller's ethically engaging subject matter and thought-provoking story line pulled my emotions in all directions. . . . Intense."

—Cheryl Wyatt, award-winning author of medical and military romance

"Redwood blends the horrors of today's headlines with the darkest side of cutting edge neuroscience in this fast-paced Christian thriller. Hang on to your heart in this gut-wrenching roller-coaster ride!"

—Jan Dunlap, author of the Bob White Birder Murder Mystery series

"Taut with danger and raw emotion. . . . The tension and suspense don't let up until the very last page."

—Henry McLaughlin, award-winning author of *Journey to Riverbend*

"Leave it to Jordyn Redwood to come up with the most perplexing, thought-provoking, and fascinating medical mind-twisters and then to reveal them in a story so compelling that you just can't put it down."

—Erin MacPherson, author of *The Christian Mama's Guide to Having a Baby*

"A white-knuckle ride to the very last page. Razor-sharp writing and trustworthy details make this heart-pumping, insomnia-inducing thriller a keeper."

—Jocelyn Green, award-winning author of the Heroines Behind the Lines series

"It's time to etch Redwood's name where it belongs, in the famed hall of suspense authors who never disappoint. *Peril* is Redwood's conclusion to her trilogy and thus far, the best. I'd tell you to hold on while reading, but sometimes it's better to let it all ride. *Peril* proves that point."

—Heather James, author of *Unholy Hunger*, the first in the Lure of the Serpent series

"*Peril* lives up to its name in this medical thriller and suspense rife with raw emotion, relatable characters, and heart-stopping moments that will leave you wondering until the very end."

—Kariss Lynch, author of *Shaken*

PERIL

Bloodline Trilogy 3

PERIL

A Novel

JORDYN
REDWOOD

Kregel
Publications

Peril: A Novel
© 2013 by Jordyn Redwood

Published by Kregel Publications, a division of Kregel, Inc.,
P.O. Box 2607, Grand Rapids, MI 49501.

ISBN 978-0-8254-4213-1

Printed in the United States of America
13 14 15 16 17 / 5 4 3 2 1

For Mom and Dad.
Thanks for teaching me that hard work
pays off and dreams do come true.

Acknowledgments

THERE ARE MANY PEOPLE who help complete a novel. Some aren't necessarily involved in the writing and editing process but are very important in keeping the author sane. Thanks to my husband, James, for doing all you can to keep me on track and helping out so much so I can finish my books. Also, Greg Johnson—trusted friend, agent, and mentor—for keeping me back from the cliff's edge, particularly in January 2013.

As always, I do a lot of nonfiction research for my novels and I want to acknowledge those books that played a part in crafting this tale. These books are thought-provoking examples of the possibility of the medical mystery in *Peril*, and I recommend reading them before deciding against the plausibility of the theory. *Mind Wars: Brain Research and National Defense* by Jonathan D. Moreno; *Gianna: Aborted, and Lived to Tell About It* by Jessica Shaver Renshaw; *The Heart's Code* by Paul Pearsall; *The Woman Who Can't Forget* by Jill Price with Bart Davis; and *Unplanned* by Abby Johnson with Cindy Lambert.

To my technical experts: Deputy Sheriff K. Mai for overall police knowledge and Detective S. Tarr for the SWAT scenario. Thank you for your service to our communities.

To my amazing editors: Susan Lohrer, Mike Nappa, and Dawn Anderson. Thank you for the time you've taken in teaching me to be a better author.

To the marketing team at Kregel: Dave Hill, Noelle Pedersen, Adam Ferguson, and Cat Hoort. I appreciate all your work on my behalf, getting word out about the Bloodline Trilogy. Nick Richardson—I get so many compliments on the book covers! Thanks for your creativity.

To my readers: You are the ones who make this journey truly worthwhile. I am honored to write and share stories with you.

Prologue

HE WAITED AT THE EDGE of the trail for her to pass, hidden in the gap where the underbrush transitioned to a mixed grove of lush aspen and skeletal Rocky Mountain lodgepoles scourged by tiny black insects.

Actually, he considered himself a kindred brother to the scourging pine beetle. Amazing little creatures. It impressed him how something so tiny could topple a stalwart of the forest—something more colossal than it could ever hope to grow. In order to reproduce, the beetle laid its eggs under the bark. When the eggs hatched, the larvae cut off the tree's circulation, consuming it for growth, and severing the life force of the specimen. This life cycle of the beetle served as executioner for the tree.

It mimicked his preferred method of killing.

He smoothed his fingers lightly over his upper arms, tracing the faces of those gone before. Usually, he kept his tiny charges tucked under long sleeves—like children with their heads plunged under bed linens to hide from the boogeyman—safe and protected under his clothing. Why take a trophy when you could have an image of the prize forever imprinted onto your body? Besides, he liked the vibrant color of the ink against the paleness of skin. And the pink burn from sitting days under the sun tracking her added to the sense of hell he had wrought upon their lives.

He eyed the vacant, hairless patch where her picture would be injected. Not one previous victim had shared his own characteristics of blond-tipped brown hair and brown eyes.

Until today.

His first tattoo had been a gift to him from a local citizen in a land of unrelenting heat, sand, and wind who thought if he curried favor with a foreign military force it would ensure his freedom. The idea of offering such a beautiful image for hope of liberty stirred something deep inside him. Why give away something tangible to get something intangible? Was the idea of freedom, even in light of certain chaotic governmental transition, of greater value than the safety of the status quo?

Being unhindered.

Wasn't he offering the same with death? Wasn't freeing the spirit from its physical entrapment the ultimate gift?

Yes—he was that generous.

Another perk of his killing—relishing the aftermath of the terror he created. Better than the act was seeing the tearstained faces of relatives as they cried for their children to be found. Television anchors didn't understand how much he cherished these moments and how they were one reason he continued on . . . to have many more of the mindless masses watch.

His ears perked at the soft tapping of running shoes against the path. Routine was every hunter's gift, and she was always generous. She was just rounding the bend, jogging steadily, earbuds in place, hands pulsing down to the beat of the music.

The air was heavy, full of the promise of rain and the odor of recently discharged *eau de skunk*. Even though he sat in the thick of it, right next to a fly-swarmed rabbit carcass, he was comfortable with the cover the stench provided.

One thing he had yet to discover was how his prey sensed it was about to meet the monster it feared lived under its bed. The very shadow that pulled parents from their slumber, groping for flashlights to assuage the blown-up, neuron-fired night creature of their child's imagination.

The world was a dark place. If only parents were smart enough to share what they knew and were constantly reminded of on the news every evening. That going to a movie at midnight could hold just as much risk as going to school, as eating at a pizza parlor, as running alone down a woodland trail. That men waited to hunt young girls who chose this form of enjoyment, by themselves, assured that nothing bad would ever happen to them.

Pride.

Relying on one's self was always the last nail in the coffin. Pride fueled a false sense of security. It ran against nature's design where things worked better in unison.

Where relationship protected against imprisonment of the spirit.

As his prey grew closer, her body betrayed her subconscious instinct that his sitting amongst the fragrant smell of decay did little to cover the scent of murderous lust that leeched from his pores. Mere feet from his position she stopped cold in the middle of the trail and looked around.

She drew her hand up and plucked out one of the earbuds. The tinny sound of music raced through the cool air. A country tune to encourage her feet to keep moving.

Something on the other side of the trail caught her eye, and he followed her gaze to a rabbit racing back into the bushes. Her chest rose as she inhaled deeply; fingering the earpiece back in place, she restarted her pace.

Like a sprinter at the starter's gun, he bolted from his position.

He tackled her, linebacker-style, pushing her into the underbrush on the other side of the trail. The only noises were her breath as it exploded from her chest and the rustle of trees that sounded more like two small animals fighting than a girl about to lose her life.

It always surprised him how little they fought. Purposefully, he rolled her over the ground a few times then stopped, his body pinning hers, his hand clamped tight over her mouth. Wide, pale brown eyes met his. Torn grass and leaves clung to wisps of dark brown hair with blond highlights. She shook her head to communicate what her lips could not and began to pound her fists against his arms. Pink, manicured nails slithered up under his dog tags, grabbed them, and snapped the chain in two as she yanked them off.

Have to remember to find those when I'm done.

He repositioned his body so her arms were trapped by his knees, which freed up his other hand to place his index fingers over his lips.

Her forehead scrunched. The unspoken promise of his mannerism increased the doubt in her eyes. The finger from his lips dropped to her neck, and he felt her pulse race unfettered under his fingers at her carotid artery. With his thumb, he found the echo of it on the other side.

Many did not understand how the act of strangulation killed. It was never about the airway but about choking off the blood supply to the brain. Just as the pine beetle larvae suffocated and starved the tree by consuming the very thing that ensured its life.

He grew lightheaded as he pressed his hand tight over her neck, the muscles in his arms bulging as they contracted under his desire. If he could apply even, tight pressure for just a few minutes, she would pass out, and the remainder of his liberating acts could be realized. Like a cat toying with a hatchling fallen from a tree.

His prey began to buck and twist her pelvis in an attempt to throw him off, but his weight surpassed hers by over one hundred pounds, and he merely smiled as the increased exertion would hasten what he ultimately planned.

She screamed through muffled lips and attempted to bare her teeth under his fingers.

He squeezed harder, pushing the mass of his upper body into the hold.

Her eyelids fluttered as her body attempted any maneuver to stay the coming darkness. Slowly, her tense muscles grew lax and her hands flopped into the dry pine needles.

He waited until her breath slowed and then stopped. This phase took several more minutes. As he released her neck from his grip, his peripheral vision caught something on the trail.

His leather wallet lay in the middle of the path like a beacon of light to any law enforcement officer who discovered the body. He would have left it where it was until he finished had he not heard voices and footfalls coming up the path. He could see their faces over his shoulder as they came around the curve.

Pushing himself off the body, he raced back over the trail and grabbed the wallet mid-stride before crashing through the brush on the other side. Just as he feared, the voices stopped. Then they began to question one another.

"Did you hear that?" *An older male.*

"You don't think it was a bear, do you?"

A scared, younger female. A possible next victim?

He shook his head against the urgency for killing that filled his mind. He turned and kneeled in the grass.

"I doubt it."

"You know there was just a sighting not far from here."

"Don't worry." A faint pat of flesh against something solid. "You know I always come prepared."

"I don't know if it's wise for the group of Boy Scouts just behind us to see you carrying a weapon."

Great. An armed, concerned male and a peace-loving, griping female.

Exactly one of the reasons he enjoyed his hobby. Definitely not something that would work in his favor. He was ready to get up and hightail it out of there when he saw his victim's pale hand stretched from the underbrush. He hadn't rolled her far enough, and the ashen extremity was easily seen against the dark green and brown of the forest floor. On the path, something had slipped from his wallet. A piece of paper. For the first time in a long time, he felt dread course through his veins.

Quickly, he flipped open the worn black leather. The essentials were present. Driver's license. Credit cards.

Was it something that could identify him?

As he backed farther into the trees, his vision obscured, his worst fear realized.

"Hey, what's that?" the woman asked.

"What?" her male companion answered.

"Don't you see it?"

"That's not a hand . . . is it?"

Quickened footfalls.

"Is she alive?"

He quietly turned and walked away.

"She's warm. I'm starting CPR. Call 911."

And he heard the rustle of her body being dragged from its cover.

Chapter 1

THE ER CREW BURST INTO the pediatric intensive care unit like a Civil War battalion trying to crash through enemy lines.

One nurse was on the gurney giving compressions. Two others propelled the bed while trying to maintain the upright position of IV poles that resembled a mechanical Christmas tree of syringe pumps pushing lifesaving medications into the patient.

Morgan Adams stood from her chair at the nurses' station and motioned to Eric Gregory, one of her coworkers. "Clear out bedspace six."

Why is it the one day I need to leave work early the PICU falls apart like a sand castle crushed under the rising tide?

They'd been alerted that this admission was coming. What they hadn't been expecting was that the fourteen-year-old girl would be coding when she entered the unit. It was too difficult to move a patient during a code onto the bed that awaited her. Better to shove the ER gurney into an empty space and continue what needed to be done to save the girl's life.

In the wake of the ER crew, there appeared to be a police detective, accompanied by a uniformed officer.

Definitely not getting off work early today.

Morgan turned to Lucy, another of her nursing cohorts. She was a woman whose skin tone was just a shade lighter than her dark brown eyes, and whose Jamaican accent worked like intravenous valium to scared children.

"Lucy," she said, "page Dr. Ayer. Eric—"

"I know." Eric said. "The code cart."

Morgan neared the patient as the ER gurney braked in position. "What happened?"

An ER nurse dressed in navy blue scrubs eyed her. "Her heart rate dropped into the twenties on the elevator."

Morgan slid two fingers under the C-collar to the young girl's neck to see if she could feel the carotid pulse. The open windows of the plastic revealed blotchy, angry patches of red and blue on each side of the neck.

That's unusual. The normal method of strangulation leaves circular ligature marks.

Faint petechial bruises, caused from capillaries rupturing under pressure, dotted the girl's face like freckles.

Except these aren't innocent sun-induced skin blemishes of her youth.

Under her fingertips, Morgan sensed the pulsatile flow of blood rushing by. "Pulse present with compressions. Let's pause to see if CPR helped her out any."

The nurse stopped. Morgan eyed the transport monitor, noting the still too-slow rhythm. The rate persisted in the twenties—a slow, faint echo of the heartbeat.

She withdrew her hand and turned to pop the lock on the code cart. "All right, continue compressions. Let's get a CPR board underneath her. Eric—"

The young man's dirty blond hair dropped over his hazel eyes as he pulled open the top drawer that housed the emergency medications. "I'll get the epi and atropine ready. Do we have a weight?"

"We're going by fifty kilos," the other ER nurse stated.

From the door, Morgan caught sight of a couple she guessed to be mid-thirties, holding on to one another.

The parents. And everything the medical team says is in earshot.

She looked Eric's direction. "After you get those meds ready, let's page the chaplain, too."

Morgan drew her eyes away from the couple and settled them on her young charge in the middle of the bed. A nurse at the teen's chest rocked up and down to stave off the grim reaper. The girl's brown hair flickered with chunky blond highlights.

The only part of her with color other than the bruising around her neck.

Many nurses thought they could understand the outright terror this girl's parents were feeling at the possibility of losing their child. She doubted they could. Morgan had lived through the death of her infant daughter, and she prayed silently for the coming darkness to stop.

There've been too many deaths. Am I even living?

Morgan grabbed a penlight from her pocket and pulled up the girl's eyelids. A ring of light brown and dilated black pupils stared vacantly back. She placed the light back into her scrubs and then tucked her blond curls behind her ears.

"Pupils are sluggish. Now, all we need is a—"

Dr. Ayer rushed through the doors. "Is this Zoe Martin? What the hell happened? I thought she was stable in the ER."

The ER nurse rolled her eyes. "She was."

There was always contention between units. Generally, all staff disliked who they received patients from and who they had to admit patients to. The ER hated EMS—particularly when they continued to bring patients despite notices for diversion. The ER hated the ICU—particularly when they had open beds but refused to take patients because they didn't have enough staff to care for the children. The PICU hated the ER—particularly when they brought an unstable patient through the doors.

Ayer yanked his lab coat straight. "Well? Can anyone here offer any insight as to why she's currently coding?"

Morgan eyed the ER nurse and gave her a friendly smile. There was nothing like being in the middle of a critical situation and having a doctor snidely question treatment. Ayer wasn't known for having a soft and fluffy side.

"She dropped her heart rate on the way up here."

"Stop compressions. Let's see what we have," Ayer ordered.

The nurse raised her hands in the air like someone held at gunpoint. Ayer had a gift of making the most seasoned nurses feel incompetent by the constant scowl on his face. The residents hated rounding with him.

He nodded after examining the rhythm. "Is there a pulse present?"

The nurse with the raised hands reached down to check. "Yes, still has a pulse."

Ayer circled a pointed index finger back at the patient. "Resume compressions." He eyed Eric with the ready syringe of epinephrine. "You weren't going to administer that without a doctor's order, were you?"

Eric shook his head. "No, sir."

"Because that would be outside your scope of practice. Looking to get fired after being here only a few short months?"

"Absolutely not, sir."

Morgan clenched her hands at her sides.

Why did he insist on doing this now? A Napoleon complex?

A good ICU nurse always anticipated what the patient needed so it was ready as soon as the doctor asked for it. How would Eric feel during the next code? Would he wait to draw up the med until it was ordered, delaying lifesaving treatment for the patient because of today's public chastising?

"Let's get her loaded with epi," Ayer ordered.

Eric approached the bedside and began tracing the line from the main IV bag down to the patient's hand, where he injected the drug.

Ayer cleared his throat and rocked onto his heels, which generally meant he was gearing up for an academic lecture. Even in the absence of a resident to enjoy the lesson, Ayer couldn't help but test those around him with his wealth of knowledge and their lack thereof.

"This patient presented to the ER as the presumed victim of strangulation, correct, Morgan?"

Morgan's heart thundered in her chest.

Can I not have one free moment to stabilize a patient without getting lectured?

Then again, Ayer had two full minutes to torture them before the next decision could be made regarding the patient's treatment.

"Yes," she answered.

"Anyone know her downtime?" Ayers asked.

Another ER nurse shook her head. "We can only guess. She was found by a couple and a group of Boy Scouts. They state they saw a man running off. She didn't have a pulse when they found her, but they felt that they had interrupted the attack so attempted to save her life."

Ayer's eyes narrowed. "My report from the ER doc stated she did have a pulse when she hit the ER."

"Yes, sir. She did," another ER nurse affirmed.

"So our fine, trusty citizens saved her life enough to put her in a vegetative state for the remainder of it. Morgan, what do you think our overall problem is?"

Morgan's vision hazed. An iron fist of grief constricted her heart. The team continued to do compressions. In the emergency department, they'd already intubated and the ER respiratory therapist now provided the necessary ventilations.

Why today of all days? Another child dying, exactly one month after my daughter's death. Is nothing sacred, God? Please spare me from having to witness another parent's grief. Please.

"I'll go make that call for the chaplain." Eric handed her three syringes—one more epinephrine, one atropine, and a syringe full of flush solution. Both meds were designed to help increase the heart rate.

Normally PICU staff wouldn't prohibit parents from watching them code their child. It often helped provide closure for families if they could see every effort made to save their loved one's life. However, in Morgan's experience, it was most beneficial when another person separate from the medical staff could explain what was happening at the bedside.

Most units overhead-paged their code events, which prompted the in-house chaplain's response. However, a couple of units managed their own codes without paging overhead—the ICUs being some of those units.

"Morgan!" Ayer shouted.

She jumped. A headache brewed behind her eyes, and she gritted her teeth against Ayer's insolence. Her mind offered many words she refused to say out loud.

Ayer took a step away from her. Still, her glare wasn't enough for him to fly off his perch and abandon the point he wanted to make.

His superiority over everyone else.

He glowered at her. "What is Zoe's problem? Why is she trying to die today?"

Besides the man who held his thumbs over her neck to deprive her brain of oxygen?

Morgan placed her heels together, shoulders straight, before she fired the heavy iron ball directly into Ayer's head.

Lowering her voice, she said, "Dr. Ayer. Zoe is likely suffering from the onset of rapidly progressing cerebral edema caused from the anoxic injury at the hands of her attacker. This is why her heartbeat is slow. She is exhibiting Cushing's triad, which is high blood pressure, widened pulse pressure, and bradycardia. This signals that her brain no longer is in its happy place and is at risk of being shoved into her spinal cord and therefore complicating her situation further, as it could lead to brain death. I would suggest that we load the patient with mannitol to combat the swelling in hopes that pulling off extra fluid will reduce the pressure. And if it is her brain causing the slow pulse, it should respond by increasing. Can I draw that medication up for you, doctor?"

Don't. Mess. With. Me.

Morgan fought the urge to keep her fingers from snapping in his face.

Lucy gave her a wink and the slight shake of her head in lieu of a sassy retort of her own. For several seconds Ayer looked at her blankly as if he'd stroked.

"Two minutes of CPR. Should we check a rhythm?" The ER nurse stopped compressions again.

Ayer checked the monitor. "Pulse with that?" The nurse gave a thumbs-up. "All right. Since it remains low, let's give a dose of atropine and load the patient with mannitol. Continue CPR." He nodded curtly at Morgan. "Nice work, Ms. Adams."

Morgan handed off the atropine to another nurse and left the bedside to grab the mannitol when the man whom she assumed was a police detective grabbed her elbow. His brown eyes were nearly the same shade of his slightly curly locks. "How's it looking?"

She glanced at the hallway. The chaplain still hadn't arrived. How could she offer any response with the parents staring at her like she was in fact the angel of death?

Chapter 2

DETECTIVE BRETT SAWYER scanned the trail where the girl's body had been found.

He started from the trailhead and inspected the dirt and grass on either side. His team fanned out behind him like a flock of birds flying in formation, making him the head of the V as they searched the ground for possible clues. He eased up when they neared the site where EMS had revived the young girl.

He believed Zoe's soul had vacated but her heart remained steady and strong, not easily convinced that death might be okay when her brain no longer functioned. That was the trouble with these situations. At least that's what the medical team told him in their fancy medical terms. *Anoxic brain injury.* He'd written it down. Had asked that PICU nurse, Morgan Adams, to spell it out for him. What he intellectually understood was the same thing that emotionally unsettled his spirit. *Zoe Martin is dead. Her body just hasn't figured it out yet.*

"Where's your better half?"

Brett glanced off the side of the trail. A uniformed officer, Trace Rutledge, motioned him to his position. He angled that direction.

"Detective Long is working with SWAT today," Brett said.

"Finally got tired of you?"

Brett cracked his best Joker smile. If he dyed his brown hair green, applied the white, pasty clown makeup and voluminous red lipstick, he might be able to make some cash on the side. Though no one in Colorado would ever hire him. James Holmes had ruined that possible side job after allegedly shooting up a local theater.

"My charm, of course, is too brilliant even for my suave, germ-freak companion. He never tires of it."

"Come on, admit it, Sawyer. You'll miss him if he switches to that full time."

Though he'd never confess it publicly, Brett didn't relish having to train a new partner to understand all his idiosyncrasies. He was like beer to a fine wine connoisseur . . . it took a while to develop that sense of taste. And he doubted there were many out there who would understand Detective Nathan Long and all of his oddities. That man could stock Office Depot if they ever ran short of highlighters.

They were two peas in a proverbial pod.

"He'll realize those SWAT guys are too by-the-book even for him. Got something?"

"I think we found his hidey hole."

Brett glanced to the left where paramedics had left remnants of torn gauze packages and resuscitation equipment littered on the other side of the path. EMS seemed to have done their best to contaminate his crime scene.

Might as well call them the evidence eradication team.

Of course, he knew they believed knuckle draggers like him couldn't possibly understand the importance of saving a life in lieu of preserving evidence. It's just that, when their efforts failed, families looked to him for resolution and what if they'd disintegrated something that could break his case? *No easy answers to that one, I guess.*

There were also a couple of patches of vomit a few paces away on the blacktop. *Guess that's where a few Boy Scouts discovered that fiction and reality aren't quite the same after all. Their little stomachs couldn't handle it.* He scanned the ground as he walked toward Trace. *Hard to tell the difference between new and old trampling.* This is when he could use one of those squirrelly, old-Western mountain men to help him track the killer.

Brett wondered if it was time to go wide with publicity about this murderer. The case of Lilly Reeves, Nathan Long's now-wife, had sensitized the department as to when it was most appropriate to give out public information related to a serial criminal. There was a fine line between proper notification and when the ensuing public panic would save lives. There'd been one recent news conference about two prostitutes who had been found strangled in wooded areas. It was surmised that their services were solicited and they'd been brought to the location of their eventual death. Naturally, a press conference about the deaths of a couple of downtown hookers didn't raise the concern of remote parental suburbanites. Why not let young Zoe go for her morning run on a familiar local trail that hadn't had a bit of trouble reported?

Well, except for the bear and all.

Brett paced a few more steps and stopped. There was a small area littered with cigarette butts and other accoutrements of drug use. "Geek squad know about this?"

"I told them. They're searching the other side of the trail."

Brett slid on a pair of vinyl gloves. He hated when his hands looked all Smurf-like. Nathan preferred to live in a plastic bubble; Brett loved the feel of dirt underneath his fingernails.

Surely, Nathan wouldn't split up their odd-couple pairing. Not after what happened the last time he'd worked with SWAT as an FBI hostage negotiator. People had died, and died horribly. Nathan still placed the blame squarely on himself. It was only after his wife's rape case was solved that Nathan had fully disclosed his horror in that experience.

And now he wants to go back?

Brett sat on his haunches. "Pictures at least?"

"Yeah, they photographed everything already."

He noted the section of yellow crime tape. "I don't think any of this is going to be his."

"Why not?"

In his gut, Brett knew this killer was not likely under the influence of drugs. Too much time waiting for the right girl. Watching her. Tracking her. Finally taking the leap to snuff out her life.

"A man needing a fix isn't going to be able to sit still long enough to do what was required here. Takes a lot of patience for someone to find a target. To wait for the perfect moment to take it out. How many successful hunters are crack addicts?"

Rutledge nodded his head. "Guess you have a point. Even if most of them are bad."

Standing and taking a few steps back, Brett turned to the side. *Might as well look around some more to see if the killer left anything behind in his hurry to leave.*

He pulled the high strands of grass apart as he walked. Nathan called it God. Brett called it cop's instinct, but something in his gut told him to keep walking this way. He glanced back to the trail. A few steps up and the perpetrator would have a better view of the bend and more room to pounce on an unsuspecting girl, especially one with music blaring in her ears.

After five steps Brett stopped.

Definitely a better view of the trail from here. A breeze evaporated sweat that beaded on his forehead. *Anything lightweight would have blown this way.* He began to scour the ground again.

More packages of torn gauze and cotton balls were stuck in the shoots of withered grass. Spring had been hot and dry and the foliage resembled the aged effect of autumn even though his calendar indicated June. *At least this area hasn't been chewed up by fire like many parts of the state.*

A small, folded card sitting about six inches up off the ground, stuck between dried, crispy weeds caught his eye. He pulled it and opened it up.

A name and a number. A hospital business card.

Dr. Tyler Adams.

Now wasn't that interesting. His fine PICU nurse had the same last name as this doctor. And they worked at the same place.

Chapter 3

Dr. Tyler Adams nearly shoved the phone off his desk as he pushed the intercom button. His clinic coordinator's voice sounded thin through the speaker. "Sir, the PICU is coding a patient. Your wife's not able to come to the phone."

He checked his watch. *One patient consult left before Morgan and I are supposed to meet.* He eyed the bouquet of flowers at the edge of his desk, each bloom losing a bit of life every minute they were denied water.

One month since their baby had died. Not an anniversary he wanted to celebrate.

"Thanks for checking."

Grabbing the patient's chart, he skimmed over his last few clinic notes. This visit was unusual. An urgent request from the patient to be seen as quickly as Dr. Adams could fit him in.

At times, Tyler wondered at the wisdom of taking on this consulting position. When he first received the call from Dr. Thomas Reeves, he'd quickly agreed to a meeting, not having any idea what the reason might be. After all, this was the same doctor who had invented MemoryEase—the first medication to show significant, verifiable progress in treating post-traumatic stress disorder. From a purely physiological standpoint, it had revolutionized PTSD therapies and brought a certain amount of notoriety to Reeves as well.

But why would a famed neuroscientist like Thomas Reeves need help from a heart transplant surgeon? Tyler couldn't wait to find out.

That dinner two years ago had been quaint, set here at NeuroGenics, right on the grounds of Reeves's private kingdom. His proposal was mind-boggling, and the money he'd offered was undeniably a gift that could help erase the debt Tyler accrued from over a decade of medical training.

He could still do his first love, transplant medicine, but consulting here did add long hours to his workweek.

When he'd approached Morgan with the idea of taking on a part-time position, she hadn't argued in the negative. But now the time he spent away from her and the tide of their grief potentiated the distance between them.

That bothered him the most.

Morgan's overwhelming sorrow over the loss of their child, and her subsequent medical complications fueled the separation. His eyes lingered on Morgan's picture just a moment, then he gathered the patient's chart and headed to the room next door.

Tyler was surprised to see a man about his patient's age standing outside the door.

"Can I help you?" Tyler asked.

"Just waiting for my friend. He didn't really want me in there during your little chat." He reached his hand out. "Dylan Worthy."

Tyler accepted the gesture. "Dr. Adams. Perhaps the waiting room would be more comfortable." A statement versus a choice.

Dylan shrugged. "I'm fine here."

There was something about Dylan that Tyler didn't like. Was it the wild, blond spiked hair? The tattoos that peeked out under his shirt-sleeves? Or the fact that the scar on the left side of his head indicated he was likely another of Thomas Reeves's patients?

Why don't I know about him?

"Sure," Tyler said. "Just not very comfortable here in the hallway."

"No worries. I'll find something to occupy myself."

Tyler nodded and gave two quick raps on the wooden door. Then he entered the examination room.

Reeves's institute tried to do a lot of things *differently*. Exam rooms were devoid of the normal vinyl-covered rectangular wooden tabletop and instead had a few comfortable chairs. His patient was Scott Clarke, a former Navy SEAL. Scott sat on the edge of the leather recliner. Tyler took the padded, dinner-table-style chair that sat near a wall off to the side. Tyler settled back in his seat, but Scott remained on the edge of his.

Most people thought of Navy SEALs in the same vein as the wrestler and ex–Minnesota governor Jesse Ventura—big, husky, and able to split a baseball bat in two with a swift karate chop. Wasn't the truth always stranger than what the mind thought of as the ideal?

Navy SEALs were trained to blend into any environment they were tasked to infiltrate. At times, getting into remote, barren wildernesses required stealthy agility. Scott was the ideal. Average height. Weight about one hundred ninety pounds. Thin. Quick reflexes. Fast on his feet. His dark brown hair still sported the military-style haircut even though he'd been honorably discharged from military service last month. The only reason Tyler remembered that fact was he'd received a letter about the change in his patient's military status the same day their daughter, Teagan, was admitted to the PICU.

"Good to see you, Scott," Tyler said, opening his patient file. "What brings you in today?"

The former SEAL leaned his elbows into his knees and tapped his feet against the floor, his face pressed into his hands. The behavior seemed more in line with a nervous ten-year-old than a trained military man.

"Scott?"

When Scott lifted his head and his steely, gray-green, reddened eyes zeroed in, his demeanor fed into Tyler's anxiety about the day.

"What brings you here?" Tyler asked again.

"I want the graft out."

Tyler sighed. "Scott . . . it's just not feasible. The graft is fused to your own cells. Dividing them out would be impossible. These cells have created a network with your own. They're intertwined."

Scott's shoulders sagged at the words. He looked as if he would slump to the floor.

"Tell me what's going on. I can only help you if you let me in on some of the things you're feeling."

The patient inhaled and went for the packet of cigarettes in his front pocket, then seemingly realized where he was and shoved it back down. "It's just too much. I can't explain it."

"Try?"

"It's painful. Not in a physical sense but . . ."

Tyler crossed his legs and set the open file there, waiting for the man to continue. The military wasn't the best at providing for the mental health needs of its soldiers—possibly because they were equally as unwilling to talk openly about thoughts and feelings. A sure recipe for disaster.

A crazed smile crossed Scott's face. "It almost works too good."

"Is that possible? Wouldn't you say these increased skills were part of the reason you were awarded the Silver Star?"

He ignored the implication. "Who would've thought these doctored-up neurons would actually do what you said they'd do?"

"Well, honestly, you'd have to thank Dr. Reeves for that. The whole protocol, the idea behind it, came from his mind."

Scott nodded. "Yeah, and he didn't have help from somebody else like we did."

Tyler frowned at the statement. Assigning a cluster of cells personal characteristics seemed odd. Like calling your kidney Fred. "What do you mean by that?"

Scott tapped the side of his head. "It's like someone else is there."

"You're hearing voices?"

He clasped his hands together and squeezed. "No. I'm not hearing voices. No reason for you to line up an admission to the funny farm. Not yet at least."

"Okay, then what?"

"Did you ever consider what the consequences would be of giving someone the ability to have . . . what is it you call it?"

"A superior autobiographical memory."

"Yes. Big words for us grunts." He ran his finger across his upper lip. "Aren't there some things you'd like to forget?"

Tyler fidgeted in his seat. Did Scott know what today was? "It depends. Although painful, some things we'd like to forget are those very things that make us who we are. The pain of the things we endure helps us to be more compassionate toward others."

Scott chuckled. "That's quite a speech, Doc. Don't think I took you for the sappy type. How's work going for you? Transplanted many hearts lately?"

"There's one young lady that desperately needs a transplant who's on the list. She'll die if she doesn't get one soon."

"What's her blood type?"

"Why, are you offering yours? Are you wanting to take your own life?"

Scott shrugged his shoulders and eased back into the chair.

"How have things been at home?" Tyler asked. "Job going okay?"

Scott's eyes narrowed as if contemplating how truthful he wanted to be. "Not so well. Haven't been able to hold down a job."

Tyler motioned toward the door. "Is your friend supportive?"

"Who? Dylan? You met him?"

"Hard not to with him just outside."

Scott nodded and then chuckled softly. "Dylan may not be the best influence. Never stays in one place too long. We served together so he gets what I'm going through."

"So he's someone you can talk to." Tyler situated the file so he could write notes in the chart.

"About some things, I guess . . . like this surgery." Scott folded his arms over his chest. "I've been reading a lot about memory lately. Probably should have spent some time doing that before I became your guinea pig."

"Scott, your type of surgery had been done before. It was just the cells that were different."

He nodded. "You know, at first, it really was amazing what the graft could do. The amount of information I could keep in this soggy noggin was like something you'd see in the movies. It made planning missions easy. I could make inferences between different intel reports—it was easier to see connections between terrorist groups that were physically separated from one another. I mean, miles and miles of bare mountain tundra."

"Then what exactly is the problem? You sound happy to have these new skills. Don't you think it helped you get the Silver Star?"

Scott's eyes darkened like a blue sky gathering storm clouds. "Maybe the graft enhanced our efforts, but we would have succeeded in that mission—even without the surgery. If that's all it was, just a great memory, I wouldn't be here."

"Then why are you here?"

Scott leaned forward and brushed his hands over his short hair. "It's hard to explain. It's the emotion that's all wrapped up in them."

"Can you try?"

He exhaled slowly through puffed cheeks. "My marriage was in trouble long before the surgery. Got a lot worse after."

Tyler nodded and remained silent, partly because he could relate emotionally to issues of marital discord Scott was doing his best to hide. Unfortunately, Scott's glossy eyes and reddened cheeks betrayed the bubbling caldron inside. The effervescence of a marriage disintegrating traveled to others like mist in the wind.

"I don't know if I can help you understand how my memory works now. It's like a running calendar of events, but also with it is the exact emotion I felt at the time. So every argument my wife and I had, not only do I remember what I said but I can see in her face how I made her feel."

"Don't you think that would happen normally?" Tyler asked. "Events that are highly charged release adrenaline into our bodies. We know this cements memories more quickly and deeply and that emotions tied to those situations erupt when they're revisited. This is the basis of Dr. Reeves's research into post-traumatic stress disorder."

Scott smiled thinly. "It's different than that. I know guys who have PTSD and it's nothing like what I'm experiencing. It's more like having your own personal analyst. You go back through these events, over and over, reliving and analyzing the bad decisions you made and what you could have done differently." He ran his palms over his pants. "You begin to see your part in the total destruction. People are so quick to put blame on someone else, but I know that I have hurt her very deeply."

"You're still together then? Isn't there hope?"

Scott leaned his chin into his hand and looked out the window. This side faced west into a broad valley just as the mountains grew from foothills to stone guardians of solitude. "I'm making some decisions now that may ultimately end my marriage."

"But you're not divorced yet. There's still a chance. There's always hope," Tyler said.

"Are we going to talk about G-O-D now?"

"Do you want to?"

"Are you a minister as well as a surgeon?"

Tyler laughed, partly at the remark and mostly to relieve the tightness in his chest. "Definitely not, but there are things I've seen . . . miracles that can only be explained by my belief in God. The human body is an amazing organism. It's so intricate that I don't think it could have ever come together in a pile of goo lit by a strike of lightning."

"You say that out loud very often?"

"It might surprise you how many people there are who work in medicine and believe in a higher power."

"Sounds very impersonal."

"How do you mean?"

"Some big presence in the sky." Scott stopped, his mouth open, his breath held in his chest. He shook his head and the icy gaze returned. "Did you know she was here?"

"Who?"

"My wife."

"When?"

"Before my surgery. A couple of weeks before."

Strength leeched from Tyler's muscles. "Do you know why she came?"

Scott kneaded his hands together. "I only know it wasn't her first visit. She'd had one a couple of months prior."

"Did you ask Dr. Reeves about it?"

"Not yet. I thought you'd know what the reason might be. Reeves isn't always forthcoming with information."

Tyler reflexively glanced at his watch; his soul cried for him to leave. *Will Morgan understand if I'm late again?*

He looked back at Scott. "One, no, I never knew that she came to visit. Two, if she was seen in a doctor-patient capacity, it would be a breach of her privacy rights for me to look at her chart since I've never provided direct care to her."

"You don't find it strange that a woman—" He closed his eyes.

What is really going on?

"Scott, what is it that you really want to know?"

The alarm on Tyler's watch toned, like the warning of a bomb about to detonate.

"I want to know why my wife was here and what Thomas Reeves might have done to her. Was she part of the protocol?"

Chapter 4

Early Evening, Monday, June 11

Morgan reached for the amber bottle. *How easy would it be to die?* She smoothed her thumb over the prescription label, calculating the number of antidepressant pills it would take to cease her existence. She eyed the full glass of water on her nightstand and felt herself breathing. *In. Out. In. Ou—*

She flinched when the house vibrated beneath her. Tyler was home. Fully releasing her held breath, Morgan took the bottle of amitriptyline and tucked it into her pillowcase.

Did Tyler make it to the grave today?

Even though Morgan's heart ached for the sweet lavender smell of her daughter fresh out of the bath, it couldn't bear going to the patch of ground that held her tiny little body. The marble of the grave marker sapped her strength with every visit. It was becoming more difficult to shake the coldness and find any light to ease this darkness creeping into her soul.

Despite her best efforts, even now she couldn't help rehearsing the pain. Morgan had suffered unforeseen complications a few days prior to Teagan's birth—complications that had caused her kidneys to go into failure. Despite her induced delivery, her kidneys continued to deteriorate over the next several weeks and Morgan was placed on dialysis.

Adjusting to a chronic illness in the same breath as trying to care for a new infant was mind-boggling. The hopes of getting her pre-baby body back quickly fell away when she'd had a catheter placed into her abdomen for dialysis. The gallon of fluid that sat in her belly for several hours to draw out toxins made her feel like she was nine months pregnant again, without the joy of anticipating a prize at the end of the road.

The doctors soon shared that it was unlikely her kidneys would recover from HELLP syndrome, and that she would need a kidney transplant, or dialysis for the rest of her life.

In her mind, she could still see Tyler as he came into the kitchen during those days. His routine was to undress in the mudroom and to put contaminated clothing directly in the wash. Teagan had been born in the middle of flu season, two days before Valentine's Day, and they wanted to ensure those viral particles didn't travel from their clothing to her newly minted respiratory system. Plus, they were at a point where they needed to keep Morgan as healthy as possible, too. Strange how such small particles could survive outside a host for many hours. Just like an organ could be outside a body for hours yet still bring life to another.

They'd sheltered Teagan for the first eight weeks of her life. Morgan had a good friend who'd volunteered to take care of Teagan when she went back to work. Quickly mounting medical bills had sidetracked her plans of staying home. Her insurance benefits were better than Tyler's, and they were going to need the extra income to cover those costs the insurance didn't pick up.

Tyler's contract work for Dr. Reeves was both a blessing and a curse. The income was badly needed, but now Tyler was hardly home.

It didn't bother her as much as it should have.

After entering the kitchen, Tyler would pick up a glass of red wine that waited for him. Oftentimes, he didn't want her to bother cooking him dinner when his arrival home was never dependable. Bad habits came quickly, and he usually got something on his way home.

It was easy to pour a glass of wine and have it waiting for him. One of the few wife-like tasks she still tried to do.

That was something she missed. Him sitting at the kitchen island in his plush, white terry cloth robe, sipping a cabernet, sharing about his work adventures. Teagan sleeping nearby in her Pack 'n Play. Morgan rummaging through the refrigerator, trying to dream up something new and creative. During her maternity leave, managing Teagan and the dialysis hadn't been too bad. She fit in extra sleep when the baby napped.

After a few stories from his day, Tyler would pick up Teagan and brush his whiskers against her cheek until her dark blue eyes opened and greeted his matching pair. He'd kiss her cheek, walk her upstairs, and get her settled to bed. By the time he was done, Morgan would have something prepared for him to eat. It never bothered Morgan that Tyler roused Teagan from her sleep; she was always quick to go back down.

If I'd known those quiet evenings with Teagan were numbered, I never would've allowed my baby to go back to sleep.

Morgan went back to work. Twelve-hour shifts weren't optimal on dialysis, but working in the pediatric ICU didn't offer any alternative and she dreaded thinking about leaving the type of nursing she loved. Her unit had borne with her even though she needed extra breaks for dialysis exchanges. Then, after a long day, she'd come home to have to set up her treatment and manage Teagan. Tyler started coming home later and later, and she gave up keeping Teagan downstairs awaiting his arrival.

After Teagan's death, Morgan had opted for a shunt to be placed in her arm to facilitate the hemodialysis treatment she currently endured three times a week. And she'd gone on the transplant list.

That had been the beginning of the distance between them. It was as if they were on opposite sides of a small, barely trickling creek. But every action—going to bed without talking, leaving in the morning without a word, and not talking on the phone through the day—was like a cup of water into the stream that eventually grew to the raging, class-five rapids that was the current state of their marriage. Tumultuous.

Churning.

She could so easily be drawn under the foaming water for a cold, suffocating death.

That evening had started like any other for Morgan.

Snow was falling softly and the grass had a nice layer, though it was melting quickly on the streets. She'd picked Teagan up from Victoria's house. The first inkling Morgan should've had that something was amiss was when she arrived late from work and her daughter was packaged up and ready to go. Normally she found Victoria with the baby cuddling in the living room. Through the sidelight windows, Morgan could see Teagan was parked by the front door and buckled into her infant carrier. In one swift movement, Victoria had swung open the door, picked up the carrier with her free hand, and shoved it into Morgan's arms, not even allowing her to come inside. It was a side of her friend that she'd never seen. Impatience. Anxiety. Victoria said Teagan had been fussy all day and she didn't know if she could continue to care for her.

Packaged infant.

Crying all day.

Wanting out.

How many times had she heard the exact same story at work? There should have been something that tugged at Morgan's nursing instinct. She should have known then, as she carried her baby to the car, that a cascade of events was brewing inside her daughter's body. Trauma that her own dear friend set into motion.

The drive home was short. Teagan hadn't stirred. It was already late in the evening, so Morgan decided to leave the baby buckled in the infant carrier while she had her dialysis fluid drained and clean solution infused back into her abdomen. *Thirty minutes tops.*

She'd pushed down the carry handle and taken a quick peek before she went upstairs. Teagan seemed to still be sleeping. After reviewing the events in her mind, Morgan now remembered how her skin looked pale.

Morgan had just finished the treatment when she heard Tyler coming through the heavy garage door that jolted the whole house when it closed. At first, her heart hammered at the sound of the break in the peaceful quiet of the house, but it was his outright scream for her help that caused her to stumble from the bathroom.

She raced down the stairs, crashing into the kitchen. Tyler had Teagan on their marble island, his lips pressed over her nose and mouth. Teagan's head was as blue as the blueberries they'd had for breakfast.

The next several hours blurred in Morgan's mind like the remnants of a nightmare. The arrival of the ambulance. Her stammering through the story of how her daughter had been perfectly fine until Tyler came home.

EMS had placed a breathing tube. They'd gone emergent to Sacred Heart.

The CT scan of her head showed the devastation. Multiple bleeds. New and old subdural hematomas. Massive cerebral edema. Rib fractures. Retinal hemorrhages.

And her coworkers looked at her like a pedophile on a playground.

She knew the mantra that played through their mind. She'd taught it to some of them herself.

Whoever was last seen with the baby—hurt the baby.

That was her. It was Tyler.

Then the horror of every parent. The police interview in the midst of knowing that her daughter had been declared brain dead by one of her attending physicians. The conversation played through her mind like an unrelenting accusation of her failure to act.

"Morgan, I know you've been under a lot of stress," Dr. Marshall had said. "You're trying to work while being on dialysis. There's the added stress of having a new baby. These things are far from easy. We can only help you and Tyler get through this if you tell us exactly what happened."

Her voice weak and thin because she'd screamed so many times. She looked at him squarely. "I did not shake Teagan. I would never hurt her!"

And then Victoria had shown up with flowers for her baby. Pink gerbera daisies had been Morgan's favorite until that day. Until she saw them proffered up like a thinly veiled plea for forgiveness.

And that's when it had all fallen apart.

All the drama of a *telenovela* and more.

In the end, Victoria confessed she was the one who'd shaken Teagan. That she'd done it more than once, to quiet her crying. That was the last time Morgan ever saw her—leaving the PICU in handcuffs.

The sound of Tyler's footfalls on the steps brought her back to the present, to this moment, but the pain she felt was just as strong as it had been one month ago.

Morgan lay on her side, looking out at the city lights that lay in the valley below their home. She used to sway Teagan in her arms at the view. Tyler crossed over the carpet, teased her blond hair back, and placed warm lips on her forehead. Only after, he laid the flowers he'd originally bought for Teagan's grave on her dresser. Pink roses, limp, with brown, curled edges.

She wanted to throw them in the trash.

Tyler set his wine glass down in the armoire that held their television and turned on the news. He always hummed nursery rhymes he'd sung to Teagan as he got ready for bed.

"Looks like both of us had interesting ends to our day."

She remained silent. The thought crossed her mind to feign sleep to avoid conversation altogether.

"Hon?"

Her eyes drew to the TV. Even the national news had picked up Zoe's story. A child's murder halted by the curious innocence of Boy Scouts was like chum in the water for sharks. Their own lawn still hadn't recovered after the media had parked on their grass. Even better than a stranger taking the life of a child was the story of a pediatric ICU nurse and her transplant surgeon husband beating their own daughter to death.

Presumed guilty before proven innocent.

"You heard about Zoe Martin's case?" Morgan asked.

He turned around and clicked off the light. "Hard not to. Everyone's talking about it. How is she?"

"You're asking as a potential harvester of her organs?"

Sadness flashed in his blue eyes.

Why am I picking a fight, today of all days?

He sat next to her on the bed and pulled her hand into his. "I'm asking because I'm curious about what happened. To have a conversation with you."

Tears leapt from her eyes and she pulled her hand from his. She closed her eyes tightly and buried them under the palms of her hands. Would this ache for her daughter ever go away? Did she regret the decision she had made? Is that why this void was never filled—because there was nothing of her daughter left to give hope to anyone else?

Tyler eased his arms around her back and pulled her tight into his embrace. He rocked her gently, but instead of comforting her, it only intensified the pain in her body, and she pushed back against him.

He held his hands up. "I'm sorry."

Morgan rolled on the bed away from him. "Do you hate me for what I did?"

"What do you mean?"

"For refusing to donate Teagan's organs."

She could hear the rush of his breath fill his chest and stop. He laid a heavy hand on her shoulder. "Honestly?"

Morgan nodded. This was the elephant in the room between them since Teagan had died. The coroner had given permission to release the body for donation, and Tyler had assumed, considering her background, she automatically would be on board.

"Hate is too strong a word. Disappointed, I guess." His hand tightened. "I know it would have helped my grief to know that part of her was helping another child."

"Especially now that we can't have any more."

He rubbed her arm slowly. A response when he struggled to find the right words to say.

"Morgan, I love you. That hasn't changed. There are these issues we need to work through. What I don't know is how you feel about me. Do you want to stay in this marriage?"

She buried her face under her arms.

The bigger question is, do I even want to stay alive?

Chapter 5

Evening, Monday, June 11

BRETT THREW HIS CAR INTO park and flipped off the headlights.

"I shouldn't have called you," he said. "I knew it would get your detective radar into overdrive. Lilly is going to kill me."

Nathan was in the seat next to him. In between picking bits of lint off his pants, he'd been reviewing two case files. One was of the aggravated assault case of Zoe Martin, and the other was the one on Dr. and Mrs. Tyler Adams. Brett's partner closed the folder and looked in his direction, the light from the streetlamp shading his face like the Phantom of the Opera.

"Come on," Nathan said. "I know you missed our witty repartee, and Lilly is working in the ER tonight anyway."

"Guess I'll need to keep you out of the line of fire for sure then. I don't want Lilly killing me for letting you catch a bullet. I'd have to start my own list of unforgivables."

Nathan patted his breast pocket where he kept the worn piece of paper. "Maybe you should create such a list."

"About things I can't forgive myself for? Honestly, I got enough to be depressed about already."

"You haven't talked much about your mother since her death."

Brett loosened his tie. "Aw, man. You know I hate to talk about touchy-feely stuff. Let's focus on you. Any new list additions?"

Nathan settled his knee against the door. "Since losing those hostages and delaying public disclosure too long in Lilly's rape case? I did add Raven Samuals to the list. I shouldn't have stopped watching over her. Maybe I could have prevented her descent into revenge. Maybe those officers would still be alive." The car was quiet for a few moments.

The silence made Brett uncomfortable. "Let's get this interview done."

"I am glad you called me about it."

"Once I saw your name on Teagan's file and the connection to the little note I found—I had a hunch you'd want to be in on this one from the start."

Nathan closed the folder and tapped it against his knee. "You were on your little hiatus when her case came in."

"Anything interesting?"

"Not after the sitter confessed. Morgan, the mother, she's a lot like Lilly in a way."

"How?"

"Just her demeanor. There's this toughness about Morgan Adams."

"Maybe we should be worried she's packing. Considering the marksman your sweet wife is. I saw her outshoot Lee Watson on the range once."

Nathan chuckled. "Don't say that in front of him when he's with his SWAT guys. I won't be responsible for what happens." He grazed the folder with his fingers. "Lilly's the only woman I know who carries a concealed weapon."

"You know she could get the draw on you."

"Probably."

"Not probably. Absolutely. Next day off—"

"Yeah, yeah, yeah. You're just hungry to get me knocked down a few. I'm not working with SWAT for my marksmanship skills."

Brett pushed his door open. "I'm glad you realize that."

Nathan hopped out of the car and closed the door. "As long as you appreciate the shortcomings of your character."

Brett affected mock disdain. "Me. I'm perfect."

"Minus the ladies' man shiner you're sporting today. Did you mistake a boyfriend for a brother again?"

"Doorknob."

"Whatever." Nathan stopped midpoint up the stairs. "Do you see these flower beds? I wonder if Adams is a closet landscaper. I've been looking for someone."

"I'm sure he's got loads of time between his doctoring and all to do your yard work."

The Adams' residence was a refurbished historical Victorian home painted in vibrant colors. Brett thought a child might have had a hand in picking out the color scheme, or at least an adult that was infatuated with McDonald's. One half was orange-red painted brick, the other side a pale yellow and the top half a sunnier, deeper yellow. The pathway lights flickered on as the sun was swallowed by the Rocky Mountains.

Nathan smiled. "You take the lead. You know more about the case than I do."

Brett's chest swelled with pride. He respected Nathan more than his ego would ever allow him to share. Lately, Nathan had chilled quite a bit. *Wonder what's going on between him and Lilly to cause such a change? Maybe they're finally trying for a family.* He rang the doorbell and pulled his credentials from his pocket.

The door opened to reveal a man, about six-foot-two, dressed in blue plaid flannel pajama bottoms and a white T-shirt. Brown hair. His eyelids narrowed over his dark blue eyes.

"Dr. Tyler Adams?" Brett said.

Confusion swept over the man's face as he nodded.

Behind him, a woman with long, curly blond hair and hesitant green eyes pulled a white terry cloth robe tighter around her slim waist. The nurse. *Why did people look so different when they were out of their uniform?* Brett flashed his badge. "I'm Detective Brett Sawyer." He waved his hand Nathan's direction. "My partner, Detective Nathan Long. We're with Aurora police. Can we come in and ask a few questions?"

"Weren't you at the hospital today?" Morgan Adams asked Brett.

"Yes, ma'am. I was the one there from the police for Zoe Martin."

She shook her head with a puzzled frown. "You know I can't give you any medical information about her case. You'd have to go through the public relations office for that."

Her husband opened the door wider. "What is this regarding?"

Brett stepped closer to the door. "Mrs. Adams is partly right. It's regarding the assault on Zoe Martin, but I'm not here for any of her medical info."

"Why don't we step inside?" Nathan suggested.

Dr. Adams showed them to a well-sized formal living area just off the foyer. The room was painted a light golden brown. Heavy, red velvet curtains and a red stuffed chenille couch popped against the more neutral tones. The main sitting area was poised in the middle of the room with a bi-level wood table facing two additional wing chairs. Adams motioned to the wing chairs and Brett and Nathan took seats. Morgan shuffled in and seemed to melt into the couch next to her husband.

Brett cleared his throat. "Dr. Adams, I'm sorry to bother you tonight. I'll try to keep it brief due to the late hour. Have you heard anything about Zoe's case?"

Tyler leaned back and folded his hands on his lap. "Just that a young girl was attacked on a local trail. Obviously I know that she was admitted to Morgan's unit."

Brett could see Morgan studying Nathan.

Guess the mothering instinct never goes away, even when your child has died. It just carries over to other children.

She leaned so far forward on the couch, she almost tumbled off. "You were one of the detectives assigned to Teagan's case."

Nathan nodded. "Yes, I was. I'm very sorry for your loss."

"You were so kind to us." She eased her hand over Tyler's but then pulled it away as if it breached some unspoken line. "I never felt like you assumed I was guilty."

Nathan nodded. "I appreciate your kind words. It was a difficult situation."

Tyler crossed his arms over his chest. "You said this was about the girl, Zoe Martin."

Evidently, further discussion on the topic was not permissible.

"Right," Brett said. "I was part of the police team that searched the park today where her body was found." From the folder, he removed the clear plastic evidence bag that held the business card. "Not far from the site where they found Zoe's body, we also found this."

Brett held it out. Tyler stood and pulled it from his fingers, looking it over on both sides before handing it back. "It's one of my business cards. So?"

"Can you account for your whereabouts today, Dr. Adams?"

"You can verify where I was with my secretary and nurse. They were with me up until thirty minutes ago. I was seeing patients all day. Every thirty minutes."

"Terrific. If I could have their numbers, that will be great. Any idea how this card would have ended up on the trail next to an assault victim?"

Tyler inhaled deeply. "Honestly, it could have been any number of ways. I must give two dozen of those out a day and who knows how many are grabbed and handed around."

Adams's body language was congruent with his statement. He sat comfortably. Arms relaxed. Facial expression sincere.

"Did you see the time and date on the back?" Brett asked.

Adams nodded.

"Do you recall anything significant about that date?" Brett followed.

"That was almost eighteen months ago. I'd have to look back into some records to see if something strikes me. Sorry, nothing stands out."

"What do the letters NPO mean? The noted time of midnight mean anything to you?"

"NPO is a medical term that stands for nothing by mouth. If I had to make an educated guess, I would say that date denotes a surgical date and this was another reminder of a procedure. Though, this is not normally something we would give to patients. First of all, this is medical lingo, and most patients won't understand what the abbreviation means. Second of all, that card comes from Sacred Heart. We don't operate on adults there."

Brett tucked the evidence back into the folder. "A couple of your medical colleagues mentioned you were doing some contract work? Where is that?"

"NeuroGenics," Tyler said. "I'm sorry. Did you think I was at Sacred Heart today?"

Wait. Wait. Wait. I should know this company.

The first true sign of discomfort during the interview didn't come from Tyler. It came from Nathan. He looked like he might Elizabeth-Taylor-faint right out of the chair.

"Doesn't the institute handle mainly private security contracts?" Nathan asked.

Tyler was beginning to pale a bit. "Yes. We're operating under a privately funded grant."

The fire of Nathan's police instinct was lit, and it zeroed directly on Tyler. "Do you know a man named Dr. Thomas Reeves?"

Brett's elbow slid off the padded armchair. *That's it! Thomas Reeves's brainchild. But what does Nathan's father-in-law have to do with . . . well, anything?*

Tyler clenched his hands tightly, his fingers jammed into the back of the other hand. "I understand what a sensitive issue this is for everyone. However, it's classified work. There's military interest in what we're doing. There's nothing I'm going to be able to disclose to you, including who might be sponsoring the contract. Nothing about the staff at this point. I'm happy to give you the names of the two women who can verify my whereabouts, but I'm going to have to talk to my medical director before continuing our conversation."

Brett stood. "We'll arrange a time for that to happen." From his wallet, Brett pulled one of his business cards. He handed it to Tyler. "I'd appreciate those names tomorrow, sir, so we can get this little matter cleared up. I would be grateful if you could look through some of your records and see if anything around that date strikes your mind."

Adams slid the card from his fingers. "Sure thing."

Brett walked around the table and reached his hand out to Tyler and then held it tight in his grip. "As a father of a murdered child, I know you understand what Zoe's parents are going through."

"Brett . . ." Nathan warned.

He smiled and Tyler's face iced over. "Don't give me reason to assume you're involved with what happened to Zoe." Brett released his hand. "I've put doctors in jail before."

Chapter 6

Noon, Wednesday, June 13

MORGAN WALKED THROUGH the PICU doors after lunch and was immediately greeted by Amy Kent's mother, Joanna. The woman embraced her so tightly that Morgan's lunch bag dropped from her hand onto the floor. Morgan reached up to Joanna's shoulders and eased her back.

"What are you guys doing here?" Morgan asked.

Tears fled down her cheeks, as if her own sadness was too much for them to take. "The LVAD . . . something's wrong with it."

The small heart pump, known as a left ventricular assist device, helped ease the workload of the heart. More recently, it had been used on an ex-vice president to maintain his life until transplant.

Definitely not good news.

"How long?"

"I don't know, but she hasn't been feeling well for a couple of days." Joanna pulled the curtain aside and Morgan stepped into the darkened space.

Amy Kent was a stunning, blond-haired, blue-eyed beauty. Surely, the envy of every other girl her age for her beauty-pageant looks, sweet personality, and wicked-smart brain. Life for her had everything going in the right direction until she contracted a nasty little virus that morphed her heart into a weak, dilated, ineffective organ.

"What's the cardiologist saying?" Morgan asked.

"That she doesn't have . . ." She covered her mouth with her hand, eyes squinting against the thought of every parent's dismal desperation.

The thought of having to bury her own child.

Joanna began to moan as Amy lay sleeping in the bed. Morgan embraced her as she eyed Amy's numbers on the monitor. Heart rate fast. BP low. She scanned the pumps. Sure enough, she was also requiring medication to support her blood pressure, and even at the current dose it didn't seem to be helping.

Morgan took a step back and used her thumbs to wipe the tears off the woman's cheeks. "Joanna, don't go there. Your baby is alive. She's in the best place. We'll figure it out. You know Dr. Marshall is the very best."

The screech of the curtain being yanked against the track brought Morgan's eyes away from the mother to her coworker, Eric.

"Dr. Leeds wants to speak with you."

The neurosurgeon on duty today. That can't be good.

"About what?"

"Bedspace D."

Zoe Martin.

Morgan rubbed Joanna's shoulders and settled her back into the chair. "Just pray. I'll try to catch Marshall and see what the plan is. We'll chat later."

As soon as she cleared the curtain, Leeds was a mere five steps away, tapping his toe against the linoleum. Even before she could greet him, he stated his case like a drill sergeant. "The Martins don't get it."

"Don't get what?"

"That Zoe is brain dead."

Morgan grabbed him by the elbow and pulled him back toward the hall near the staff lounge, away from the bionic ears of PICU families. "You can't say something like that in the middle of the unit. Everyone hears you."

He sighed. "Morgan, give me a break. I need you to get them to understand so that we can withdraw care. Legally, she's dead. Further care is unnecessary and futile." He'd tried to explain the findings in the Harvard-type spiel of a literary professor. They simply hadn't understood the language.

"Even coming from you, don't you think that's a little harsh? They are losing their child. She was murdered."

"They've already lost her." Then a spotlight of recognition gleamed from his eyes. He stroked his bald head several times and then tugged at the cuffs of his lab coat. "Sometimes, I don't know why I ever did peds neurosurg. There's always so much bad news you have to deliver. 'I'm sorry your child has an inoperable brain tumor.' 'I'm sorry, you did kill your child by letting them ride an ATV without a helmet.' 'I'm sorry . . .'"

Never had she seen Dr. Leeds with any feeling, let alone the weight of Zoe's case that suddenly brought all these emotions to the surface.

"I just don't think I can do this work anymore. I don't know if I *want* to do this work anymore." A hint of redness colored the edges of his eyes. He reached up too quickly, embarrassed, wiping away tears that had yet to fully form. "Too many kids I've watched die. More often than not, what I do seems to make little difference."

Morgan's knees began to shake at the reality of what she was witnessing. A single man, no children—had latched on to these children as surrogates for the ones he was never able to have. Leeds was known as an obsessive worker. Tough on the residents. First one in—last to go home. One of the worst bedside manners; but if a family needed a miracle, his name was at the top of her list.

Morgan was at a loss for words. "Dr. Leeds— "

"Michael," he said. "Please. My name is Michael. Why do you call every other doctor by their first name but not me? No one does."

His shoulders sagged. The image of a beaten man. His life's work had taken the final toll, and Morgan knew in her heart that Zoe was likely his last case. There was a limit to the amount of sadness and grief a human could carry, and this man's tank had overflowed.

Morgan exhaled through the burning in her chest. *What hope can I give? An amazing clinician at the end of his rope?* Not long ago, she would have offered him what she considered everlasting hope and peace.

But since Teagan's death, that well for her had long gone dry.

"Dr. Leeds . . ." She shook her head. "Michael. You and I have worked together ever since I was a new, baby nurse. You've taken my head off so many times, you could become the envied twin of Henry VIII."

He shoved his hands deep into the pockets of his lab coat, looking away from her down the hall.

"You're not my favorite doctor to work with." She swallowed the saliva that collected in her mouth. "But, you are the one I would call first if a kid needed a miracle." She leaned against the hallway wall. "I'm sorry for all of us and for the toll this job takes on our lives."

He straightened his shoulders. "I know I shouldn't ask you to do this, but I am." He eyed her, the color of his irises a shade darker with the weariness he carried. "Convince them she's gone."

Morgan glanced at the two anguished parents. After two days, the firestorm of media continued to crawl over the campus of Sacred Heart Children's Hospital like ravenous dogs looking for a meal. A slow ache crawled through Morgan's gut. It was a community that she'd never dreamed she would belong to—parents of murdered children.

Morgan nodded to Leeds. "What about your fellow?"

"If you think I'm bad—"

"Fine. I'll do it."

She'd never seen a man exit the PICU so fast.

Morgan proceeded to Zoe's bedspace, pulled a chair to the foot of her bed, and stretched the curtain closed behind her before she took a seat.

Julia Martin searched Morgan's eyes as she placed her hand over her daughter's limp, pale one. This was one of the most difficult aspects of nursing—explaining death when the machines that kept Zoe "alive" mimicked real life so well.

Morgan motioned for them to sit. They would understand more if she explained each nuance in language they used every day. Interpretation took time.

"Do you remember Dr. Leeds doing all those strange tests to Zoe? Like brushing cotton against her eye and injecting cold water into her ears?"

The father, Ian, nodded while Julia stared at Morgan wide-eyed and fearful.

"He was testing for some basic reflexes that all of us have. These are generated from the brainstem. This is the part of the brain that regulates the heartbeat and breathing." Morgan swallowed hard. "Zoe doesn't have any of these reflexes present. She doesn't have any sort of sedative in her system that would prevent her from having these. Because of that, Dr. Leeds wanted to do a brain flow study."

"That's what she went to radiology for," Ian clarified.

Morgan nodded her head and began to feel a vibration at the center of her chest, a playback of when she first heard the news of Teagan's brain flow study and what it ultimately meant. Unfortunately, her job knowledge gave her instant understanding, whereas these parents struggled on a thin tightrope—clinging to the hope that somehow their daughter would return to the way she had been.

Morgan pulled her lower lip between her teeth before continuing on. "During a brain flow study, a radioisotope that can be seen on X-ray is injected into the blood. After that, pictures are taken of the brain."

Straightening her back, Morgan rested her hands over the two pictures she held on her lap. Nursing was about education—about hitting each individual learning style to somehow let the truth of a situation sink in.

Morgan flipped the first picture up and her stomach began to ache. Even needing these pictures as teaching tools seemed sacrilegious. "This is what a normal brain flow study looks like. This is *not* Zoe's study, but just to show you the difference." She peered around the front, like a librarian reading to a group of eager children.

Yet the eagerness on these parents' faces was not one of joy but of apprehension. Morgan pointed to the plumes of dye—evidence that it had been pushed through the bloodstream via the body's internal highway system. "You can see here how the injected dye was carried by the blood vessels into the brain."

A slight nod of affirmation from the father. The mother continued to sit still.

"Wherever blood goes, oxygen goes. That's how organs stay alive. Without blood flow, there is no oxygen delivery and that organ will die."

Morgan switched to the other X-ray. "This is Zoe's study." The uneasy vibration had changed to pain, and it traveled along her muscle fibers like electricity. Everything about her body began to feel heavy. "See how there is no indication of blood flowing up to her brain at all?"

As she waited for her statement to sink in, her heart heaved with adrenaline. Morgan placed the pictures side by side. The sting of coming tears threatened to overwhelm her. Maybe what her coworkers said was true. *Why do I keep doing this work? Why do I keep submitting myself to other families' grief when I don't have a handle on my own?*

Her voice cracked as she started. "See the difference? Zoe's brain isn't getting any blood flow and therefore has died. Zoe is what we call brain dead. She has died. I'm really sorry."

Ian dropped his face into his hands. A piercing pain struck Morgan's chest. She quickly blinked back her own tears as she bit hard into the inner side of her cheek to keep from breaking down; the copper taste only increased the roiling in her gut.

The curtain that was pulled closed around the bed wouldn't keep Ian's weeping from the other families who were visiting the unit. Julia's eyes glossed over as she clamped her lips together to quell their trembling.

"How can you say that when I can see her chest rising and falling? Her heartbeat is up on that monitor!"

Morgan set the pictures down. "I know this is very confusing. The breathing machine delivers oxygen to her lungs. Because of that, her heart continues to beat. However, another test we did on Zoe even before we took her to radiology looked at whether she would breathe if the machine wasn't helping her."

The woman came up out of her seat. "And did she?"

Morgan clenched the pictures on her lap and shook her head.

"You're lying!"

Julia grabbed Zoe's shoulders and began to shake her daughter in the bed. The child's straight brown hair, still with remnants of dirt and leaves embedded in the silky smooth fibers, tousled against her pillow. "Zoe Marie! You wake up right now!"

Ian looked dazed. His own processing of the situation paralyzed any ability he might have had to comfort his wife. Morgan came up off the chair to the mother's side of the bed. She gripped the woman around the waist and began to move her back from her daughter's body. And then it came, the torrential sobbing of grief as the woman latched her arms around Morgan's shoulders, barely able to keep herself standing.

Through the edge of the open curtain, she could see Detective Brett Sawyer waiting in the wings. His eyes widened, and she simply shook her head as she brought her hands up and held them against the woman's back.

Ian's voice brought her attention back. "Can we donate her organs?"

Julia pulled away from Morgan. "How can you think about that right now?"

"Because I want something good to come of what happened. I want part of her to still be alive."

Morgan assisted Julia back into her chair. "It's possible. We'll have to clear it with the coroner considering the circumstances. They've done it in the past."

"Why do you have to clear it with them?" Ian asked.

Morgan looked at the detective again and he motioned for her. She couldn't verbalize the answer to Zoe's father's question. Her mouth refused to form the words.

Because now, the detective can amend the charges to murder.

Chapter 7

Afternoon, Friday, June 15

TYLER PLACED TWO FINGERS on the inner aspect of Amy Kent's wrist, feeling the pulse generated by her new heart. Morgan bustled around him setting medication pumps, listening to heart tones and breath sounds as another nurse documented vital signs.

It was these moments when his once strong faith stirred for revival inside of him. Amy's blood type had matched that of the, officially now, murder victim. Was it God's providence or his restoration through an evil act? Was God good in all circumstances? Why did one family have to carry tragedy at the same time another family rejoiced? Zoe Martin's heart was now beating in Amy Kent's chest.

There wasn't any feasible way for those two families to avoid crossing paths in the PICU. It was an inherent flaw in the building design. An open unit. A large waiting room. Harried parents with nothing better to do than to share their experiences with the other families in the same holding cell.

And it was that scene that broke his heart. Not from sadness, but from a vacuous awareness that he had missed out on such a moment. The possibility that he could have used his daughter's organs to save the life of another parent's child.

Instead, Teagan was a mire of nothing in the cold, dark earth.

He'd witnessed the moment this time. The curtains had been pulled away from Zoe's bed as the organ team was getting ready to take her to the OR. Joanna Kent had waited for Zoe's parents to emerge from the cocoon of their corner.

She'd raced across the unit and enveloped Julia Martin in an embrace that only two mothers in that circumstance could understand. A quiet hush settled over the unit. People bowed their heads, the only way they could offer privacy in such an intimate, emotion-wrought stillness in time shared between two souls passing on either side of life and death.

And the words that Joanna Kent whispered to Julia Martin over and over were simply . . . I'm sorry.

The idea of sacrifice had always been close to Tyler's heart. It was what amazed him about Christ's death. No matter what you could say about his life on earth—that he was crazy, that he was a liar, that he was in fact God—didn't matter when what the man believed led him to give up his life in the most horrendous way: voluntarily.

Just as Zoe's parents had given up her heart, voluntarily, so another child could live.

Tyler wondered, in a soulful, universe-gazing way, if these earthly lessons were designed by a good God to give humanity glimpses of what he'd done for each of them.

And he wondered if Morgan still believed it anymore.

Death and life in the same day. One family's grief is another family's joy. The best and the worst day tied up in one messy, bright bow.

He watched Morgan as she busied herself with her coworkers to get Amy settled. Common procedure was to admit a transplant patient directly to the ICU after surgery instead of going to the post-anesthesia care unit. These children required more than one-on-one nursing care. They typically had two or more nurses in attendance for the first few hours after surgery, watching the monitors closely, assessing their patient's body systems for the slightest signal that something was going awry.

Really, it still amazed him to watch nurses in action. There was something about them. They could be both compassionate and stern in the same moment. They could laugh and cry with a family as they moved from one bedspace to another, all the while watching for those subtle clues that their patient was taking a turn for the worse. Forget about the complexity of pediatric nursing. Caring for an infant, a toddler, a teenager, each required a different approach. Plus, the appropriate medication dose for a high schooler would kill an infant.

And he'd been lucky to find Morgan.

They'd first met at the beginning of his pediatric cardiothoracic fellowship. She'd been singing softly to a child who'd just received a pacemaker, trying to entice the youngster with toys, the ultimate assessment of a child's pain level. Active play—excellent. Not interested in playing—the child wasn't feeling well. She'd been straightening the girl's stray curls with her fingers, offering up her own curly, blond locks as entertainment when it seemed the child got a sudden burst of energy from her sugary, orange Popsicle and grabbed Morgan's hair, entwining her sticky fingers in the locks and pulling hard.

Morgan cried out and stayed the girl's hand as her vibrant green eyes searched the unit for help. Yelling in the PICU was reserved solely for emergencies, and toddler's sticky-fisted hair-pulling was a definite nonemergency.

Tyler raced to help her. At first he drew his trauma shears from his pocket to cut her free but she offered a look of *Are you kidding?* and he'd raced to shield them back in his pocket.

The first words his future wife ever uttered to him: "Why is it you surgeons always want to cut something up first?"

He couldn't help but smile. "It's the fastest way to a cure."

Morgan laughed in return. Ten minutes later, he presided over a pile of orange, gooey washcloths that had separated fist from hair. The patient was smiling and playing. He'd patted the bundle of dirty cloths at the end of the bed. "Cutting would have been faster than this, but I do like your long hair better than the short cut I would have given you."

"Surgeon and hairstylist?"

"Where do you think Scarlett Johansson gets her great style from?"

"Scarlett Johansson?"

He'd held his hands up in mock surrender. "All right, you know my darkest secret. Now I can take you out for dinner."

"Where?"

"I might be able to afford the cafeteria."

———

Amy's monitor toned and brought his attention back to his current patient. A jealous tug pulled at Tyler's heart as the attending cardiac surgeon sidled up next to Morgan at the patient's computer, reviewing the initial numbers. He nodded and laid a gentle hand on her shoulder. One thought crossed through Tyler's mind.

I want to be that close to her again. Have that easiness.

Would he ever get over first thinking about Teagan's death when he entered this unit? Would Morgan?

Chapter 8

TYLER FLIPPED THROUGH THE nurses' notes and reviewed Amy Kent's information—a now-active, healthy child begging her mother to bring her to the playground every day. Post-op transplant visits were some of Tyler's favorite patient appointments. A child who once buried dreams now had all the hope of growing into adulthood.

Both the child and the family.

He knocked twice and then popped inside the room. It had been one month since Amy's surgery, and it was a blessing to see the family on this side of things. Happy. Peaceful. Starting to get past the feeling of the dark cloud constantly looming.

Which was why Tyler frowned when he saw the distressed look on Joanna Kent's face.

The new crop of worry lines aged her ten years. *What's going on?* He reached to shake her hand in greeting. When he tried to release his grip, she held firmly, and tugged gently so he would look at her. "Can we talk somewhere private after her exam?"

His heart sunk. That type of "talk" was just like a girl saying *We need to talk . . .* when she was just about to break off a relationship. It was the asterisk of preparation in something that Tyler didn't want to hear.

He was sure of that.

Medically, Amy was vibrant. Her color was pink. Distal pulses easily palpable. No puffy ankles. Strong, steady heartbeat. But Amy's countenance echoed the sense of foreboding that her mother had. She perched herself on the end of the exam table, tense fingers digging into the vinyl.

"Amy, you look great. How have you been feeling?" Tyler asked.

The child shrugged her shoulders. Joanna stood from her chair and simply said, "Now."

Not a question. A statement of urgency. Tyler patted Amy's knee. "Your mom and I are going to talk outside. Be back in a jiffy."

The girl nodded but momentarily reached for him as if to clasp his hand, then dropped her arms back to the table.

Even before Tyler could fully close the door and walk the mother down the hall a few paces, the words tumbled out of Joanna like dice rolled onto a table. "She's having nightmares."

Relief washed through Tyler. His heart rate calmed. "That's not unusual considering what she's been through. All the anticipation of waiting for the heart, the actual surgery, can be traumatizing for patients."

She shook her head. "No, that's the wrong word. They're not dreams . . . they're memories."

A nurse walked by, one eyebrow raised at those words. He laid a reassuring hand on Joanna's shoulder. "What I said still applies. She's been through a lot. It's just her mind processing the events."

Tears ran down Joanna's cheeks. "You don't get what I'm saying." She pushed his hand away. "She's having memories of Zoe Martin's killer."

Tyler's stomach flipped and he leaned a shoulder into the wall to steady himself. "What makes you think so?"

"She describes the attack." Joanna fumbled for a crumpled tissue in her handbag. "I want to go to the police. Do you think they'd believe her?"

The sobs overwhelmed her. Tyler was rarely in a position where he was the one to provide comfort. Usually in this situation, post-transplant, families were never in such a grieved state unless there was concern the organ was being rejected. He glanced around for a little feminine support. When he found none, he wrapped one arm around Mrs. Kent and she fell into his chest like he'd rescued her from drowning.

Tyler patted her back to calm the intensifying trembles. "We'll figure it out. It's going to be all right."

"She's not my little girl anymore."

"Of course she is."

"No!" Her eyes widened at the rise of her voice. She inhaled deeply. "Amy's not sleeping. She was always so happy. I called her my little piece of sunshine. That joy is gone. Every night, I wake up to the sound of her screaming. She's a shell of who she once was. It's terrifying."

"Okay, let's set up a consult with a psychologist versus going to the police. Get her talking about things. See if that helps."

"I want her back on the list."

Tyler eased back. "What do you mean?"

"I want you to cut that heart out of her chest and bury it with Zoe's body. It's the only place it should be."

Chapter 9

Late Morning, Monday, July 30

THE INTENSITY THAT RADIATED off Joanna Kent was partly contained rage and partly fear for her daughter's safety.

"You're sure she's going to be all right?" she asked, choosing to pace in front of the two-way mirror instead of sitting in the chair Brett offered her.

"Amy's safe in there. If what you say is true, it won't be any worse than what she's been going through. I trust these two. They'll get to the bottom of this."

"What if he knows? What if he finds out that she's a witness?"

He being the murderer.

"I don't think that's possible. Let's not worry about things we can't control."

This was one of the strangest meetings Brett had ever participated in. Last week came the call from Dr. Adams. Honestly, after getting the good doctor's alibi for Zoe Martin's murder, Brett never thought he'd hear from him again. Not that Brett ever suspected Adams of any real wrongdoing, but after working with Nathan on the Lilly Reeves rape case, Brett had learned to keep his mind open to unexpected possibilities. Even when they flew in the face of all logic and reason.

Needless to say, the call from Dr. Adams shocked him. The physician claimed that the girl who'd received Zoe's heart was having memories of her donor's murder. Could even provide a description of the assailant.

At first, Adams had reassured the mother that nothing insidious was going on. What she termed "memories" were likely just dreams, or some strange form of post-traumatic stress. He explained that no matter how her mother tried to protect her from the story, Amy likely heard of Zoe's case and was smart enough to infer she was the recipient of her heart. It was conceivable considering Zoe's parents were on the news most nights trying to keep Zoe's case fresh in the minds of the press. What better way than to highlight the fact that part of Zoe was still alive through the transplant they'd agree to give?

What prompted Dr. Adams to call Brett was the urging of his wife. Morgan Adams had a long history with Amy through her frequent visits to the pediatric ICU, and Joanna had called Morgan when Dr. Adams had dismissed her worrying. These visions Amy was having were beginning to affect her health negatively, and Morgan worried that Amy's body would reject the heart transplant if the amount of stress the girl carried wasn't reduced in a hurry.

After talking it over with Nathan, Brett had taken his partner's suggestion and called Derrick Vanhise, a Boulder-based psychiatrist. Vanhise suggested having Keelyn Watson interview the child, too. Keelyn was a body language expert and forensic interviewer and was developing quite a reputation for getting kids to disclose the heinous things done to them. Keelyn had special insight into police protocols as her husband, Lee, was a SWAT commander.

Small world.

So, now Dr. Vanhise, Keelyn, and Amy sat in a police interrogation room, not for the fear factor but for the use of the recording equipment. Keelyn wanted to review the tapes afterward, so she could slow down body movements for analysis.

Vanhise sat next to Keelyn, his thin frame smartly dressed in khaki pants and a bluish-green plaid shirt. Brett was surprised he hadn't shown up in his usual beachcomber attire, which, even for Boulder, bordered on strange. His black hair was combed and graying beard trimmed. For a young girl, his dress would exude the quiet calm of a professional there to help.

Keelyn's brown hair was pulled up into a sloppy bun. The harried readiness of a mom with a toddler at home. Keelyn's hazel eyes sparkled joy behind her reading glasses. Her black skirt and teal pullover seemed too warm for summer. Then again, she didn't have any extra fat on her to help maintain her temperature.

Eight-year-old Amy seemed so small slumped in front of them. Blond hair in a ponytail and dressed in denim shorts and a glittery t-shirt with a unicorn on it. A blue-black hue tinged the skin under Amy's eyes. Joanna said they were from environmental allergies and a complete lack of sleep.

Allergic shiners. Amy's hands were folded in front of her. Eyes warily scanning the room as another officer finished hooking up the recording equipment.

Vanhise nodded toward Brett through the two-way glass signaling it was time to begin recording. In his hand, Brett held his field notes and Zoe Martin's file so he could do some fact-checking against Amy's story.

"Amy, my name is Derrick, and I work with people when they are having trouble. Although I am a doctor, I don't work with people when they are sick like when you needed your heart to get fixed. I work with people like you, Amy, when they are having trouble sleeping because they are remembering something bad that's happened to them."

She nodded her head but kept her eyes downcast.

Vanhise motioned to Keelyn. "Amy, this is my friend Keelyn. She's here to help me talk with you because she's a girl, and you know sometimes boys don't get what girls think. Plus, she has a little girl at home, too."

Amy looked up. "You do?"

Keelyn offered a warm smile. "I do! Her name is Sophia. She's a lot younger than you though. Hasn't started preschool yet. How's your summer been?"

"Not good. I don't feel like doing anything."

Keelyn nodded. "I bet that's very hard for you. I'm sure you miss your friends."

The girl kicked her feet out in response. Vanhise looked Keelyn's direction.

"Amy, who lives at home with you?" Keelyn asked.

"Me, Mom, Dad, and my brother."

"Do you have any pets?"

"Just one crazy dog."

"Oh, I'm jealous. I always wanted a dog. Why is yours crazy?"

Amy looked up at Keelyn with a little brightness in her eyes. "He always steals my shoes!"

"No kidding!"

"We call him the Shoe Thief. You just can't leave them anywhere. You'd think he'd have grown out of it by now."

"That does sound silly. What's your dog's name?"

"Muffin."

"Is he a small dog or a big dog?"

"Mmmm . . ." She shrugged her shoulders. "Medium, I guess. He's a cocker spaniel. Looks like chocolate, but dogs can't have chocolate, which is weird to me."

"Why is that weird?" Keelyn asked.

"That something people can have can make someone else sick. Like my heart is making me sick."

Derrick and Keelyn exchanged glances. Vanhise cleared his throat. "Can we talk about that, Amy? Why do you think your heart is making you sick?"

"Because I wasn't having nightmares before I got my transplant."

Vanhise crossed his legs. "Can you tell me about the dreams?"

The girl hugged her arms around her body, clasping her hands on each shoulder. "I don't think it's a dream."

"Why not?" Keelyn asked.

"Because I see him when I'm awake."

Brett settled his hand against the wall as acid roiled in his gut. "What happens?"

"It's like I'm not me anymore. I'm in someone else's body. Her world."

Brett eyed the man at the recording equipment. "Some sort of flashback?"

The officer gave a contemplative nod. "Could be, I guess."

Keelyn's voice drew his eyes back. "Can you describe what the world changes to?"

Amy grabbed onto both sides of her chair, as if she sensed an earthquake coming. She began to kick her legs out, mimicking stationary swinging. "I'm running in a park. I don't even like running."

"Do you recognize where you are?" Vanhise asked.

"No." She tossed her hair over one shoulder. "That's what makes it all really weird. That it's not like it's me doing these things. It's like someone is taking my body and I'm just along for the ride."

Brett massaged the taut muscles in his neck.

"So, you're running in the park and then what happens?" Keelyn prompted.

"Something shoves me off the path. At first, I don't know what it is. It feels like what must happen to my brother when he plays football. He's a quarterback, you know."

"That's great. You watch his games?" Keelyn asked.

"All the time. It was just like that. He'll be getting ready to throw the ball and someone he can't see kind of sneaks up on him and takes him down."

"Can you see who it is? This person who pushes you off the path?"

Amy started to cry. "Not at first. It's like I get hit." She took her fist and popped it into her other palm. "And then I'm rolling. I'm so dizzy I want to throw up."

Joanna reached for Brett's elbow. "When that happens she'll literally fall down. It's almost like a seizure. She'll stop what she's doing, put her hands up to her head, and then crumble to the floor screaming. It breaks my heart to see her so terrified."

"Amy, what do you see when you're not dizzy anymore?" Keelyn asked.

Amy braced herself into the back of the chair. Her voice a whisper. "I can't say it out loud. Do I have to say it?"

Keelyn leaned forward and placed a hand on the girl's knee. "We're here to help you make sense of what's happening. We can only help if we know what you see."

She fidgeted in her seat and tears coursed down her face. Derrick handed her a tissue from a nearby box. "Amy, sweet child, you're safe here. Your mom is just outside. You're in a police station. All the people here would die before they ever let anything bad happen to you. Plus, that horrible man would have to get through Keelyn, and I know she's one tough cookie."

"What about you?" Amy asked Vanhise.

He leaned forward and wiped the tears from her eyes. "I'd be with you, hiding behind Keelyn, of course."

A faint smile. "You're silly."

He smiled back. "I know. This is hard stuff, and I'm glad you're willing to let us help you. Is there someone you see when you're not dizzy anymore?"

A moan escaped from her lips, and Brett's heart ached right along with it. It was the first moment he believed the girl might be telling the truth. He'd interviewed hundreds of criminals and probably a thousand victims in his tenure as a police officer. There was something unmistakable about a soul in trouble and how it expressed pain that it thought no other human being could survive. It came from deep inside . . . the center . . . the soul, some would say.

That's what it sounded like. Haunted. Spiritual. A cry for help from a soul in such distress it would rather die than continue to live through the trauma it faced.

Amy's sharp rasp of air into her chest focused his vision. "Please, don't make me."

Keelyn got off her chair and kneeled next to the girl. "Amy, you are safe here. It's going to be okay."

Her eyes bulged. "He's big. So much bigger than me, and he sits on top of me and he's so heavy that I can't breathe anymore." She gasped and reached for her throat. "He's got weird hair. Sharp and spiky like that guy on Food Network Channel."

Keelyn gently took Amy's hands and eased them back down to her lap. "Shhh . . . you're okay. It's okay."

"There are these things around his neck. Shiny squares that bounce the light into my eyes and now I can't breathe or see!"

"Okay—"

"I reach up and pull them off and grip them in my hand. I don't want to let them go. His thumbs squeeze my neck, and my chest is burning like it's on fire!" A scream peeled through the room, and Vanhise nearly left his seat at the sound.

Keelyn rubbed her hand over the child's back, then embraced her in a one-armed hug.

"And all I can hear is a girl singing, 'All you're ever gonna be is mean. Why you gotta be so mean?' and everything goes dark."

Brett's own lungs flamed at the last statement. He quickly leafed through his notes back to the interview with Zoe Martin's mother. *Yep, there it is.* For her birthday the day before, Zoe had gotten a new iPod. The only thing on her player the day she went running was an album by Taylor Swift.

He grabbed his phone and pulled up iTunes. Quickly searching for the name of the album mentioned in the report, he cued the most popular song titled *Mean*. One minute into the lyrics, Amy's statement was verified.

Now what do I do?

Joanna eased herself into a chair at hearing the words. "It's true. It's really true. She remembers what happened to that girl. Is she haunting her?"

"Does Amy like Taylor Swift? Has she ever heard her on the radio before?"

Joanna shook her head. "She's homeschooled. We don't listen to secular radio. She's only eight years old. She doesn't own any of her own albums. She doesn't have a phone, a music player . . . nothing! What is going on here? You believe what Amy is saying, right?"

Brett shrugged his shoulders. "I don't know. I don't know if I believe in ghosts, but I do know I'm headed back to the park."

"To look for what?"

"For whatever Zoe pulled off her attacker's neck."

Chapter 10

Early Afternoon, Wednesday, August 8

THE WARM METAL OF THE bleachers cut through the chill in Morgan's legs as she sat next to Tyler.

He covered her hand with his, fingering her wedding ring. She looked into his blue eyes, a shade darker than her green ones, and swept a few strands of dark brown hair from his forehead.

"Still cold?" he asked, tightening his free arm around her shoulders, a smile on his lips.

"Tired." She leaned her head into his chest.

He raised his arm and pointed to a figure in the distance. "See that guy over there?"

Morgan squinted. "Barely, why? Do you know him?"

"Hard to tell for sure at this distance, but I'd swear he's one of the men who participated in the research protocol. Scott. He was at the clinic a few months back."

"I thought most of them were overseas now."

"He's discharged from the military." Tyler shrugged and turned his attention back to the field in front of them. "I'm surprised you wanted to do this, considering you had dialysis this morning."

"I like to watch baseball."

Tyler nudged her with his shoulder. "You aren't very good at lying. And you hate baseball."

"I like to watch your nephew play."

"Our nephew."

Tyler was the youngest of seven children. All his older siblings, three each of boys and girls, had children of their own. For three months, Tyler's parents could boast a baker's dozen, but Teagan's death had brought them back to an even number. From the moment Morgan learned of her pregnancy, her mother-in-law had been concerned about the thirteenth grandchild. Morgan could relate to her apprehension, as she tended to lean toward the superstitious herself.

In the weeks following Teagan's death, an open wound festered a distance between her and Tyler. And now, considering her current state of health, it was doubtful that she'd be able to carry another pregnancy. Her love for Tyler was strong, but her will to hold their marriage together waned as illness sapped her strength. Did she even have the fortitude to stay alive? To stay on her treatment plan until the ultimate solution became available?

Near the dugout, she could see her brother- and sister-in-law waiting for Seth to come up to bat. A tall, lanky fourteen-year-old, her nephew swung the lathed stick to and fro and tapped his cleats one against the other as he approached home plate. Puffs of dust echoed from his shoes, playful in the breeze.

Tyler hugged her close to his side. "Game's almost over. You'll be able to rest when we get home."

"Need to stop by Mom and Dad's house first. They say they have news."

"Good news, I hope. Maybe they know if one of them is a match for you."

Morgan eyed Seth as he took a few practice swings. A dread set in her chest. *Why am I feeling this way?* When she got those tight fingers around her heart at work, she began to ready emergency equipment to ward off the grim reaper. She tried to shake the bad omen.

"Why not just tell me over the phone?" she grumbled.

"Want me to call them and see if you can stop by tomorrow instead?" He pulled her toward him, a clinical appraisal in his eyes. "You look awful. Are you sure you don't want to leave?"

"Thanks for trying to boost my ego." She looked back toward the field. "I just don't have a good feeling."

The first pitch was wide. *Ball one.*

"About what?" Tyler asked.

"About . . . anything."

The second pitch. A swing and a miss.

"Strike one!"

He fingered her long blond curls. "That's cryptic."

"Sometimes I think my illness is God's penalty."

"God is punishing you?"

"For not donating Teagan's organs." She felt the explosive exhalation of his breath against her cheek. Why did she have to ruin a perfectly fine day by dredging up one of their biggest conflicts? "I'm sorry. I know you don't want to talk about it."

His eyes drifted back to the baseball field. Cool fingers spread in her gut like worms writhing out of the dirt. Seth readied the bat. The pitcher wound up and hurtled the ball faster than Morgan imagined a teen could muster. Seth swung early. And the white projectile slammed into his chest.

The first thing to fall was the bat from Seth's hands.

Then a look of utter shock crossed his face, like a knife had been thrust and twisted into his heart.

Seth grabbed his chest.

Morgan was on her feet, scrambling down the rickety aluminum bleachers as Seth crumpled onto the hard-packed dirt. Tyler pushed her along with a heavy hand in the middle of her back.

The run onto the field drained the last bits of her strength. Her knees slid into the dirt as she neared Seth. Her sister-in-law was already at his side, wringing her son's hands within hers. Seth's coach and father stood a few steps back, seemingly perplexed by what had just occurred. Morgan gripped the boy's shoulders and shook him hard.

"Seth! Can you hear me?"

No response.

She slid shaky fingers into the groove between his Adam's apple and neck muscles.

No pulse.

Lord, please. We cannot take another child dying in our family.

She looked directly at the coach. "Do you have an AED?"

"A what?"

Morgan bit into her lip to stem what she wanted to say. "A machine that will shock his heart."

The man's eyes widened, a hint of the emergency at hand settled into his face.

"Where would I get one?"

"Call 911!" Morgan ordered. He felt his pockets for a cell phone. Coming up empty, he took two slow steps back before he turned and ran for the dugout. Seth's teammates hovered a few yards away. Other parents began pulling phones out.

"Tyler, help me."

Tyler dropped to his knees beside her. The baseball pitch that struck Seth's chest appeared to have come at the exact moment in his cardiac cycle when his ventricles were resting . . . recharging. During that vulnerable phase, a blow to the chest could cause chaotic electrical activity that overrode the heart's normal conduction system and arrested the heart's beating.

Morgan's nephew was clinically dead.

She stacked her hands, one over the other, and began to compress the center of his chest.

"What are you doing?" her sister-in-law screamed, her shrill question the only noise in the gathering crowd.

Bile clawed up Morgan's throat. Morgan looked up and tried to place a look of professional calm on her face. Emergencies were easier to handle when it wasn't your family.

"Lisa," she said, "Seth's heart has stopped. We need to do CPR until the paramedics get here."

"What?" She turned to her husband and he barely caught her as she caved into him. "Dave, she couldn't save her own child's life, and now she thinks she can save Seth? Get someone else to help him."

Tyler's eyes narrowed. He placed one hand on his knee to stand up. Morgan reached out and grabbed his pant leg. "Not now. I need you to do CPR. I'll do the breathing."

Dave grabbed Lisa by the shoulders and pulled her back. "Let her help! This is what she does."

It was everlasting minutes before the hint of sirens broke the stillness over the field. Tyler stopped another round of compressions; Morgan blew into Seth's mouth, and saw the rise of his chest as confirmation that his lungs had inflated. She eased her fingers to his neck again.

She shook her head at Tyler. He fisted up his hands and started again. "It's been over four minutes."

Of course Tyler couldn't leave his medical knowledge aside. As a transplant surgeon, his livelihood centered on incidents like this one where his patients waited for others to succumb from the effects of lack of blood flow to the brain. When blood flow stopped, neurons were injured. When cells were injured, they swelled. When they swelled, even if blood flow was reestablished, the pressure could be too high for the oxygen-hungry nerve center to be fed, and then it would be too late.

Brain death.

Lisa's sobs tore at Morgan's soul. Neither wanted to share the grief of a dead child.

"Tyler, we're his heartbeat. He's going to be okay."

Despite Morgan's response, the look from Tyler's blue eyes was not one of shared reassurance but of clinical certainty about the outcome. Morgan shook her head. "I've seen miracles. We don't know what will happen."

A team of two paramedics, followed by an additional two firefighters, ran onto the field.

"Hey, guys, I'm Drew. What happened?"

At first, Morgan couldn't take her eyes away from the line of tattoos normally covered by his flight suit that ran the length of both of his arms. He was one of Sacred Heart's new flight paramedics. *Must be moonlighting today.*

"He took a baseball to his chest and then he collapsed. We've been doing CPR."

"Man, you guys are amazing." He turned to his cohort. "Let's get the defibrillator ready."

Drew eased Tyler off Seth's chest. A quick flash of trauma scissors sliced up his baseball jersey. The other paramedic peeled the backing off the thick adhesive patches and put one on each side of Seth's chest. A firefighter edged Morgan away and began to assist Seth's breathing with a mask to his face.

The ECG tracing came up on the machine. Morgan's stomach plummeted. His heart was in a chaotic rhythm. Lisa's wails echoed the fine whine of the machine as it charged.

"Everyone clear."

Drew pressed the button. Seth's chest muscles jerked.

"Back to CPR. Let's get a line in. Chase, let's get a dose of epi ready."

Soon enough, IVs were placed in each of Seth's arms. Morgan grabbed the bag of IV solution as an extra set of hands while the EMS team continued to do CPR.

The proceeding two minutes seemed like two hours. A pause at the chest and another look at the monitor.

No change. No pulse.

Another shock. More CPR.

A dose of adrenaline through the IV line.

Morgan cleared her throat. "He's going to need amiodarone."

The paramedic lifted his eyes. "And you know that how?"

"I work at Sacred Heart in the PICU and I'm an ACLS instructor. You need to load him with amiodarone."

A cordial smile crossed Drew's lips—an effort to ease the tension. "Guess we haven't met yet. Don't worry, I know the protocol. Chase, let's get the drug out of the kit. Next break let's load it in."

Another two minutes.

Drew checked the monitor. "Still v-fib. Charge to 360 joules."

Morgan lost sight of Dave and Lisa. She began to pray. The words, once so commonplace and easily whispered, now like a foreign language on her lips. The distance between her and God larger than the one she suffered in her marriage.

How can I pray to an entity that is handing out punishment for my misdeeds?

She felt like a prisoner asking a jailor for mercy.

Morgan squeezed the fluid bags between her hands. The more fluid, the more it could aid the medication in reaching Seth's heart.

His chest leapt from the dirt again. A different man at the chest for compressions, followed by a syringe full of the antiarrhythmic drug into Seth's veins.

Lord, I know we haven't spoken over the last few months, but please, do not extend my punishment to Seth. Please, save his life. I know you are caring for Teagan. She does not need her cousin to be there with her.

The prayer did little to ease her fear about what the ultimate outcome would be. Tyler was on the phone.

Who is he talking to?

Drew placed a hand over the arms of the firefighter who was doing compressions. "Everyone stop. Let's see what we have."

A quick pause. The answer came at another charge of the defibrillator. Morgan looked away. A faint slap of noise as Seth's body came back into contact with the ground.

More CPR. Another two-minute segment before they would know if the drug to stabilize his heart rhythm had worked.

Another pause. The tattooed paramedic shielded the face of the monitor from the sun. "Looks like we have a normal sinus rhythm."

Morgan exhaled. "Is there a pulse?"

Drew nodded. A huge smile on his face.

"He's still not breathing," Chase said.

The smile faded a bit. "Let's get him intubated."

Tyler placed his phone in his back pocket. "He'll need to be transported to Sacred Heart. He fits the research protocol for hypothermia therapy after cardiac arrest. It's the best shot to save his brain."

Seth is going into my PICU?

Her sister-in-law shouted, "Absolutely not! That's the last place he should be."

Chapter 11

Late Afternoon, Wednesday, August 8

MORGAN PULLED UP TO her parents' place and parked the farthest to the left of their three-car garage.

Her childhood home had a lopsided appeal with the white car doors to one side and the main home on the right. The home's base was structured from river rock in tones of brown and gray. Above that was light, tawny stucco with chocolate-brown shutters flanking each of the windows. One large picture window framed her mother's waiting silhouette.

The door opened and Sally Meyer welcomed her as always, with a tight bear hug. "Where's Tyler?"

Morgan stepped over the threshold. "He's at Children's."

"Didn't you both have the day off? You were going to a baseball game." Her mother eased the door closed and waved Morgan to follow. "Sounds like you could use something to drink. I made a fresh batch of sweet tea."

Her mother busied herself gathering glasses, ice, and the pitcher of tea. This was by far Morgan's favorite spot in the house. Echoing the gray tones of the river rock in the front, the kitchen spanned hues of white to slate. Seating herself at the peppered black and ash granite island, she pulled a coaster toward her and awaited her mother's delectable concoction.

Sally was a self-taught, fabulous cook who'd experimented her way from charred grilled cheese to restaurant-quality dinners in the span of five years. A smile tugged at the corners of Morgan's lips as she thought back to her early years of food refusal and her mother's love expressed in every new dish she tried to add meat to Morgan's thin frame. The spicy vapors from chili smoldering on the stovetop were softened by the rising cornbread in the oven. The low hum from the electric ice-cream maker soothed Morgan's nerves as her stomach rumbled anxiously.

"Where's Dad?"

Her mother tucked a stray blond hair into her bun that was marbled with dove-colored strands. "Upstairs rummaging. He'll be down in a little bit. Gives us girls a chance to catch up."

Sally handed Morgan her drink. The cool, sweet liquid chased away the sand from the ballpark field that still coated her throat.

"You don't look good. How'd dialysis go?"

Morgan shrugged. "Same as always."

"Is there something you're not saying?"

Morgan couldn't bear to look in her mother's questioning eyes. "Dave and Lisa's son, Seth, is very sick."

She put her fingers to her lips. "What happened?"

"He arrested."

"As in, his heart stopped?"

Morgan sipped again, her own heartbeat slowing at the sorrow in her mother's eyes. She looked down. *If I fall into that well, I won't be able to climb out.* "He was hit in the chest by a baseball. It was quite a while before we could get his heart started again."

"Oh, Morgan. That's just awful! How is he?"

Morgan bit into her lip. "Alive. Tyler called a PICU intensivist that we work with. He's eligible for this research protocol where they cool the body down to spare the brain any damaging effects from not getting blood flow. They'll sedate him and keep him in a coma for a couple of days."

Her mother reached for her hand. "But why aren't you there?"

Morgan wiped a confessional tear from her eye. "You know my history with Lisa is not chummy."

Sally smoothed her hand over Morgan's arm. "Look, my instinct is always to protect you. It angers me how she blames you for Teagan's death."

"She has every reason to."

"That's ridiculous."

Morgan leaned back into the high white chair. "Teagan was shaken more than one time, Mom. There were three different-aged bleeds in her head."

She shooed Morgan's comment away with a wave of her hand. "I don't care. Why would you ever suspect that a good friend of yours was shaking your daughter?"

"I'm an expert in abusive head trauma. I was published."

"You were not Teagan's nurse, you were her mother."

"Exactly." Morgan pulled her eyes to the window. The bright, cheery day was a direct contrast to the darkness that smoldered within her. "Why did it never cross my mind that her symptoms could be abuse? I was the one who should have saved her life. Not because I'm a nurse but because I was her mother."

For the longest time they sat, Sally's hand soft on Morgan's knee.

Finally her mother grabbed the pitcher and refilled Morgan's glass. "I know you're thinking more about this because the three-month anniversary is coming up. Did you see that doctor I told you about?"

"The psychologist? No, I'm not ready."

"Maybe it's just the right time then. We should often do things when we're not ready because if we don't, we'll never get there. What you put off today you really have no intention of doing."

Is that a veiled reference to my absent church attendance?

Her parents' faith was a stalwart of their family, and Morgan had been raised in the tradition of those tenets. Unfortunately, her unanswered prayers to spare Teagan's life left her questioning how the God of love could take away what she loved most. In light of that, she'd practically abandoned the faith of her youth.

"Where is Dad?" she asked again. "Why hasn't he come down yet?"

Her mother's body sank deeper into her chair. She twirled her tumbler nervously on the smooth surface of the counter.

Come to think of it, Morgan noticed, *Mom's behavior is off today. Her hairstyle—up in a bun versus the loose, let-down curls. Her clothing rumpled when it is usually pressed.*

Her glass sans coaster.

Dad absent from this conversation.

"What's up with you?" Morgan finally asked, the pressure in her chest causing the words to stumble somewhat harshly.

"I'm not sure this is the best day to talk about this. Considering—"

"Mom, please. Is Dad all right?"

She swiveled her chair toward Morgan and gathered her daughter's hands. There was something in her mother's brown eyes. The darker brown flecks that normally comforted Morgan's spirit today lent to a feeling of spent exhaustion hiding something secret. Her eyes glossed over with the threat of coming emotion.

Uneasy tingles crawled up Morgan's spine. "Mom, are you all right?"

She squeezed their hands tighter until Morgan's nerves numbed under the tension. "Your father was tested to see if he could be a donor for you. He's not a match."

The tightness eased from Morgan's chest. "Okay, that's fine." She pulled her hands away. "Why all the drama? It's not that unexpected. I'll just have to wait my turn on the list."

Her mother shook her head, more hair falling from the loose bun. The look of a crazed mental health patient came to Morgan's mind.

"I have something to confess to you."

Morgan pushed back into her chair. The look on her mother's face stilled any words on her tongue.

Sally Meyer kneaded her hands, distraught. The only other time Morgan had seen her in such a state was when her aunt died, her mother's only sibling. Even Teagan's death hadn't risen to this level. "You know I love your father very much."

"Yes."

She placed a heavy hand on Morgan's cheek. "And he loves you. He would give you his heart if it would save your life."

Morgan pulled her hand down. "I know."

Her mother inhaled deeply. "Early in our marriage, we were having some trouble."

The distance between her and Tyler crossed her mind. Maybe their issues were present before but just intensified after Teagan's death. "Why are you bringing this up now?"

"I should also say I would have never told you this if my confession didn't bring up the possibility of saving your life. Your father is your father and always will be."

Morgan's mind raced. "What are you saying?"

"During this time when your father and I were having trouble, I had an affair. I got pregnant—with you."

"You're saying Dad is not my biological father?"

A plea for forgiveness bled from her mother's eyes. "I'm sorry."

Morgan grabbed at her shirt with her hand, her heart now thumping painfully. "Why would you keep this from me for so long?" she cried.

"What good would it have done to know?"

She slammed her hand onto the cold granite. "You're the one who always talks about speaking the truth."

Sally blew a stray hair from her eyes. "I know. I'm not perfect. I never claimed to be."

Morgan fanned her hand against her chest to calm her rapid heartbeat. "Does this other man even know that you had his child?"

She could merely close her eyes and shake her head no.

"How long has Dad known?"

Her mother took a heavy hand and back swiped the base of her nose. "Only after the tests came back."

"You kept this from him all these years?"

Morgan began to rise from the chair, but her mother clamped two hands on her knees. "You listen to me. I know you're confused and hurt."

"Try betrayed." Morgan seethed.

"This doesn't change what you have with the man upstairs. You are his child. He'll never leave you."

"But you denied me a relationship with my biological father. How could you even think to do that?"

"I know you may never understand my choice, but it was to spare you. To ensure you still had a happy home. My hope in telling you this is now you have another potential donor."

Morgan laughed out loud as the bitterness in her heart fought for release. "Mom, you're delusional. How exactly did this play out in your mind? I knock on his door, introduce myself as his long-lost, unwanted offspring and then ask if he'll offer up a blood sample or a cheek swab so someone can slice his back open and yank out a kidney to give to a daughter he's never known?"

Waves of hysteria began to wash over Morgan—second only to the moment when Teagan's heart tracing flatlined and she knew her baby girl was never coming back. Would she ever feel the same way about her family again?

"He was a selfish man."

Morgan came up off the chair, inches from her mother's face. "Perfect! Now you want me to ask a selfish man to donate his organ."

Her mother's hand came up to Morgan's chest. "You have every reason to be furious with me, but I am still your mother and I will not have you speak to me with such disdain." She pulled her hair from her eyes. "I came to find out he'd deserted a woman and her young daughter a few years before we met. His career, his discoveries were all that mattered. I was merely a side attraction."

"Who is he?"

"Thomas Reeves." Her voice suddenly went soft. "Dr. Thomas Reeves."

"As in the famed neuroscientist?"

"Yes."

"As in Tyler's boss?"

"Yes, the same man."

Then Morgan's mind traced back the conversation. Something tugged at her heartstrings. Something she desired to always have that had been a constant hole in her heart.

He left a woman and her young daughter.

Morgan swallowed. "Wait . . . I have a sister?"

Chapter 12

Evening, Wednesday, August 8

THE FORTY-FIVE-MINUTE drive to Vanhise's Boulder home gave Brett time to contemplate the known facts of his murder case. He drummed his fingers against the steering wheel, ticking the points off in his mind while the sun began to descend behind the Rockies.

Fact One: Amy Kent claimed to have memories of Zoe Martin's murderer.

Fact Two: Amy had given details that only the murder victim could have known. Taylor Swift playing on the iPod hadn't been released to the press. Brett believed Amy's mother when she claimed Amy didn't know anything of the popular singer.

Fact Three: He'd found a set of dog tags. Surely, these were the shiny rectangles Amy had referred to in her interview.

In the days since Amy's interview, Brett had trampled the ground of that park more days than he cared to admit. What was it about these young girls that drew him in so much? Zoe and Amy. One life tragically ended. Of course, it was his duty to find justice, to nail her assailant to the wall. Literal nailing was his preference, but he'd be happy to let the court ferret all that out.

Was it the fact that he'd divorced before he ever had children of his own? Normally, he wasn't touchy-feely about his life. But had he missed out on what family—a real, loving family—could offer?

He pulled into Vanhise's driveway, shut off the car, and made his way up the narrow walkway. Derrick opened the door before he knocked, patting him on the back as he ushered him inside. His decor wasn't quite the surf-skiing attire of his office but had a warm, lived-in feel. He eased the door closed behind him.

"I was surprised you'd want to visit, Detective Sawyer." Vanhise motioned him to follow.

"Please, call me Brett. No need to be so formal."

They walked a short distance to the kitchen. A small farmer's table sat to one side of the wall. Derrick lifted a pot of freshly brewed coffee from the counter and Brett gave a quick thumbs-up.

"Black?" Vanhise asked.

"How'd you guess?"

"You don't seem like the cream-and-sugar type."

Brett took a seat as Vanhise placed the cup in front of him. "It's not foo-foo coffee, is it? Someone tried to give me raspberry flavored once and I almost booked them into jail just for the shame of it. I hate that stuff."

"Simple, basic, Folgers."

"That's music to my ears." Brett lifted the steaming mug. "Cheers."

"Whisky?"

Brett smiled. "Not tonight. But I appreciate you being so thoughtful."

Vanhise stirred sugar into his cup and took a seat as well. "What brings you all this way? You were vague over the phone."

Brett pulled the evidence bag from his pocket and set it on the table. "These."

With one finger, Derrick pulled the plastic his way. "Dog tags?"

"They belong to a Dylan Worthy. I found them at Zoe's crime scene."

"The rectangles bouncing off the light she referred to in her interview. After all this time?"

"It took me a while."

"How can I help? Looks worth pursuing."

"Oh, absolutely, I'll be hot on Mr. Worthy's trail. But I wanted to ask you . . . do you think it's possible? Transferring memories between people?"

Vanhise eased back in his chair. "A doctor has to be open to things sometimes that don't have clear, concrete answers."

"So it is possible."

A gray-muzzled chocolate lab lumbered into the room, sidled up to Derrick, and laid his huge head on his leg.

"Do you like dogs?" Vanhise asked.

"Not a fan of animals really. A dog I could take. Cats . . . I don't go out of my way to provide assistance if they're up a tree. Just don't have the time to take care of them."

Vanhise motioned for the dog to lie down. The animal groaned displeasure. "Always wants a treat," he said. Vanhise patted his head a few times as he settled. "As to your question and the reason for your visit, I would say there's enough anecdotal evidence to consider that it is a real possibility. Memory is a funny thing. We don't really understand how the brain does it biologically, or even how young a person can be to form memories."

"Have you ever known a patient with such an experience?"

"To be truthful, I've taken Amy on as a patient."

"Is she the first person you've counseled with this kind of problem?"

"No, not really. I did counsel one particular patient who I believe formed memories in utero."

"What made you think that?"

"Well, when she was growing in her mother's womb, a medical error caused hypertonic saline to be infused into the uterus. As a result, she was born very prematurely. Her skin was horribly burned by the salty solution. She was hospitalized for months and continues to have chronic medical problems because of it." Vanhise sipped his coffee. "She and her mother began to see me when she started elementary school because she had suddenly developed an irrational fear of fire. I mean a horrible, paralyzing fear. Would dream of her skin being burned off. Well, in fact, she had suffered this injury, but no one ever thought she would have been old enough to retain any memory of it."

"So that's what you decided? She remembered the injury and it resulted in a paralyzing fear of fire. How is that possible?"

"Brain waves can be measured at eight weeks in a fetus, and the brain is fully formed by twelve weeks. Some theorize pain can be felt by this time. I dated a NICU nurse once during my residency. She'd been taking care of a baby with a femur fracture—obviously inflicted. Well, the baby would fuss and cry every time the mother's boyfriend came toward the Isolette. He ended up confessing that he caused the injury."

"The baby pointed the finger at his abuser?"

"The infant's reaction to this man became so remarkable to the nurses that they began to make notes every time it happened. There are lots of unexplained phenomenon in medicine, but if the brain is fully formed and functioning, why can't it process and store memories as well? Particularly traumatic ones?"

Brett tapped the table. "Has anything like that held up in court?"

"I don't know," Vanhise said, setting his cup down. "But if those dog tags ultimately reveal your criminal, I guess you'll find out."

Chapter 13

Morning, Thursday, August 9

TYLER PULLED ON HIS lab coat then sat at the bank of computers to check how the research subjects had progressed overnight. He could only stay an hour before he had to be back at Sacred Heart to check his pediatric cases. Considering how late he'd stayed there to sit with his sister, he'd let the finer activities of his morning routine fall to the wayside. He rubbed his hand over the stubble on his chin while he glanced through each patient's chart.

Concentrating proved difficult. How could he erase the vision of Seth, slack-jawed, a breathing tube snaked into his throat, the hiss and whine of machines keeping his shell alive?

Is that really what I think? That Seth isn't a part of his body anymore?

Tyler put his palms together, leaned forward, and closed his eyes.

Visions of Teagan coalesced behind his lids, her sweet face and extra-chubby cheeks. Perhaps not shaving today was more than lack of time, more like a subconscious attempt to remember his baby girl. His coarse whiskers tickling her feet would always bring bright smiles to her face. In fact, the first time she'd ever really smiled was when he rubbed her foot over his cheek after he'd skipped shaving one morning. It had been just the two of them. Morgan had been scheduled to work the weekend, leaving daddy alone with his new infant daughter.

He opened his eyes in hopes the bright overhead lights would flush out the vision. Moments when he allowed himself to dive into these memories never ended up with a good place to land. It was difficult to experience the good memories without the terrifying ones creeping in.

So much in him wanted to pray, to return to the place where he'd once felt comfort and solitude. The place he'd never thought he'd leave, especially in a moment of crisis. There'd been something of that in Morgan that drew him to her. Of course, her beauty struck the eye of most men, but there was this quiet peace about her that was like warm salve on an open wound. Her spirit expressed contentment and his life had never been calm until they were together.

Most of his childhood had been spent trying to get the attention of his parents amongst the clamor of his older siblings. He was used to running the race: achieving good grades to get scholarships for medical school and getting the best transplant internship. With Morgan, less of that began to matter, and he found that his relationship with her had eased his sense of wanting it all for himself.

Their daughter intensified it.

And then she was gone.

The words on the computer screen fuzzed before him, and he blinked several times to bring them into focus.

An unexpected sound of a man screaming demanded Tyler's sudden attention. A clamor of poles falling. Glass breaking. Tyler stood from his desk. A nurse ran by.

"Dr. Adams! We need help down here."

He ran down the hallway after her.

The scene in the room was a confusing blur of blue scrubs, arms and limbs flying. The nurses were wrestling with the writhing body of Brad Winters, a volunteer for the research protocol.

How did he get out of bed?

The patient's head was shaved, a half-moon-shaped incision down the left side of his skull. A row of staples gave it a railroad appearance. One nurse was on the floor, Brad's head cradled on her lap, as another held him up on his side and provided oxygen through a mask held inches from his face.

"What happened?" Tyler asked. He kneeled down onto the floor next to the battered crew.

Grace shook her bob of two-toned hair. "I don't know. He was seeing things I couldn't see. He complained about not being able to use his left arm. When I came closer to the bed, he jumped out and lunged at me. Then he started to seize."

Tyler placed two fingers on Brad's wrist. It was difficult to find his pulse under the movements of his uncontrolled muscle contractions. "Let's give a dose of Ativan for the seizure."

Seizures weren't uncommon among neurology patients. During his pediatric residency, epilepsy was a common condition he dealt with. What concerned Tyler was new onset seizure in a patient who just had a neural brain graft—one a high-priced security firm was paying for.

An additional nurse popped open a yellow tackle box. They kept this emergency kit for just such situations. After a quick tap of the syringe to push out the extra air bubbles, she grabbed the young man's hand and pushed the med through his IV line. She followed it with a quick flush of saline. A few additional moments and the tonic-clonic movements abated.

Tyler gathered Brad Winters in his arms and hoisted him back onto the bed. The nursing staff reattached his bedside monitor. The patient's vital signs looked stable. His oxygen level held despite the respiratory depression that the antiseizure medication could have caused. A quick check of his pupils confirmed they were equal and reactive to light.

"We're going to need to CT his head," Tyler said. "See if he's developed a postsurgical bleed." He turned to the nurse. "You think he was hallucinating, Grace?"

She shrugged. There was so much important information for a nurse to gather at the same time she provided emergency treatment for a patient. What body part did the seizure affect first? Was there any type of aura? If the seizure started in one part of the body, did it extend anywhere else? How long did the seizure last? Did the patient stop breathing? Change color?

Tyler knew the skill developed after years of providing care, and Grace was one of their younger additions. He clamped his mouth shut and waited. *Just allow her mind to mull through the events as they happened. My screaming at her will do little to help me gather the information I need.* Meanwhile, his mind reeled at the implication of what this seizure could mean for Brad.

"I don't know how to make sense of what happened. He's been fine all morning." She pulled herself off of the floor.

"Take your time."

"We were having a normal conversation about his family. It was like something came over him. This change washed over his face. He began to complain about his left arm. About how he couldn't move it anymore." Her eyes glistened under the harsh lights. "Then gibberish came out of his mouth. He looked horrified when he heard himself talk. I thought for sure he was having a stroke. I came closer to the bed and that's when he just came after me, like he wanted to hurt me. Then he started to seize and fell to the floor."

She rubbed her hand over his bald head, and Brad reached up with his left hand to shove it away.

"He seems to be using it now," Tyler noted.

"I'm not sure if he had use of it just before the seizure or not. I never got a chance to do an assessment."

"Let's get him in the scanner. See if we can determine a cause for the seizure."

"You know he's not the first patient to exhibit these symptoms." It was the nurse who'd drawn up the Ativan. She hovered at the door.

Kennedy. The charge nurse. Older. Wise. Seasoned.

"I know," Tyler said.

She pressed her pink frosted lips together. "Maybe it has something to do with the graft."

Tyler narrowed his eyes. He knew not everyone on staff agreed with the protocol. He wondered why some of them stayed, but in light of the bad economy, even nursing jobs were scarce.

"What are you saying exactly?"

Kennedy tucked her gray hair behind her ear. "I'm not saying anything. I'm making an observation. Other patients have had these types of symptoms. Complaints about not being able to use an extremity. Seizures. Hallucinations."

Tyler's nerves tingled. "Before we jump to conclusions about the protocol, let's see if it's a common postsurgical complication like bleeding. Can we do that?" Tyler hated to be dismissive, but he wasn't in the mood for an argument.

Kennedy pushed away from the wall. "I'll call radiology."

It was unusual for Tyler to let any clinical situation get his ire up. Perhaps it was concern for Seth that caused his laid-back demeanor to take the stance of a pit bull.

Or was it his own growing concern over the protocol itself?

He marched down the hall back to his workstation and entered the order for the scan. With this current patient's symptoms on his mind, he continued to read through the nurses' notes on several of the other protocol patients. Something was going on. Something he didn't understand.

Nightmares. Symptoms that mirrored post-traumatic stress.

He wouldn't find these symptoms unusual in a recruit who had served an active combat mission. Problem was, some of the men experiencing these symptoms hadn't ever been shot at, some hadn't even left the US to serve on the front lines. Dr. Tyler Adams let his clinical mind take over, sorting through all the unhappy possibilities.

It wasn't long before Lt. Colonel Markel crossed the desk in front of Tyler. His icy blue stare held Tyler's shocked gaze as he marched toward Dr. Reeves's office. It was hard to resist the urge to duck for cover. He neared Reeves's door and entered without knocking.

Surely Markel's not here because my patient suffered a seizure?

Though the words were muffled, the rise in voices behind Reeves's office door evidenced a heated exchange. Why would the highly decorated officer be angry? Particularly when the military wasn't directly involved in the protocol anymore? They'd been working through an intermediary, giving the government plausible deniability.

Another bang as the door flew inward against the wall. The colonel shot past, barely a look in Tyler's direction.

"Adams!"

Tyler rose from his chair and entered the luxurious space of Reeves's office. Lucrative security contracts could reap plenty of benefits, though Reeves had been a man of wealth before he'd hit the big time with the Department of Defense.

"Sir?"

"The next group. When will they be ready for training?"

"Three just had their surgeries. The other three aren't scheduled until next week."

"We need to think about moving up the next group's OR dates."

Tyler's heartbeat kicked up another notch. "Sir, I don't think that's a good idea. The graft recipients are having complications."

"Such as?"

"I'm not sure it's anything to worry about yet, but one seized this morning. A nurse mentioned that others have been having nightmares, nonuse of limbs—"

"You're going to let a bunch of nurses concern you?"

"Sir, their observations are relevant. They spend the most time with these patients. We don't want to send unstable men into the field."

"Who says we've done that?"

Tyler shook his head. "I've heard rumors that one of your first participants to get the matched graft killed a young girl."

Reeves tossed a hand in front of his face. "First off, his name never got out—not even to you. Second, he was kicked out of the military. Third, who says his actions, if verified, can be traced back to the graft?"

"I'm not saying they are, but it doesn't shed any positive light on what we're doing here. If any of these individuals are tied to criminal acts, it won't be long before the media starts to snoop and figures out what we've got going on here."

"The media and everyone else will cave when they realize what I've created. People will be standing in line and paying untold sums of money for this technology. They'll be fascinated by it. These patients will be heroes—real life superheroes."

"Do you think they'll want to be sick and famous?"

"Fame surpasses everything."

Tyler rubbed his palm hard over his chin.

His most difficult climb was overcoming Reeves's ego.

Chapter 14

SALLY MEYER STRAIGHTENED her clothes before she knocked on Thomas Reeves's door.

It had been just over twenty-eight years since they'd talked. Their brief, tumultuous affair had given her such a gift in Morgan, yet so much heartache.

In some aspects, she felt free and weightless. The burden of suspicion about Morgan's conception that she'd carried—hoped against—had been lifted in the most awful way. Once they'd learned her husband wasn't a match for Morgan, the possibility that there was another donor for her ailing daughter consumed her thoughts. Late one night, it was as if providence had spoken to her through a news report about home DNA test kits. She couldn't get past those thoughts, and it spurred her into acting to find out the truth.

Now she had to face the man. She had to see if he'd be willing to save her daughter's life.

Our daughter's life.

The clinic's receptionist had pointed her the right way. She knocked on the door to his office and waited for a response, hoping her son-in-law didn't breeze around the corner before she was allowed in. In the wake of her confession, Sally couldn't be sure Morgan had disclosed to Tyler the secret she had shared.

The door flung open, and the initial annoyed look melted into skeptical searching, followed by soft recognition.

"Sally?"

Not knowing the correct protocol for dropping in on a previous lover, Sally held out her hand. "Thomas, it's good to see you."

He took her hand, pulling her inside.

They both fumbled through the first introductory words of pleasantry.

He motioned her to a chair, and she kneaded her thumbs as she waited for him to seat himself.

"Sally, to say the least, it's a shock to see you here."

"Thomas, it really is amazing to see how far you've come. They say you've practically found a cure for post-traumatic stress disorder. All those lives you've helped."

He brushed his palms over his desk. "Well, I don't know that I would go so far as to say a cure. But an adequate treatment plan can go a long way to ease suffering. I didn't know you were following my research."

She settled her hands over the arms of the chair, trying not to grip them. "It's hard not to notice some of the media attention you've gotten for your success."

He brushed her comment off. "Been years since the news people cared to talk about me. And actually, I prefer it that way nowadays." There was an awkward silence. "It means a lot to me that you would stop by to give me your well wishes."

In his eyes, Sally could see there was something more he wanted to say, but he began to tap his teeth together instead. Something he always did when he wanted to avoid a conversation. Old mannerisms died hard.

"I don't know any easy way to say this, so I'm just going to put it out there. You have a daughter."

He seemed to melt with relief. "Of course. Lilly. Do you know her?"

Sally released the arms of the chair and brought her hands to her lap. "No, I should have said *we* have a daughter."

His eyes narrowed and he didn't speak for several long seconds.

"Why are you telling me this now? Are you here for money? I mean, it's been almost, what . . . thirty years? You can't honestly expect me to give you anything for an adult child."

Sally felt weak all over. She doubted she'd have the strength to storm from his office. *How can that be the first thing he asks about? Money!* Her assessment of his character, the rumors of his selfishness, they were all true.

"You misunderstand the purpose of my visit. Morgan is a wonderful girl. She works at Sacred Heart Children's Hospital. She's a charge nurse in the pediatric ICU. Has worked her entire nursing career to save kids."

Reeves leaned back in his chair. "That's great, Sally. But why tell me now if it isn't money you want?"

"She's sick."

"My work is pretty limited right now to the brain, and I'm more of a researcher. I don't really do primary care, but I can refer you—"

Sally held her hand up. "Can you please just stop and listen to me? Morgan needs a kidney transplant. None of her close family is a match. That's how I found out Morgan is your daughter. My husband turned up with an incompatible blood type. They said he and I together couldn't have had a child with Morgan's blood type."

At first, Sally couldn't understand the look in his eyes. It was as if she had spoken a foreign language; a look of confusion overwhelmed his features. He was wide-eyed; fearful even, his features held like a silent-movie scream.

Then he shook his head, the look of dread dissolving into frank astonishment. "I can't believe it. What they say about irony is true."

"What are you talking about? Will you see if you can help her?"

He placed his arms on his desktop and leaned forward. "You know I don't have the best track record. Our being together was out of loneliness. But what you don't know is I was the architect of my own misery. My daughter—Lilly Reeves. She's an emergency physician over at Blue Ridge."

"I'm sure she's a lovely—"

"Lilly sees me as responsible for her mother's death."

Sally's heartbeat kicked into overdrive.

"I did learn about them when I was pregnant with Morgan. That you'd left them."

"If only that was my most terrible sin." Reeves templed his hands. "Lilly's mother needed a kidney transplant. I was a match. To make a long story short, I refused to go through with the surgery. I left them because I didn't want to take care of a chronically ill wife and needy child."

Pain burst through Sally as though her chest were being split open. How could a doctor withhold a lifesaving measure—for his own wife?

"She was never able to find a donor. After years on dialysis, she didn't want to live that way anymore, and her depression fed into that. She gave up on treatments. Even with a daughter, she didn't have the will to live."

Sally bolted from her chair, nearly knocking it over. "How could you do such a thing? Leave a woman to die such a horrible death?"

He rubbed his hands over his face. "I deserve anything and everything you would say to me, but you don't have the right. You don't have any claim over my life. Trust me, I've felt the pain of that decision for years. Lilly and I are estranged. I've made some small steps to try to change that but we've got a long way to go."

"Maybe this would be a step in the right direction. Do what you should have done years ago. Just get tested . . . that's all I ask."

"Sally, though it was fine to see you again and hear of your news, this isn't something I can do. I'm under contract for a very complicated research protocol, and I simply cannot be laid out for surgery, even assuming I'm a match."

"How can you refuse? Put aside the fact that you are her biological father. What about the doctor in you? Don't you value life?"

He exhaled heavily. There was something he wanted to say. She could see the burden of confession pull his eyelids closed, a tortured look set into his face.

"Sally, if you knew me . . . really knew me, you would know that valuing life has nothing to do with my job. I wish you and your daughter the best."

Chapter 15

Early Afternoon, Thursday, August 9

SALLY KNEW THIS was a bad idea.

She had misgivings from the moment she pulled into the parking lot of Blue Ridge Medical Center. For several minutes, she sat in her car, battling the pros and cons.

After Thomas Reeves rejected her request, his revelation of his daughter's place of employment brought only one thought to her mind.

Maybe Lilly Reeves isn't as obstinate as her father.

Maybe she was a mother. Maybe she'd been gifted with compassion, even though that seemed to be genetically absent from her father.

The thought of Morgan's death finally propelled her from the car. She entered the emergency department and walked to the admissions desk. The clerk looked up from her computer. "Can I help you?"

How could she explain in a few simple words? "I'm here to see Dr. Lilly Reeves. I'm a friend of her father's. He sent me here."

How many lies will I tell to save Morgan's life?

"Sure. Let me see if she's busy. You might be in luck. It hasn't been too crazy today."

After a short phone conversation, the woman ushered her back into an examination room. At first, Sally sat on the paper-covered table, but it didn't take long for the annoying rustling under her fidgeting extremities to make her move to the chair. *What am I going to say exactly?* At least with Thomas, even though it was in the distant past, she had a relationship. An open door to at least begin the conversation. With this woman, there was no easy way to start. How much history should she give?

There was a soft knock.

"Come in," she called. Her voice sounded high and tight.

Lilly Reeves was striking. Long black hair. Deep blue eyes. She strode right in, held out her hand in a formal welcome. "Dr. Lilly Reeves. And you are?"

Sally let the woman's hand close over hers. "Sally." She cleared her throat. "Sally Meyer."

"Well, it's a pleasure to meet you, Ms. Meyer. What can I do for you today? The unit clerk said my father sent you?"

Lilly pulled a gray rolling stool that was housed under the counter to the center of the room and sat down, those piercing oceans of deep blue begging a confession from Sally's lips. Her mouth opened but no words spilled out. Shaking her head, she started again. "I did just come from seeing your father, but he didn't send me here. I came on my own accord."

The woman crossed her arms and edged back from Sally a little. "You're a friend of his?"

"*Was* a friend would be a better way to phrase our current relationship."

Silence hung in the room like an unwelcome friend. Why wasn't she saying anything?

"Are you a mother, Dr. Reeves?"

At the question, her lovely blue eyes darkened. A heavy sigh escaped her lips. "I never know how to answer that question."

Sally bit into her cheek. Lilly's response didn't shed any light on her situation, but sadness painted a haunted darkness to her voice.

Salty blood crossed Sally's tongue as she released the inside of her cheek from her teeth. "I'm sorry. There seems to be something painful there. I'm here because of something painful I've done."

Lilly slid her stool to the left and leaned against the wall. "Ms. Meyer, I'm sure you're one of the nicest women ever. But I'm not a psychiatrist and you haven't signed in as a patient. Is this a personal matter for which you really need a mental health professional?"

Sally clasped her hands together. How could she phrase the next sentence so the good doctor didn't unleash a troop of well-muscled men carrying a white straitjacket? Did they still use those? "Dr. Reeves, your father and I had an intimate relationship at one point in time."

Her eyebrows rose slightly then a professional coolness erased the hint of surprise. "Ms. Meyer, I'm not a priest either, but I can get someone from the chaplain's service to come and talk with you."

Dread sank its hooks into Sally's flesh. She was losing this woman, and the crazy house was certainly the next step.

"Dr. Reeves, the reason I asked if you were a mother is that I'm here to ask for your help in saving my daughter's life. I don't know if you've ever been at the point of desperation at saving a child who is close to you, but it's why I'm risking telling you something your father probably doesn't want you knowing."

Sally stilled, waiting for a response. For many moments, her eyes focused at some point on the wall, Lilly Reeves sat there, quiet—contemplative. What was it about her that pulled at the edges of Sally's memory? She'd visited this ER a couple of times but never remembered this woman caring for her.

Finally, she turned to Sally. "Okay. I'll hear you out. But only because I do know what it's like to have someone threaten a child close to me."

The swell of triumph nearly brought Sally's fist up in a chorus of alleluias. Now, for the next risky move. "Your father and I had a child together nearly thirty years ago."

"What?"

"A girl. Her name's Morgan Adams. She's a nurse."

"Here?"

"No, at Sacred Heart. She works in the pediatric ICU."

"You're saying this woman is my sister."

"Well, I guess half sister would be the correct term. But, yes."

"My father knew this for how long?"

"Honestly, I just told him today."

"Why after all these years?"

Sally settled her hands on her legs. "Denial, I guess. When I found out I was pregnant I silently hoped it was my husband's. We'd gone through a rough patch and I strayed. Timing was close enough I didn't really think to worry about it. After Morgan was born, my husband fell madly in love with her. In my heart, I knew he'd be the best father, even though it needled me to think he possibly was not her biological father. Why upset a happy home and childhood?"

Dr. Reeves tilted her face up ever so slightly. "Except that it ended up being a lie."

Of course, she's right. Morgan's anger is a testament to that.

"Yes . . . and I don't know if I can repair my relationship with Morgan," Sally said, "but I will try until my last day to prove to her how much I love her."

A posed smile set on Lilly's face. "I respect that. I can say that's something my own father has never made a priority."

"So, you're not close?"

"His selfishness put my mother in her grave. I've not forgiven him."

"I'm sorry to hear that."

"He never had to worry about taking responsibility for anything. My mother's sister took me in after that."

"I see."

Lilly hugged herself. "Enough about me. Water under the bridge as they say."

Was it, really? Her demeanor oozed the sense of weighted regret bound around her neck. To Sally it seemed she did want a relationship with her father.

"What does Morgan need to be saved from?" Dr. Reeves asked.

The sentence focused Sally's thoughts. "She's in kidney failure."

"I'm sorry to hear that."

"Neither my husband nor I are a match for a kidney transplant. When I learned that, I decided to find out for sure if the man Morgan knew as her father really was in the genetic sense. The test came back negative."

Lilly laughed out loud. Not a that's-hilarious type release but more like an if-you-only-knew-the-irony rupture. "So you went to my father asking for a kidney?"

"If I had known about his previous actions, I wouldn't have approached him. I never knew about what happened to your mother."

"Would it have made a difference?"

What was this? A character test? "What do you mean?"

"Would it have stopped you from having the affair?"

The hollowness in Sally's gut said no. Could she speak those honest words and still have the hope that Lilly would give permission for a drop of her blood to be tested to see if she could save Morgan's life?

"No, I would have done the same thing. Back in those days, I wasn't thinking about anyone but myself. And asking for your forgiveness now would seem like an insincere attempt to garner favor for my next request."

"Let me guess, my father declined to be tested."

"He did."

The lack of surprise on her face spoke volumes of the true distance between father and daughter. "And that's why you're here now? To ask me if I'll help? Because we're related?"

Sally folded her hands together. "Yes. It is why I'm here. I can't bear the thought of her giving up. Morgan's not had the easiest life of late. Being on dialysis has sapped her strength. After her baby girl's death, I think it's all becoming too much for her."

The vision of Morgan in a coffin brought tears from her eyes. Sally groped in her purse for Kleenex. Lilly stood and opened a cabinet and pulled out a small cardboard box. She tore away the perforated top and offered the box to Sally.

"Morgan lost a child?" Lilly asked.

Sally pulled a couple tissues free. "Yes, a daughter named Teagan."

Lilly slumped back onto the stool. "I know a little bit about that."

Again, that quiet haunted look took over. What was it about her that Sally should remember? "About losing a child?"

"Two, actually. They're not dead . . . they're just no longer mine. I gave them up for adoption."

The vividness of the memory struck Sally full force. Lilly Reeves was the woman who'd been hunted by one of the most maniacal serial rapists on record. Her story had been all over the news a few years back.

Lilly now pulled a tissue from the box and began to shred it between her fingers, some of the thin fibers floating to the floor seemingly as substitution for the tears she couldn't cry. Sally understood a barren well where unspoken despair was all that was left.

"I don't know what it is about ER rooms, but I've had the strangest experiences in them."

"Like what?" Sally asked.

Quietly, she rolled the remaining tissue into a ball. "I had a visitor once, at another institution. Of all things, he shared a story about when Adolf Hitler was a boy. About the angel of death saving his life."

"Seems counterintuitive . . . the grim reaper saving a life."

Lilly's eyes held hers. "Unless that one life is responsible for the death of millions."

Sally tipped her head, her mind stilled at the theoretical implications. Even death always wanted more.

"After that, I began to read heavily about Hitler's life to see if I could find a reference for this tale. I never did find absolute confirmation, but I did come across an interview with a Jewish woman who was working as a nurse during World War II." Lilly gathered up the bits of tissue that lay on the floor. "There was one night she was caring for a soldier who had pneumonia. In those days, treatment was limited. As a doctor was rounding on the patient, he made a comment that the young man was going to die by morning. Well, this young man overheard the doctor's statement and began to panic. The nurse went to his bedside. His one request of her was just to sit with him so he wouldn't die alone."

"Morgan often gets asked why she didn't become a doctor. That's really the main reason. Time with her patients."

Lilly smiled at the statement. "Well, this nurse sat with this soldier all night. Comforted him in his loneliness. Early the next day, just as the sun rose over the horizon, the man woke up. The nurse pulled the curtains aside, letting the sun fall on his face, and said to him, 'This is your sunrise. A gift has been given to you.'"

A soft knock pulled Lilly's attention to the door. A male figure motioned for her to come out. She held up a hand with five fingers.

She turned back to Sally. "The war progressed and things became very dicey for the Jewish people. German soldiers would block off both ends of a street in Jewish neighborhoods and go through the buildings room by room, gathering up people for imprisonment . . . or worse. She'd been hiding in a closet when she was discovered by a soldier who'd been sent to kill everyone in sight."

Sally's heart knocked against her rib cage as she imagined her daughter, a nurse, and what Morgan would do if her life were ever threatened in such a way.

Lilly's eyes widened. "The soldier yanked the nurse from her hiding place, drew his weapon, and held it to her head, his finger against the trigger, but his eyes searched over her face. After several moments, he holstered his weapon and said to her, 'I am the soldier you sat with all night. Now, I return the favor to you. This is your sunrise. Now go quickly. I'm setting you free.' It's a story that's always stuck with me. How one sacrificial act can spread like ripples over a calm surface and forever change what was common before."

Tears fell down Sally's face. "That really happened?"

Lilly stood from the stool. "Because another woman cared for my children and gave them a home when I couldn't, I will do this for you. I'll get tested to see if I'm a match for Morgan."

And with those words, she left Sally alone.

Chapter 16

Late Evening, Thursday, August 9

With a quick snap of his wrist, Dylan Worthy let the knife fly from his fingers and sink into the red center of the bull's-eye. The metal sinking into wood gave a satisfying groan. He grabbed another knife from the table and pulled it slowly through his fingers.

"I dare you to stand in front of it."

Scott Clarke pulled the weapon from the target and walked his direction, setting it down next to the others. "We have other things to discuss. Another round?"

Dylan nodded and motioned to the waitress. He began to place the hunting knives back into their carrying case. "You never enjoy the little things."

"Haven't you killed enough? Why keep practicing? You're not in the military anymore. Don't you think it's time to move on?"

He smiled. "Considering what we're planning, I think practice is still necessary."

"Why are you living in Grand Junction? Staying in Denver would make this a lot easier."

Dylan tied the leather strap and set the bundle next to him in the booth. "There are reasons I need a little distance between me and Denver right now. Plus, you don't have to be local to listen in on a wiretap. You heard about Brad?"

Scott eased into the booth on the opposite side as the waitress slid two mugs of beer onto the table. "I heard."

"Should I keep a tab running?" she asked, a voice that could only be smoothed out if bathed in oil.

Dylan gave her a contemptuous look. *Rode hard and put away wet would be a compliment for her looks.* Brittle, store-dyed copper hair. Vacant brown eyes. He guessed too much smoking and heroin were the main culprits behind her emaciated features and considered doing her a favor, ending her misery after she got off work. But he had other concerns at present, so he threw forty bucks on the table instead.

"Keep 'em coming until this runs out," he said.

Scott slid the drink his way and gulped a third of it before setting it down. "You must have something if you asked me to drive all the way out here."

Everything in him wanted to draw this conversation out—to absorb every nuance of the tortured look on his comrade's face. The urge for blood was becoming strong again. He brushed his fingers over his newest tattoo. "I have a way for you to bring Thomas Reeves to his knees. A way to bring the whole city to its knees."

"What did you find out?"

"He has a daughter."

"We already know that. Lilly Reeves. I decided not to go after her because of her cop husband."

Dylan leaned forward. "No, another daughter. Morgan. Morgan Adams."

"What's the benefit of going after her?"

"Because she's Dr. Tyler Adams's wife."

Scott's eyes widened. "You're serious?"

"I didn't just bug Reeves's office. I did Adams's home as well. I know for sure she's his daughter."

"And exactly how is this information going to crumble a city?"

Dylan smirked. "Know your enemy's greatest weakness."

"Which is why I don't see what you're so excited about. We know Reeves isn't a chummy family man. Another reason I decided not to go after Lilly. He's too driven. Work is his god. I like my plan better. Just blowing NeuroGenics up."

"Of course a munitions guy like you would want that. But we don't want to incinerate evidence either. If we're ever going to find out what's causing our trouble, we need that place intact."

"Then explain to me why this other daughter is so attractive to you," Scott said.

"For one, she works in a pediatric ICU."

"So?"

"We're going to take it hostage."

Scott slumped back in the booth, grabbed the other two-thirds of his beer, and drank it without breaking Dylan's gaze.

"I've already got Jose working on some interior photo shots. I'm monitoring dispatch. We'll need to disable the helipad so they can't come at us that way."

Scott tapped his empty beer mug in thought. Mission leaders always took too long to weigh all the odds. It was their supposed strength.

Dylan continued. "No one is going to be able to tolerate kids and nurses being held hostage. The media exposure will bring Reeves down."

"He's going to disclose top-secret research because of media pressure? Reeves is more worried about the government than the media. I already tried to leak some of his documents and that didn't work."

"You can't call conspiracy websites the media. People in power don't give any credit to those. Plus, who can understand all the scientific mumbo jumbo in those papers? It's not personal enough to people."

Scott broke Dylan's gaze.

Not tough enough to do the dirty work. Always been his problem.

"I'm stunned you don't see the brilliance," he said. "The pressure isn't just going to be on Reeves. You're forgetting about Dr. Adams. He won't be able to tolerate seeing his wife in danger. His sad, debilitated wife who needs a kidney transplant. He's the one that'll cave. He'll give us everything."

"You're talking about kids. Sick kids."

"Exactly."

"We're not going to get sympathy. We'll be viewed as more evil than the devil. Especially after Sandy Hook."

"Do you want it to stop? This research and what it's doing to us? This will put an end to it."

"But it's also going to end us. We might as well buy burial plots right now."

Chapter 17

TYLER FLIPPED ONTO HIS stomach, pulling the covers over his head, Morgan's news like a can of Red Bull. She'd taken a call from her mother—even though Morgan preferred distance because she didn't know how to handle all the emotions that came with the recent revelation. Reeves was her father. His mother-in-law had asked him for a kidney. He refused.

His pager toned. Another patient had seized and been rushed to CT.

The first patient's post-seizure scan had shown a mild bleed that could have precipitated that event. This time was different. The radiologist insisted that Tyler come personally to view the second scan. He had summoned Dr. Reeves as well.

Now Tyler knew for sure this night wasn't going to be a good one, particularly when the need for Reeves wasn't for his insight into the protocol but for his surgical skills.

And Tyler had to face him knowing he'd potentially denied saving Morgan's life.

The radiologist scrolled through the computer images, and Tyler's stomach ached as acid spilled into his gut. How could this have happened?

"It's a big mass," the radiologist said.

Reeves's hands were fisted at his sides. "A tumor? Somehow he developed a baseball-size tumor in the span of a few days? It's not medically possible."

The radiologist shrugged his shoulders. "His presurgical scans were clean."

Tyler's eyes hazed the black-and-white brain images into gray. "You're sure about that? Are you absolutely positive you didn't miss something that was there before?"

Reeves cut him in half with his glare. "Are you serious? A first-year medical student could clearly see a tumor that size in this young man's head. It's not exactly a subtle finding."

Now I'm the enemy?

Reeves shoved his hands deep into his lab coat. "We'll need to biopsy it. Schedule him for the OR first thing tomorrow morning."

The man turned on his heel. Every sane part of Tyler's mind begged him to keep his mouth closed, but his concern for the safety of his research participants pushed the words from his mouth. "Sir, what about the others?"

Reeves turned as if he'd been thumped on the back of the head. "What are you asking, exactly?"

Tyler clenched the patient's chart tighter. "Well, we know that this mass is where the graft was implanted."

"Your point?"

"This could be the graft . . . malfunctioning."

"A biological specimen doesn't malfunction. It's not a computer chip we put in the man's head. They are cells."

"Yes, but we know that immature cells have a way of misbehaving. They tend to wander and grow other places. Or they grow faster than the normal cells they're replacing. Other research using harvested cell lines have already shown this."

Reeves inhaled and held his breath, his face reddening. Then he released it audibly. "Although young, these were already neural cells. We didn't make them from scratch from fetal stem cells. What do you want me to do?"

"Until we know what's happened to this participant, I'd recommend we hold off on the other surgeries. No more grafts until we get this figured out."

Reeves closed the distance between them. "I liked you . . . in the beginning. But now you are losing sight of the game plan here. We have a contract to fulfill—"

"Respectfully, sir, it's not a contract to produce a certain number of viable specimens. It's a research study that has military implications funded by a private security firm. But you don't want that to get out, right? The military part . . . that's really who's using these men. All the other is just cover."

Reeves seethed. "Fortunately or otherwise, our first few subjects performed markedly well. More than any of us thought possible. In light of that, do you think we can just stop?" Reeves tapped at the screen images. "Right now, we don't know what that is. Everyone sees a big, white something in someone's head and automatically assumes the worst-case scenario. You and I both know that it could be a dozen other things, and I am not going to end a successful study on the assumption that we have a man with a malignant tumor in his head until I have solid facts."

Tyler stepped back and crossed his arms. "This finding isn't my only concern. The morale among the subjects is beginning to drop. It's not just this mass. Others have been suffering seizures, nightmares, and heightened sensitivity to noise. I alerted you to this."

"You said to not be concerned, yet. Plus, that could all be battle related."

"Except not all of the patients having these symtpoms have experienced battle, sir. For those who haven't, there would be no reason for them to experience symptoms that are akin to PTSD without having suffered a traumatic event."

"Well, maybe we just need to start them on the first drug I invented. See if that clears the issue up."

Tyler shook his head. "No, that operates outside the protocol. We can't do that. I'm just asking for a day. Let the pathologist type whatever this is and we'll move on from there. You don't want it to leak out that you willfully disregarded the health of these men, even if they volunteered for the surgery."

"Are you threatening me?" Reeves asked, his eyes narrowed, as he leaned into the gap between them.

Tyler held firm. "No sir, just trying to ensure nothing sullies your reputation for ensuring that the US military, or this private security firm, or whoever, retains the best fighting men there are worldwide."

The man eased back, his face softening. Ultimately, stroking the tiger by massaging his ego was the best medicine Tyler had found.

"Very well. We'll go with your plan. By the way, are you aware of the happy news?"

The words did little to ease Tyler's tension. Normally, when good news was shared, there wasn't a look of utter distaste plastered on the announcer's face.

"Sir?"

"About your dear wife, Morgan."

Cold spindles spread down Tyler's arms and he began to wonder if there was a threat of him turning up pleasantly missing someday. "Not sure what you're referring to."

"That I'm her father?"

"Yes, I did hear that piece of news."

"There's nothing you want to say to me?"

Tyler remained silent. These exchanges with Reeves could go either way. More often than not, they were bait at the mouth of a steel trap.

Reeves continued. "About my refusal to be tested as a donor?"

Cold vapor from the air-conditioning evaporated the tiny rivulets of worry that flowed down Tyler's neck. "It's a personal decision, sir. You need to do what's best for you."

Reeves twiddled his thumbs. "What if she dies? Will you still feel the same way?"

Could you loathe and respect a man at the same time? In Tyler's mind, one was beginning to outweigh the other. Had success and wealth eroded what little humanity Thomas Reeves had, if any?

"I hope that doesn't happen. We haven't exhausted all our options yet."

Tyler looked down, away from the intense glare Reeves used to annihilate others from questioning his actions. His rapid heartbeat measured the minutes and he looked up, trying to match the gaze.

"Are you happy?"

Reeves snorted at the question. "Of course."

"Really? Who is there for you at night? What do you do when you're alone? There isn't a single person you can turn to who hasn't bought your attention with the promise of some artificial, ego-boosting payment. Once you stop delivering the goods, they're out of your life, and when all this"—Tyler flung his arms wide—"begins to disappear . . . there won't be anyone to help you pick up the pieces."

"Even you, Tyler? You won't be there either?"

What was it about the change in his voice? A sadness at the realization of the truth Tyler spoke? Or a hardness that said Reeves was completely fine going it alone? He'd started from scratch before. Why not do it again?

Tyler squared his shoulders. "If you allow my wife to die when you had the power to save her . . . why would I offer a hand to help save you?"

Thomas Reeves said nothing as he walked away, leaving Tyler alone to grapple with his thoughts.

Is that truly the type of man I want to be?

The confrontation with Dr. Reeves had Tyler still seething when he left the NeuroGenics facility. He nearly jumped out of his shoes when he heard his name called from across the parking lot. He was even more shocked when Detective Sawyer began walking the distance between them.

Tyler faced him squarely. "Are you following me?"

Sawyer pushed his hands into his pockets. "I have a few questions for you."

"They can't wait until business hours? It's the middle of the night."

"You're a busy man, Dr. Adams. I have to take these opportunities as I can—especially when I'm trying to find a child murderer."

"I thought you were satisfied with my alibi."

The parking lot lights brightened the detective's face as he neared. "This visit isn't about you. It's about one of your research subjects."

"I'm not going to be able to discuss any part of that and you should know it. Unless you happen to have a warrant on your hands."

Sawyer stopped a few yards short of his position. "I think we can talk without your disclosing any private information. I'm looking for the whereabouts of a Dylan Worthy."

Why is that name familiar? Tyler adjusted his satchel to his other shoulder.

"I'm sorry . . . I don't know anyone by that name."

"Are you sure? Sources I've interviewed tie him to this institution."

And then it struck Tyler dead center. *Scott Clarke's mysterious friend.*

Detective Sawyer continued on. "Tied to whatever is going on here. They say he came to NeuroGenics for medical appointments. I believe that's why your name was found at the Zoe Martin crime scene. And why you use your Children's hospital cards with all your patients. You don't want anything to point this direction." Sawyer paused, apparently trying to gauge Tyler's reaction. "I can't imagine Sacred Heart is going to be very happy to hear about that. You using them as cover for something nefarious, I mean."

Tyler swallowed hard. "Why are you interested in finding this man?"

"I'm going to say this to you in confidence. We found a set of dog tags with Dylan Worthy's name on them. They are associated with the murder of Zoe Martin. I'm sure you don't want a child killer running lose, do you?"

"Of course not."

Sawyer nodded comfortably. Tyler turned away from him.

Did Dylan Worthy do this? Was Scott Clarke involved? And what will the media do when they found out Reeves might be creating murderers here at NeuroGenics?

Chapter 18

EVERYTHING ABOUT THE dialysis room at Blue Ridge Medical Center attempted, somewhat in vain, to make an unnatural process feel totally normal.

The room was painted off-white with lots of natural light from the open blinds. Cozy, cobalt-blue recliners were fashioned in a circle. Beside each chair sat a behemoth machine that replaced the function of her fist-sized kidneys that no longer worked. It was one thing that marveled Morgan about the human body; its utter efficiency when it was well, and how big the technological replacement was when it malfunctioned.

A ventilator for the lungs. An ECMO machine, which functioned as long-term bypass, to let the heart rest. A dialysis machine.

Was this how life was intended to be at the end?

Morgan's left arm rested on the cool vinyl. Two large needles accessed the fistula in her lower arm where a surgeon had cut into her flesh and used one of her veins as a conduit between an artery and another vein. It had taken time for the fistula to be able to withstand the pressure of the treatment, but for her, having a belly full of dialysis fluid and carrying it around for several hours only reminded her of the infant she had lost. And of those children she would never be able to carry.

From the large-bore metal needles, her blood coursed to and from the machine, the fine whine of the gears turning incessantly over the hours, sapping her strength as the natural hypnotic churning lulled her heavy eyelids closed. The more hours she was into the treatment, the heavier her eyelids became.

A drab cotton blanket draped over her legs. A two-week-old *People* magazine lay on her lap, opened to the latest news about whether Brangelina were or were not getting married. Whether she was pregnant. Was it twins again?

Morgan flipped the page. *Why does life come so easy for some people? Money. Fame. And why couldn't I do the one thing I know how to do best for my own daughter?*

Save her life.

A cacophony of raised voices drew her attention away from the recent plights of the various Kardashian sisters to the check-in desk of the dialysis unit. A woman in a full-length lab coat was arguing with the charge nurse. *A doctor-nurse disagreement*, she supposed.

Morgan smiled to herself and eased back, thankful not to be in the thick of a physician dispute. Some days, dialysis was worth it to stay out of the fray. Morgan sneaked another peek at the new doctor. *How does she keep the lint off that beautiful black dress? And stay comfortable in those high heels all day seeing patients?* Morgan needed flat-to-the-floor tennis shoes to keep her feet happy.

The voices grew louder—the conversation easily overheard by the patients.

The nurse's shoulders rose and she fisted her hand, holding it tight with the other as if to remind herself she was never to intentionally harm another individual.

"I don't care who you are," the nurse said. "You don't have unrestricted access to this unit and to the patients unless you have some direct reason to visit, like you're managing her case or are family!"

The woman edged back, slipped a finger through the loose waves of her hair and tucked them behind her ear. She turned Morgan's direction, her eyes as deep and bright a blue as Morgan had ever seen. Without turning back to the nurse she said, "I *am* family. I'm her sister."

A full inhalation caught in Morgan's chest. Not until her lungs begged for fresh air did she exhale in a ragged, shuddering staccato. Her pulse hammered in her ears. *Is it possible? This is my sister? Why come to see me? Why here?*

Morgan laid the magazine down on her lap and waved the nurse's direction. "It's okay. I asked her to be here."

The nurse swooped her hand Morgan's direction with all the flair of a put out maître d'.

The woman's heels tapped against the tile, a light clicking that drew several pairs of eyes Morgan's direction. What else was there to do but watch the action unfold? All Morgan could think to do was tug the blanket up over her head and hide. What kept her from tunneling under was just how starkly beautiful the woman was, pale skin tinged with a light pink hue to her cheeks. Her only makeup a hint of black mascara and red lipstick.

Just a few steps shy of her recliner, she stopped. "Morgan? Morgan Adams?"

Somehow she nodded. She was afraid her words would not come forth when her mind tasked her vocal cords with uttering them.

She held out her hand. "I'm Lilly Reeves. It's nice to meet you."

Morgan brought her free right hand up and Lilly clasped both her hands around it. She took a seat in the nearby wooden rocker, perching herself on the edge, her eyes searched every inch of Morgan's face.

In her chest, Morgan's heart buzzed like it had suddenly sprouted hummingbird's wings. Ever since her mother's confession, thoughts of this sister had consumed her mind. She even dreamed of her last night . . . of what she might look like. Would she like Morgan? Just tolerate her?

Could Lilly love her like she imagined a sister would?

Morgan eased her hand from Lilly's. The touch of her hands, the swollen sadness in her eyes, the pensive smile on her face pulled tears down Morgan's face.

Lilly reached to her and quickly wiped them away. "You're so beautiful. You have the prettiest eyes I've ever seen."

Morgan laughed, the tension easing from her chest. "Me? Have you been without a mirror?"

Lilly smiled in return and eased herself back into the rocker. "I'm afraid I have a confession to make. Once I learned your name from your mother and that you were getting dialysis, I searched medical records to see if you might be a patient here."

Morgan understood the implication. "I won't tell anyone of your little HIPAA violation."

"Trust me, I'm fine with the repercussions considering I did find you. This wasn't very nice of me sneaking up on you like this, but I figured you'd be trapped and couldn't run away."

Morgan sighed. "I wondered if this moment would happen."

Lilly leaned forward. "I want to know everything about you and your life." She reached over and fingered Morgan's wedding ring. "And about the man you married."

"How did you find out about me?" Morgan asked. "Your father?"

Sadness scrawled over Lilly's face. "No, certainly not. Thomas Reeves is not a man who's known for being forthright and honest. That's for sure."

Morgan pulled her lip between her teeth. Perhaps her mother had been right to protect her from having a relationship with such a man. After all, this woman, her sister, could barely hide her contempt.

Lilly shivered, her body shedding bad thoughts like a dog shaking off sewer water. "Your mother paid me a visit."

If she'd ever doubted her mother's love for her, this was the moment those thoughts died. Clearly, Sally had risked everything to approach Lilly. Considering what little Morgan knew of Thomas Reeves, Lilly didn't seem to be swooning over the father she herself hadn't grown up with. Morgan reconsidered her mother's position. Still, uncertainty tainted her willingness to forgive. Did she have to hide the truth? Wouldn't there have been some point to disclose who her real father was, even if there was a hint of a question? Wasn't knowing the truth always better?

In her awed silence, Lilly filled the void. "Your mother . . . she loves you very much."

Fresh tears welled in Morgan's eyes. "I know."

"Sally didn't explain much about how you ended up here. It's unusual for a woman your age to need a kidney transplant. I'm a doctor . . . don't know if you knew that. So, of course, I'm going to ask you all those inappropriate questions that should never be asked until at least the second visit."

What was it about Lilly Reeves that seemed so familiar? "I feel like I know you . . . like I've seen you somewhere before."

"I work here at Blue Ridge, in the emergency room. Used to be at Sage. Maybe you were a patient there at one time."

"Never."

Lilly smoothed her lips together. Her perfectly applied lipstick not crossing the boundary of her lips despite the motion. "I guess if I'm asking you to tell me the intimate details of your life, I can at least begin with one of my own." She folded her hands tightly against her stomach. "Only fair, right? Me being your older sister and all."

Those words, *older sister,* so foreign yet so full of meaning and possibility.

"My life was splashed across the news a few years back. The Drake Maguire case?"

Morgan nodded slowly as she pulled the story from her mind.

The serial rapist.

"I was one of his victims."

There was a brief silence between them and then Lilly reached out and clasped a hand over Morgan's.

"Now, what's this business all about?" She motioned to the medical equipment.

Morgan's throat swelled with thoughts of Teagan, how her illness would be worth every moment if her daughter were still alive. "I got sick when I was pregnant. HELLP syndrome. I developed kidney failure and there was no reversing it."

"I'm sorry."

"Did my mother tell you about my daughter? Teagan—" Morgan choked over her name, the tide of emotion suffocating her like she'd been shoved underwater, her blame the hand that held her under.

Lilly's eyes glistened. "Yes."

What had caused Morgan to immediately march down that path? Was it to test Lilly's resolve? Shove her away from a relationship because Morgan didn't plan on staying on planet earth that long?

Lilly held her hand tighter. "I know what you're doing. I've done it myself."

Morgan turned her eyes away. Lilly's hand over hers was too much, like a fire lit into the darkness that swallowed her soul. Her skin burned under Lilly's touch.

"I had a friend . . . a good friend . . . I tried to drive away because I thought I could handle my whole mess of a life better on my own. The man who attacked me murdered her." A sigh escaped her lips. "We can't hold ourselves responsible for others' actions. I felt for a long time I should have saved Dana's life." A tear rolled down her cheek. More echoed from Morgan's eyes. "I know as mothers we hold ourselves up on this pedestal of belief that we can prevent all the bad things from happening to our loved ones. It's just not true."

Lilly pulled a tissue from her pocket and dabbed Morgan's cheeks. One glance, then Morgan couldn't pull her gaze away. Lilly's face mirrored the prison of her own life. "At some point, we have to give it up and know that the reason for such things may never be known to us."

"I can't do it . . . get to that place of forgiveness."

"Forgiveness can be a hard road. Personally, the closer I am to God, the easier it's become. How about you? Do you have faith?"

Morgan rubbed the heel of her hand against the pain in her chest. "I did once—now I don't think I could ever have it again."

Chapter 19

THOMAS REEVES READ OVER the pathology report for the third time before he slapped it back down onto the table. Tyler's assessment of the situation was correct. The cells in the neuro graft were growing at an uncontrolled pace.

Early in Reeves's medical career, at medical school to be exact, he'd been surprised to learn what cancer really was. For most of his life, it had been the boogeyman in the closet. Both of his parents had died from the disease when he was fairly young. His mother from breast cancer and his father from a brain tumor.

And here he'd given a fit young man the disease he had once sworn to cure.

That pathology class had been a real eye-opener. All cancer was, in the end, was a cell that had lost control of itself. The reproductive mechanisms ran amok, dividing rapidly into a mass of nonfunctioning cells, crushing out the viable ones, preventing them from doing their work. At times, their havoc spread to distant areas of the body: *metastasis*. When that occurred, they grew wildly in other places and pushed those normal cells from completing their bodily duties.

One cell, the building block of every organ, gone awry.

Cells unhinged. Drunk with the power of a life without limitations.

And somehow it spoke to him on another level. What would that kind of life be like? One without boundaries? One without consequences?

Neural grafts were a new field. Previous physicians had attempted to use transplanted neural grafts in Alzheimer's and Parkinson's patients to see if it could cure those disease processes. Well, it had succeeded in abating some patient symptoms, but on a very small scale.

After his success in treating PTSD, the brain continued to be an ultimate fascination for him. How could he actually improve the organ, tinker with the biological supercomputer? He'd read autobiographies of people with picture-perfect memories. More than just photographic, they could remember things with such detail that it could supersede physical maps, plans, and tactical details.

Super soldiers.

Creating these men would garner military interest, he figured. Then he could live a life without limits. Military applications set everyone free. Once the power of a nuclear bomb was realized on the poor souls in Japan, everyone else feared one detonating on his territory and stayed in line.

Now, the perfect spy. The perfect soldier. Able to gather data without recording equipment. Memorize battle plans at the drop of a hat. And he could make that happen. He was sure of it.

At first, the government had shied away from the idea of actual brain surgery, but when he relayed the practical military applications, they were eager to get on board. Under the cover of another company, of course. No direct link between Reeves and the military for the media to sniff out.

But something now was horribly wrong with his life-limitless experiment. And if he didn't figure it out soon, his plush life of endless possibilities was going to evaporate before his eyes. He would likely end up with something worse. Revocation of his medical license was a definite possibility. Time in jail? He never wanted to see the inside of a cell again.

He glanced at the report and then out the window.

He'd *given* someone cancer.

The problem had to be the cells' genetic basis and not his doctoring of them. Young, immature cells were known to behave this way. It had happened in other studies. So, were more mature cells the answer? As much as he hated to admit it, adult cells did behave better, knew their limitations.

Was that the problem with a limitless life? There was ultimate destruction at the end? His mother, before her death, had talked about the Ten Commandants as the constraints that give you freedom because they keep you out of trouble.

He shook his head to dislodge the image of her wasting body from his mind. What did she know anyway?

But perhaps this is what those immature neural cells needed—a way to have limits put on their infantile behavior. Could mixing in some adult cells help?

But what adult would readily give up his brain cells, particularly if it meant he or she could die.

What's the way around that little problem, Thomas?

Chapter 20

Lilly Reeves knocked on her father's door.

She gathered the striking young man sitting at the nurses' station reviewing charts was Tyler Adams. From Morgan's description, it fit the man to a T. Brown hair with streaks of dark blond. Polarizing blue eyes. There was definitely something brewing behind them as he quickly leafed through the several notebooks stacked beside him.

Beneath her touch, the door opened, and the coolness of Reeves's inner sanctum drew her feet forward. He stepped back, a moment of shock and hidden amusement halting his pace before he beckoned her forward and closed the door behind her.

"Quite a surprise to have you visit me today. Are you going to sit or just stand and continue to look like you're going to claw my throat out?"

Lilly eased into the chair, crossed her legs, and settled her hands onto her lap. "You say you want to have a relationship, right? Did you plan on ever telling me about her?"

He brushed invisible particles from the desk blotter. "One, I've only known for a day. And two, what would the point of that have been?"

She tapped at her cheek as her eyes narrowed. "You don't think I'd be interested in knowing I have a sister?"

His eyebrows rose. "You want to meet her?"

"I already have." Lilly leaned forward. "She needs us. And you turn her mother away?"

"That surprises me."

"What?"

"That you'd want to have a relationship with her."

"Why?"

"Because the only part that relates her to you is my genetics."

"Maybe that's why . . . to see if there are any redeeming parts in your DNA."

He smiled but his eyes flared with subtle anger. "What brings you here today? Other than to question me about why I didn't immediately call about Morgan?"

Lilly intertwined her fingers and bent them backward until her knuckles popped under the movement. "Why do you refuse to get tested to see if you could be a match for her?"

He set his folded hands on the desk. "Why is it so important to you that I do? Surely, she'll have lots of possible donors."

"Her blood type is a rarer one."

"So?"

"I don't want to see her travel down the same path my mother did. I see it in her. She wants to give up. The life of living hooked up to a machine is too difficult. And her baby died. Murdered. It's not easy to get past that type of pain. Sometimes, it's easier to give up."

"You know what amazes me about the human body?"

The tension shortened the muscle fibers in Lilly's neck. She watched him stroke his brown-gray, speckled beard as he ruminated over sharing his years of overeducated wisdom. Thomas Reeves was brilliant, but sometimes keeping him on the straight and narrow path of a conversation proved difficult.

She didn't entertain him with a response.

"Neurons, your happy microscopic brain cells, are amazing engines, aren't they? Somehow, that gelatinous glob they form—the brain—sits in a liquid bath of spinal fluid and neurotransmitters form what we call memories."

"Is this going somewhere? I did go to medical school. I know how the brain functions."

"But, dear daughter, you didn't specialize in neurology. That's what's so amazing to me about this field I'm working in. How all this Jell-O in our head is the most intricate, speedy computer that was ever made."

Lilly tilted in her chair. "Like maybe it had a Creator?"

"Maybe, yes. At one time. But he's left it alone for millennia. Don't you think it's time to improve it?"

"What's your point exactly?"

"Sometimes the stories that surround transplant patients are scary.

Have you met your brother-in-law, Tyler, yet? The stories he could tell you are fascinating. Recipients developing cravings of things the donor loved. I mean, where would a young child develop a taste for one particular brand of beer her donor imbibed when not a drop of alcohol ever crossed her lips?"

"I don't know, Thomas. How would that happen?" Why not entertain the foolishness of his musings? Maybe she would learn something endearing if she stayed and listened long enough.

"Most shy away from these anecdotal reports, stating they're not scientific enough to hold any merit. No one knows for sure how something like this could happen. But we know that some patients experience these types of phenomena. They retain the memories of those from whom they've received organs. Heart transplant patients in particular. One boy developed a sudden love for Yankees baseball. Imagine his shock when he found out his donor was a former player on that team."

"What does this have to do with Morgan? With her situation? Can't you view it as a way to redeem your miserable life?"

"Don't you think I've done enough with my life to make up for that one mistake? Inventing a drug that nearly eliminates the symptoms of post-traumatic stress?"

Lilly looked toward the ceiling, a break from the intensity of his gaze. Why did his past actions have such an effect on her? Why did she allow it?

"You know what I think of your drug. It was a ruse for you to forget the painful things of your own history." She leveled her gaze back at him. "Surely you saw me standing there. In the middle of the street. Crying for you to come back."

He pulled down the sleeves of his shirt. A diamond cuff link shimmered in the light. "Perhaps you're right. My invention of the drug was to ease my own conscious of the wrongs I had done to you and your mother."

"This is what you would term *karma*, but what I would call God offering you a chance at having a real family life. If you do this for Morgan, it would do a lot to rebuild our relationship."

"You know why I won't get tested for Morgan? Because if she is a match, I would never give her my kidney. Because if I gave her that"—he tapped his forehead—"perhaps she'd become aware of all the secrets I keep."

"So?"

"If you think your half sister is suicidal now, imagine what she'd be like if she became privy to the things I know. It would be torture. You don't want me leading to another family death, do you? Wasn't your mother enough tragedy for one family?"

Lilly stood. "If you refuse to be tested to see if you can save her life, any hope you had at having a relationship with me is over."

Reeves pushed his fingers over his furrowed brow. "Haven't you forgiven me yet? What will it take exactly, Lilly?"

Lilly shoved her fists into her lab coat.

Isn't this the biggest part of the faith I now profess? Or is church just a check mark on my to-do list? How does my belief translate into action?

She couldn't do it. Not today.

"Get your blood drawn," she said, "or this will be our last conversation. Ever."

Chapter 21

Early Evening, Friday, August 10

Tyler sat parked in the garage of his house for several minutes. He'd spent most of the day at Sacred Heart performing surgeries. Then what was meant to be a short stop at NeuroGenics turned into an hour-long meeting. Reeves constantly challenged his proposed notions as to what was happening to their patients.

It all boiled down to something the man didn't want to accept. *We need to stop the protocol.* Too many subjects were having complications, life-threatening side effects like this newly found tumor. According to the pathology report, the mass was comprised of all their engineered cells— and it was going to cost this man his life.

They'd created cancer, one there was no known treatment for. They didn't know how it behaved. Would it even respond to conventional treatment?

Then there was his nephew, clinging to life like Han Solo in a refrigerated coffin. Were they saving Seth's life? Were they giving him a chance to return to the life he knew? Or was he just the victim of a new generation of scientists running amok with the human specimen?

Tyler knew in his gut that was a kind of doctor he didn't want to be. But how could he stop? The pay was amazing. With Morgan's condition deteriorating, she'd have to stop working at some point. They needed him to stay where he was.

Was it, in the end, beneficial to sell your soul to the devil for benefits delivered to the flesh?

He gathered his briefcase and patient files. Two quick steps up and he pushed through the door into their kitchen.

He stopped cold.

On top of their light, speckled, autumn-toned granite was a pool of blood dripping down the side of the white cabinet. A silver cutting knife dropped on their cherry-planked floor. It pointed toward a trail of blood that raced from the kitchen and up their back staircase. No evidence of meal preparation in sight.

Has she done it?

No . . . no . . . no . . .

Tyler's briefcase thudded to the floor. He shot up the flight of stairs and into their master bedroom. Blood pulsed at the tips of his fingers as he heard the crash of something against the shower door.

He tested the lock, found it stubborn in his grasp. He took three steps back and shouldered through the door. Wood splintered along the door-jamb as he tumbled through the entrance to find Morgan, his sweet wife, wrapping a fluffy white towel around her water sheathed body.

"Tyler!"

He raced to her and captured her, one arm around her back as his other hand raced up her neck and cupped a handful of tangled, wet curls. He drew her against him, the scent of citrus heavy in his nose. He relished every moment of it. Of her warmth against him. Of her heart beating rapidly against his. Of her breath panting softly on his shoulder. He could feel her muscles relax in his embrace and for the first time in a long time, she eased into him instead of pulling away.

Tears rushed from his eyes and he squeezed her tighter. He couldn't help it. What would he ever do if something happened to her? His mind still raced, half crazed from fear he would find her limp and never be able to bring her back.

Slowly, she raised her arms and her fingers massaged his back, hushing his distress with the firm motion of her hands.

He couldn't get her close enough. The water on her body soaked into his clothes. "You can't scare me like that again." He eased away and placed his hands on either side of her cheeks. He shook his head, trying to dispel the fright and anger so that all she could see was the depth of his love for her. "I'm *so* scared. You are killing me with this thoughtlessness you have for your life."

"You found the knife?"

"Yes, I found it! And blood dripping down the counter." He grabbed each of her hands and caressed his thumbs over her pulse points of uncut skin.

"It's not my blood."

"Then whose is it?"

"Our neighbor's. There was a package delivered here for her while she was working. She was so excited to open it she grabbed one of our knives from the butcher block and laid into it. Sliced right through the webbing of her thumb. I had stepped out of the room. I heard her screaming and came back to find her holding it out. Then she just freaked out and started reaching for me. There was blood all over my skin and clothes."

"And if I ask her?"

"You don't believe me?"

He combed his fingers through his hair. "Morgan, it's as if you're holding on to the cliff with one hand and lifting your fingers up one at a time."

She brushed past him and headed into the master bedroom. "I wouldn't have done anything today."

And just like that, all the tightness in his chest returned. "Just today? What makes today different from any other day?"

"Because I met my sister. I wouldn't want to do anything tragic on a day like this."

"But other days are wide open?"

She shrugged and his heart froze. He fisted his hands at her nonchalance. "Morgan, I'm this close"—he shoved his thumb and forefinger at her measuring off about a quarter of an inch—"to dragging your butt to the ER and having them put you on an M-1 hold."

Her green eyes filled with sadness as she sat on the edge of their bed. "You'd have me involuntarily committed?"

Tyler slumped beside her and took her hand, cupping her cheek with the other. "To save your life I would do anything. I just feel like this recklessness is a dare to God. That you don't think you need him anymore. And you're going to show it by seeing if he'll save you from yourself. To see if he'll show up this time."

Her lips quivered. "Tyler, I just can't make any promises right now. I'm trying every day to hold onto this life . . . but, I just want to find where Teagan's gone."

He kissed her fingers and squeezed her hand. "Maybe that's the problem. Both of our issues. We're holding on to Teagan too tightly. Maybe in order to live, we just need to let her go. Let go of the life we thought we were going to have. Surrender it all to the faith we once had. Maybe it's the only way we can have a strong marriage again."

"I'm sorry. I just can't."

Chapter 22

Night, Friday, August 10

THOMAS REEVES STARED OUT his window as the sun set over the Rockies. It always amazed him how the mountains looked when the sun dwindled in the sky. They almost resembled a child's construction project where the toddler had torn mountain shapes from different hues of blue and pasted them together against a dusky backdrop. It fascinated him how something so large and majestic could become diminished and two dimensional with just a change of light.

Lilly's visit had unnerved him. Was she worth enough to him to do as she asked, even though it was extortion? But then again, what was good for the goose, as they say.

His mind drifted toward the more pressing problem. Was the light going down on his career? These unexplained symptoms his subjects were having were strange at best.

It took years to find the right candidates, not only from a military perspective but from a donor one as well. The first few transplants of the young neural cells had shown the recipient could have reactions against the graft. That had resulted in his first few deaths. Of course, disclosing that would have shut him down right then and there, but he told the military the subjects had suffered a post-op brain bleed. Why give up money for something that could theoretically be fixed?

After that, he deduced that the donor and recipient had to be an HLA match. Just like any other transplant candidate. Which was why he added the family questionnaire to the potential prospects form. Why he recruited a transplant surgeon like Tyler. Someone young and hungry, with the expertise he needed but the wherewithal to keep his mouth closed if paid enough money.

Sill, finding donors was a huge obstacle.

Reeves reasoned women in distress wouldn't mind a monetary contribution to give him what he needed. When they presented for medical treatment at his newly opened clinic, he merely offered them compensation for what he asked. Unfortunately, it took hundreds of screenings to find the right one. Then an alternative crossed his mind. Why not increase his chances dramatically of ensuring a possible donor by looking for a relative? That should solve the pesky matching problem.

Scott was the first one to receive a perfect donor match. And the graft had performed miraculously. Everything Reeves dreamed came to fruition. Doctored neural cells could increase memory. Make it superior to what God—if you chose to call him that—created.

He'd heard once that God laughs when people name his laws after themselves. Well, was God laughing at Thomas Reeves now, or in awe of his work like everyone else?

The phone rang, drawing him out of his reverie.

A quick explanation from the clinic's charge nurse summarized the situation. The on-call doctor had fallen ill in the middle of a procedure. They were at risk of losing the donor unless someone filled in. Could Reeves come immediately?

Above all, he didn't want to lose the graft. Months of work and screening would go down the drain. Once the graft was obtained, it took several weeks to doctor the cells before he could transplant them. He bathed them in a mire of salt and sugar solution along with his special witch's brew. That would enable those neural cells to fuse into the recipient's brain by sinking their hungry tentacles into the patient's hippocampus.

He grabbed his lab coat and headed for the back stairs. Having an all-inclusive facility had been his plan from the beginning. It was less of a risk for the graft if his team harvested it, kept it in the same place, and then transplanted it a few weeks later.

Nearing the harvest suite, he knocked softly on the door and heard the permission of the lead clinic nurse to enter. He hadn't yet participated on this end of the protocol and couldn't say that he was all that anxious to do so now. Still, stardom, as well as science, necessitated sacrifice. Taking risks made a person rise from ordinary.

The patient appeared to be sleeping, but some trauma must have befallen her because normally the patient was awake during the retrieval process. Her face was red and blotchy, and thick black smudges down her cheeks alluded to makeup pulled down by tears. Another nurse held oxygen to her face. The quiet beeping of the patient's ECG monitor echoed her sedated heartbeat.

"Why is she unresponsive?" Reeves asked.

"We had to sedate her."

"What for?" Reeves unbuttoned his lab coat and laid it neatly on the Corian countertop.

"She caught sight of the ultrasound images. Was nearly up off the table before we could get the drug into her."

"She did consent for the procedure, correct?"

"Yes, absolutely. I have her signed form in the chart. Most don't want to see the images, but she became insistent. Then hysterical."

Reeves pulled the ultrasound machine closer and made a few sweeping passes over the patient's belly with the transducer. "What in heaven's name went on in here? The specimen's left arm is clean off. The blood in the cavity is making it hard to see."

The nurse looked at him, her eyes wide at his dismay. Not a look of abject horror but incredulousness over his comment. "It's not unusual for that to happen when we're trying to get to the part that you want."

He positioned the transducer and introduced the surgical element into the amniotic sack near the base of the donor's skull. Suddenly, there was a flash of movement across the screen.

The donor had repositioned itself and was now grasping his instrument with the hand that remained.

Acid clawed up Reeves's throat.

It's not possible.

In response to the vacuous hole in his gut that seemed to be yanking his intestines into it, his face broke out in a sweat. He blinked rapidly against the image and pulled the metal sheath out and set it aside, wiping his forehead with the back of his gloved hand.

He swallowed heavily against the bile his stomach was now forcing up his esophagus.

"Dr. Reeves, are you okay?"

He closed his eyes and inhaled deeply. He nodded in the affirmative against what his thoughts were telling him. Against what his scientific, logical mind refused to accept as his heart screamed in terror.

Localizing pain was a higher brain function. Something they looked for in trauma patients to know if they were lightening neurologically. Physically crossing the midline of the body to remove a painful stimulus, actually latching on to it, meant more than just the brain stem lived. The brain's cortex was alive. The part of the brain that science claimed was the cell layer that gave a person their *humanness.*

"Dr. Reeves, we better finish. You'll lose the graft if the donor bleeds out."

"Of course."

Reeves introduced the sheath again and adjusted the angle on the transducer. Aiming the instrument at the base of the neck, he drew it back to puncture the base of the skull. The donor rolled *toward* it, and again, with its available hand, tried to *push* it away.

Reeves stood quickly, knocking over the gray stool as he threw the sonogram transducer onto the machine, thick warm gel splattering up to the screen, and again he set the instrument aside.

He then turned and vomited into the sink.

Chapter 23

THERE WAS SOMETHING frightening about the beginning of that day. Morgan Adams perceived it in her spirit—a rift between the peacefulness she longed to experience once again and the unsteady undercurrent that disturbed her heart. It began the moment she buckled her seatbelt to drive to work.

It was a palpable warning, a portend of what the next twelve hours would bring, like being alerted to road conditions on a hazardous weather day.

Today would be wrought with black ice. Some would navigate hairpin turns well. Others would pitch over the guardrail and land impaled on pine trees.

Her gut ached. *Maybe I'm coming down with something.* Morgan traced her fingers over the face of her cell phone where it sat in her cup holder. She contemplated the wisdom of calling in sick thirty minutes before her shift was scheduled to begin—especially since she was today's charge nurse.

She backed out of the garage but stopped her vehicle in the driveway and watched the heavy door clunk down the tracks. When it settled, angry caws of black-bodied crows smothered the joyful chirping of chickadees as they fluttered about the trees. Morgan gripped the steering wheel and briefly considered pulling her car back into the garage, closing the door behind her, and leaving the engine running.

If her husband had not still been asleep, she might have been too weak to deny the attractiveness of that option. Surely, all this trepidation was related to it being the anniversary of *that* day. Three months since her daughter died. The face of her phone brightened as it displayed a text from her mother. Tensions were still high between them.

You have to go to work.

A statement. Not a question. Even in their disagreement, did her mother sense her weary heart? Had Morgan's pain pulled her mother from the comfort of her bed hours before she normally rose?

Why? What are you doing up so early?

For Seth. He'll need you today.

Why today?

Morgan's body felt heavy with the thought of surviving the next thirteen hours. Her short, clipped, unpainted nail clicked against the phone's frame.

She texted back. *Lisa doesn't trust me. She thinks I'll hurt him.*

The cursor blinked back in mocking silence.

Morgan, please. Go. It will help to be where she was.

Her heartbeat touched up a notch as her fingers tingled against the cool glass. Strange. Her mother was usually the one to support her feelings and let her cave in to the depression when it overtook her. Better to rest than push it, particularly when Morgan was ill herself. She tightened her right hand over her left lower forearm and felt the pulsatile flow of her blood as it rushed through her dialysis shunt.

Morgan?

Gritting her teeth, she jabbed at the phone's face. *I'm going!*

Those first moments of walking into the pediatric ICU heightened the dread in her soul. There was a flow of energy that came from a mingling of wounded souls that would speak right to her nurse's intuition, whispering soft secrets of which child threatened to sever the binds of the physical body to pursue the freedom of the ethereal one.

That's how it felt as soon as she swiped her badge over the access reader and crossed the threshold into the secured unit.

Someone was about to die.

After she entered the staff lounge, Morgan plopped her heavy tote on the table, remnants from the night shift dinner break still present. She grabbed the empty food containers and stuffed them into the overflowing trash can. From her bag she pulled a set of scissors and hemostats, two black pens, and a calculator for determining drug dosages.

Morgan secured her bag in her locker and made her way to the nurses' station. The night charge nurse, Phillip, approached her. She looked over the counter to the wide space that held the unit's twenty beds.

"Man, I'm glad you're here."

His normally combed, sandy-blond locks stuck up in tufts of pulled anxiety.

Looks like last night was stressful.

"What's happening?" Morgan asked out loud.

"Well, for one, we got two admissions. A thirteen-year-old female, victim in a motor vehicle collision. Bad head injury. She was the only survivor and right now she's just hanging on. ICPs have been high so they put her in a pentobarb coma. And we had to intubate an eighteen-year-old male. Asthmatic."

"That's never good," Morgan added.

"Don't I know it. He's already popped a lung. So chest tube, vent . . . medically paralyzed and sedated."

When Morgan had left the unit a couple of days ago, they'd had two patients.

"How's Seth?"

He shrugged his shoulders. "Hangin' in there. They plan on bringing him out of the hypothermia today. We've been weaning down his sedation through the night. The problem child has been the one you affectionately call *little miss sweetheart*. Bree."

Morgan's heart skipped a few beats. "What happened?"

"She looks a lot worse. Cap refill is bad. Blood pressure kept falling through the night. Had to go up on her vasopressors. Cardiology is worried she won't make it to transplant."

Morgan grabbed either end of her stethoscope with her hands and pulled the tubing into her taut neck muscles. "Why not? She's not even on a vent yet."

"Won't be long until she is. It's her blood type and her size that are the problem. She has the rarest kind and she's barely twenty-four months. An adult heart is not going to fit into her chest."

Morgan's stomach sank. Though she knew the truth, hearing it was like setting it in a granite marker. The uphill climb for families as they waited for organs was emotionally draining. She knew that from experience.

Eyeing Seth's corner of the unit, she was relieved that her sister-in-law hadn't arrived yet. "Who's on today?"

"Lucy, Trudy, and Izabel."

A decent mix.

Trudy was a seasoned nurse. That meant she was knowledgeable, but at times set in her ways—something that often annoyed her much younger coworkers. "Okay, let's close the unit and start report. Get this day going."

From the bank of windows that faced the nurses' station, two police cars at the main entrance caught Morgan's eye. The hospital was L-shaped, so from the PICU's end position on the seventh floor, it gave easy view of the front drive. A police presence wasn't unusual except that it was early in the morning, there was more than one car, and they weren't in the ambulance bay, where they were more prone to park. Usually at this hour people were already under arrest, in lock-up, and sleeping off the previous night's misguided activities.

Phillip laid a comforting hand on her shoulder. "How are you feeling today?"

"I'm not sure how much longer I'll be able to do twelve-hour shifts. Dialysis really takes it out of me."

His hazel eyes softened, glossy. "No, I meant the other."

Her throat swelled at the sudden threat of tears. Phillip had been the one caring for Teagan when she came off life support.

His hand fell from her arm. "I'm sorry. I shouldn't have asked. It's just that I think about her, too."

Morgan swiped escaped tears from her cheeks. In her selfish hold of her grief, she rarely considered how Teagan's death affected others. Her husband included.

Before Teagan died, the high rate of divorce after a child's death rarely crossed her mind. Little was known to the staff of a family's welfare after a child passed. Families didn't return to the scene, and healthcare privacy laws stymied the nurses from getting follow-up information unless they had directly provided care to the patient.

Morgan hugged him. "I know. I forget that, but I never forget how amazing you were with her."

He eased her back, his eyes searching hers. "Morgan, why do you still work here? Isn't it awful to look at her bedspace and be reminded of her death every shift?"

Phillip possessed one of the most aggravating character traits of ICU nurses—blunt confrontation. His probing was like a scalpel to her heart.

That was the question, wasn't it? Was it a form of self-torture, or a hope that during some part of the day she might feel Teagan's spirit whisper a kiss on her cheek? A lips-parted, full-of-baby-slobber kind of kiss.

"I haven't figured it out yet. Something pulls at me to be here."

"Teagan?"

Morgan gave a halfhearted smile. "Of course I should say yes. But, no, something different. I can't explain it. An unfulfilled need. Like I haven't accomplished the thing I'm supposed to do yet."

Phillip smiled back. "Well, let me know when that happens. Surely, there's got to be happier areas of nursing."

"Are you thinking of leaving?"

He sighed. "Not today. I don't know about tomorrow."

Morgan noticed three police cruisers at the front entrance now. *Maybe there's a gunshot victim in the ER, and the back lot has run out of space?*

Excluding visitors from report time was meant to afford patient privacy, since the open unit allowed conversations to be overheard. After Phillip's charge nurse report, she returned to the staff lounge where her team of three nurses awaited their assignments. Typical ICU patient load was two patients per nurse. This left Morgan open to take the first admission. Once she divided the children among them, they would go to the bedside and receive report from the night-shift nurse.

The whole process generally took thirty minutes.

While the staff gave report, Morgan made the rounds to each child's bed. It was part of the process of being a charge nurse, at least her process. Getting a visual on each child to get her own impression of their current condition. Which one dangled precariously on the ledge with his or her life?

She approached Bree's crib and lowered the yellow metal rail so she could reach her. ICU cribs resembled tiny prisons more than comforting places to slumber. They were designed to keep children from climbing out, and had transparent sheeting that dropped down from all four sides to prevent curious minds from going over the top. Due to Bree's sickened heart, she didn't have the strength to attempt escape, and her upper safety components were left in the raised position.

The toddler reached up for Morgan's index finger, her grip weak as the tiny fingers encircled her larger one. "Hey, little miss sweetheart," Morgan cooed. "How you feelin' today?"

With her free hand, Morgan swept the moist, chocolate curls from Bree's face and looked into her big, sorrowful brown eyes. Even at rest, her heart worked in overdrive to keep her alive. Being symptomatic during little activity was a sign her heart could give up at any moment. She leaned down to kiss the tiny girl's fingers, the blue hue and clubbed tips another sign of her failing organ. The child suffered from dilated cardiomyopathy, which meant her heart was huge and weak and would eventually cease beating.

The question was when.

She slid her finger down the girl's nose. "There's no dying today. Promise me?"

Morgan tried to ease a toy into her hands. Bree dropped her hand back to the bed and closed her eyes. After pulling her gown up, Morgan examined her work of breathing. Normally, a child's torso was quiet. However, with each breath, the skin between Bree's ribs pulled in, revealing the skeletal outline of her chest. Even her heartbeat was prominent to the left side where the enlarged left ventricle pushed against its protective housing. With a stethoscope at her chest, Morgan heard the distinctive crackles that proved her lungs were filling up with fluid, another sign that her heart wasn't contracting with a lot of strength.

Morgan placed gentle fingers over the girl's puffed cheeks. "Need to ask the doctor if some Lasix would be a good idea for you. Dry those lungs out a little." She eyed the oxygen flow meter. Up to three liters. She needed to transition to an oxygen mask from the nasal cannula.

Lisa's voice carried through the unit before Morgan heard the clicking of her high heels against the tile. Time to check on her nephew.

Chapter 24

MORGAN APPROACHED SETH's bedside, holding the bell of her stethoscope and the ear pieces together in front of her chest, a shield against what might pop from Lisa's mouth. When she neared, she placed her free hand on his bedrail. Lucy, Seth's bedside nurse, was busy at the next bedspace assessing a two-month-old infant with meningitis who had been extubated through the night.

The pressure waveforms on Seth's monitor told a tale of a body at quiet rest. Each color represented a different parameter. The cool blue sloped waveform his oxygen level. The spiked, steady viridian green his heart's electrical conduction. The square white hills how much carbon dioxide he exhaled.

"How was his night?" Lisa asked, her voice low but sharp. That steely edge echoed everything about her sister-in-law. Her dyed, platinum hair pulled tight in a ponytail. The black eyeliner heavy on both upper and lower eyelids stark against the light blue eye shadow and garish red lips. A white blouse tucked into a wrinkle-free gray skirt with knee-high black leather boots.

Morgan had always admired Lisa's fashion sense but marveled at how she could keep it going with her son critically ill. During Teagan's stay, Morgan hadn't strayed far from a comfortable set of holey sweats.

A tired ache spread through Morgan's chest.

"He did well," she replied. "They've been decreasing his sedation through the night. The plan is to warm him back up slowly through the day and then turn off the sedation."

Lisa's blue eyes captured her, the vulnerable fear struck right at Morgan's core. "Do you think he'll wake up?"

Morgan swallowed hard, her own grief mirrored in the sadness of her sister-in-law's face. The motherly anxious trepidation of wanting to know if the treatment had worked paired with the weighted dread of what it meant if the medical efforts failed.

"I hope so." Morgan reached out and ran her fingers through Seth's towhead locks, the silky threads almost as white as the starched pillowcase they rested on. The night nurse had spent time washing his hair—a difficult feat with a person in a medically induced coma.

"I didn't ask you what you hope. I asked you what you think."

Morgan inhaled and held her breath to stem the flood of adrenaline. Lisa's anxiety shot over Seth's bed like electrified harpoon darts tagging her skin. The flesh on her arms rose as the confrontational nature of Lisa's glare fed into her body's defense. She pulled her hand from Seth and gripped the side rail with both hands.

"Lisa, though I appreciate you asking my opinion, I don't know what to expect. My prayer is that he will wake up. What I know is that the research protocol Dr. Marshall put him on is the best chance he'll have at sparing his brain from the effects of his arrest."

Lisa leaned over the bed in Morgan's direction. "Talk to me like a mother!"

Morgan edged back from Seth's bed. She clasped her hand over the bell of her stethoscope as her mind sifted through several options.

Parental outbursts were not unusual in the PICU. Stress caused normal societal mores to fall away. When a child hovered over the cavern of life and death, all bets were off. Normally, she would round the bedside and offer tactile comfort. Sometimes the physical touch of another human being was what was needed to diffuse the situation. In response, the parent would often dissolve into uncontrolled crying, the outburst a substitute for the fear of having to make funeral plans.

However, Morgan checked that option with Lisa's icy stare.

"I'm sorry" was all Morgan could say.

"You're sorry? That's all you've got for me? What does that even mean?"

Having grown up as a single child, Morgan thought joining Tyler's happy family of so many married couples would afford her the sisterhood she longed to have. But none of them understood her, and her relatability to Tyler's clan had always been hard to come by. Especially with Lisa.

"Just what I said. I'm sorry that you're going through this. When Teagan was sick . . ."

The syllables of her child's name as they crossed her lips caused the words to stick in her throat. The charge nurse pager vibrated at her hip. She turned without a word and went back to the nurses' station. As she passed the windows on the way, she noticed more police cars at the front entrance. Even Lisa's eyes were captivated by the action.

She dialed the number. "This is Morgan. Someone paged me."

A harried voice punctured her ear. "Morgan, thank heavens you're in charge."

The nursing supervisor.

"Kathleen, what's going on?"

"I need nurses with a level head today. Have you looked outside?"

"The cop cars? Why are there so many?"

"There have been reports of three men roaming the hospital. They might be military types."

"Why is this causing concern? We're right next to a military hospital."

"One person thought they might be carrying weapons."

Morgan pulled over a chair and sat down. "Kathleen, it's too early for this kind of paranoia."

"Morgan, it's serious. Clarence was found barely alive. Gunshot wound to the chest. They're trying to stabilize him in the ER right now."

A vision of the older security guard came to her mind, his kindness well known throughout the hospital. Always a smile on his face. Even during the dark times, he was that little ray of sunshine.

Morgan blinked as Kathleen's voice continued. "We're in lockdown. I need an account of who is up there with you right now."

Morgan scanned the unit. Lisa was the only parent in so far.

"Six patients, four nurses including me, and one family member."

"No one in or out of your unit," she ordered.

"Even parents? That's not going to go over so well."

"I'm making one exception. The ER had an infant being transported from another facility. They've talked to Marshall. They're going to direct-admit her to the PICU."

"What's the diagnosis?"

"Abusive head trauma."

Morgan's heart sank. Shaken, just like Teagan.

Chapter 25

RED FLUID TRICKLING DOWN the infant's body pulled Drew Stipman's eyes to his patient. The transport paramedic's heart rate picked up speed as he reached forward to turn her arm over to check for the source of the bleeding.

At the space inside little Scarlett's elbow, and at each needle stick site where the community hospital had attempted to place an IV, their one-month-old tiny charge now oozed blood. Short acronym: DIC. Long name: Disseminated Intravascular Coagulation. What it meant was that Scarlett's blood no longer had the ability to clot. Some thought it was related to the actual brain injury—the process that happened during shaking. Others felt it was related to a build-up of acid in the blood. What it boiled down to right now was uncontrollable bleeding everywhere.

Drew cleared his throat to get his transport nurse's attention. "Emma," he called.

She placed an X-ray back into a large manila folder. "Breathing tube is in good position."

The father, and likely the perpetrator of the child's abuse, stepped closer to her. "Don't you need the doctor to read that?"

Her glare was like the whir of a lawnmower blade as it sliced a thin shoot of grass. "No, I am more than capable—"

"Emma!" Drew called again, both to keep her from crossing a line and to draw her attention to his attempts to stem the bleeding.

Her face paled.

"Roy, we need to go, now!"

Their pilot had been a quiet presence at the door as they got report. Now he scurried off to get the helicopter warmed up.

Drew yanked the transport gurney closer to the ER bed. Emma watched IV lines and tubes as Drew lifted the limp, ashen body and placed it gently on the thin frame. One small blanket, several seat belts, connection to the transport monitor. Her IV fluid had already been changed over to their equipment. Emma pulled her end of the gurney toward the door. Drew grabbed their hastily-thrown-together trauma pack. He wished there'd been a transport Isolette available. They ran down the hall, into the early morning, and loaded the gurney into the back of the helicopter.

Considering the distance, the travel to the hospital would be a short fifteen minutes. Emma's voice crackled through his head gear. "We're going straight to the PICU."

Drew nodded but his eyes remained fixed on the rise and fall of the infant's chest. Transferring a patient from one place to another was the leading cause of tube dislodgement. The last thing they needed was this little one's breathing tube to slip out of place. Intubating a patient, particularly a very small one, in a moving helicopter was difficult at best.

Emma's voice again, a tinny sound in his ears. "Someone was shot."

Drew nodded again. *Taking a critically ill infant straight to the PICU isn't all that unusual. Why does Emma feel the need to explain a busy ER?*

She patted his knee. "Drew, a hospital security guard was shot."

He looked up at her as his stomach tightened. She hadn't meant a pediatric gunshot wound. An adult gunshot victim wouldn't go to Sacred Heart.

Unless it's one of their own staff.

"Seriously?"

The helicopter banked, and Drew noticed a slew of police cars at the main entrance. His side tipped down, and the landing site was in clear view. Drew's heartbeat ticked up a notch. "Where is everyone?"

Normally, when a helicopter landed, at least two additional staff came out to help off-load their tiny charge. Extra hands helped the management of all the tubes and lines to ensure nothing slipped out.

The helicopter skids settled on the rooftop. "They're in lockdown. Maybe they can't meet us," Emma said.

Drew's heart sputtered. "You didn't say anything about that."

She worked at gathering up the IV bags. "Sorry. The PICU attending mentioned it. You know these things never turn out to be anything serious."

Drew gripped his fingers on the patient's airway to keep it steady as they began to unhook the gurney. "Lockdown? That's definitely new. It's not like a fire alarm. Did you see all those police cars out front?"

Emma shrugged. "Not really paying attention. Worried about this little one."

A figure emerged from the doorway, dressed in casual street clothes, followed by another two just behind him. He shouldered a weapon and aimed it straight for the helicopter.

Drew's heart hammered in his chest. He keyed his mike. "Roy! Up! Up! Take off now!"

"What are you doing?" Emma yelled.

Drew slammed the gurney back into the locking mechanism. "There're armed men on the tarmac." He slammed his fist several times into the top of the craft, not sure if the sound would translate to the front of the compartment.

Roy's voice was calm in his helmet. "Steady yourselves."

The helicopter lurched to the side, knocking Emma back into the window. The sound of a sudden hailstorm hit the craft.

Gunfire.

He grabbed the front of Emma's flight suit to yank her down as the craft took a dizzying full circle turn. Black sludge marred the windows. A hole appeared just above their patient's gurney.

"We're leaking fluid," Roy said. "We're going to have to set her back down."

There was a heavy thud that thrust Drew's stomach into his throat. A quick check on the infant's monitor showed normal, steady patterns. He eased his head up to check out the window and saw the lead figure advancing to the aircraft.

Drew keyed his mike. "Roy, you don't happen to—"

"No, I can't carry at work."

Emma's shaky hands grabbed at his helmet, her voice muffled. Why wasn't her mike picking up? "Drew . . . "

He eased back and noticed a dark, wet circle spreading through Emma's blue flight suit on the left side.

"Oh no, Emma . . . "

Without thought or permission, he plied her flight suit zipper down and yanked her white undershirt up. A hole gaped in her lower abdomen. He pressed his hand against it and turned her toward him.

No exit wound.

A bullet in the left side could mean a spleen injury and rapid blood loss.

Drew pulled off her flight helmet to rid the suffocating effect it could have on her breathing. "Emma . . ."

She looked at him, her eyes glossy with both fright and shock. "I'm really hit?"

He eased his helmet off and smiled at her. "You know, you're supposed to let me handle the heavy fire."

There was a rap at the door. Roy's voice was thin through the partition. "Guys, they want us out. We're stuck here."

"Roy, Emma's hit! We need to get her to the ER."

Clearly audible were the swear words that flew from Roy's mouth. "I'm out first. Hang tight."

Drew grabbed a bucket package of 4x4 gauze and placed it to Emma's side, the bleeding more of a gentle oozing than a brisk flow. At her throat, he placed two bloody fingers and assessed the strength and speed of her heartbeat.

Thready and weak.

"How is it?" she asked, her pale lips in a nervous smile.

The trouble with treating medical personnel was they knew the purpose of every little mannerism and what it meant. They also knew the platitudes that were often said to keep a patient calm in light of grave injury.

He shook his head. "It's not as bad as I thought."

"You're lying."

"I'm not."

"Then I don't need a line?"

"Well, I wouldn't say that. I just don't know—"

The back clamshell door opened. What Drew saw at first was the metal tip of an automatic weapon. Instinctively, he raised his hands in surrender.

"Out!" The weapon motioned, as if to magnetically pull him from his protective cave. "Listen! I said out!"

Drew glanced at Emma, at the baby unconscious on the gurney. He was the only one left capable of protecting them. He gripped her hand. "It's going to be all right. I'll figure it out."

She shook her head, unbelieving. There had been an attraction developing between them. He could see the wish of hope fading in her eyes, thoughts about what they could have been.

He kissed her cheek quickly. "I know. I should have asked you before now about that date."

The man's military cut matched the hard edge of his voice. His gray-green eyes spoke of a life lived on the same thin razor.

Drew eased out the back door with his hands held high. "I'm Drew." The man seemed perplexed at his statement, as if he hoped for some pleading in light of Drew's current endangered state. "I have a sick infant in the back. My flight nurse was hit when you opened fire. She needs to get to the ER."

The man's eyes narrowed. "Unload the baby. The woman stays here. Once we're in the PICU, the ER staff can come up here to get her. We'll leave the pilot back to help."

Drew shook his head. "She needs prompt medical care. I can help her. Let me stay."

"This is not a negotiation." He cleared the sweat from his forehead. "Off-load the baby now."

Drew did as he was told. It was going to be difficult managing the child on his own. He disconnected the transport ventilator and began assisting the infant's breathing by hand. "I need someone to hold these up."

The lead man motioned to one of his cohorts. That man shouldered his weapon and grabbed the bags of IV solution. Drew stepped out, guiding the gurney with one hand, bagging with the other. His eyes trained on the chest to ensure rise and fall were present, a sign that he was inflating the lungs. As he pulled the load to one side of the helicopter, a third cohort came into view. This one had an assault rifle trained on Roy. The look in his eyes was hidden behind mirrored sunglasses, but Roy's clenched fists spoke of barely contained anger.

"Emma needs—" Drew started.

"I'll take care of her, Drew. I promise."

The nudge of the weapon at his back propelled Drew forward.

Clearly, they wanted entrance into the pediatric ICU. *For what purpose?* This was the unknown risk. Damaging the helicopter meant they weren't hoping to use it as a means of escape. Not wanting to leave meant they had a clear agenda of what they wanted to accomplish. Voiding their means of escape meant death could be the welcome possibility of an out.

Why hold a group of sick children and nurses hostage?

They neared the elevator that would drop them down one floor to where the PICU was housed. Drew eased in with the man assisting. The other two backed in ahead of him, their weapons trained on Roy until the doors closed.

Drew continued to bag, intentionally slowing down so he didn't provide the infant too many breaths from the adrenaline that pumped through his veins. He felt part of his life flash before him. He'd spent years in prison, an innocent man serving time for his twin brother's crimes. Even then, he'd never been this fearful about what the next moments would bring. When men were angry against men, their behavior was predictable. When men were steely, armed, and quiet—the outcome was almost always a mystery.

"When we get to the PICU, you're going to badge us in through the doors," the leader said.

Drew doubted these were hospital types. The comfort their leader had in using the names of the units heightened Drew's concern. They'd definitely planned this out. It wasn't some random event.

The doors eased open and one of the men yanked the end of the pram to pull it from the elevator. Drew clenched his hand down on the frame. "Easy, you're going to dislodge my airway."

The man held the elevator door open and eyed Drew evenly. "Do you know Morgan Adams?"

Drew shrugged his shoulders. He knew that nurse's name, had helped save her nephew's life, but he didn't see any reason to increase the chance of her being a target. "Never heard of her."

"How about Dr. Lilly Reeves?"

Now, why would they want to know about her?

Chapter 26

THE PICU DOOR SWUNG open to reveal the flight paramedic flanked by three armed white males dressed in casual clothes, their automatic weapons readied and pointed into the unit.

At first, confusion stymied Morgan's usually clear thought pattern. *What exactly is happening?* Tingly fear buzzed at her fingertips as they glossed over the raised buttons of the phone at the nurses' station. No connection to law enforcement could be made with the receiver to her ear and another person on the line.

"Morgan?" Dr. Marshall said.

She swallowed hard. "We've got trouble. They're in the unit."

Just silence.

From her position at the central station, she had a clear view of every reaction by her staff. Over the rhythmic hum of life-support equipment, she heard a collective gasp as horror throttled each of her coworkers' throats. Lucy, the nurse, gripped a bed rail and eased herself to the floor. Morgan's sister-in-law, Lisa, placed a firm hand over her comatose son's shoulder.

The door closed, the one patient entrance in and out of the unit, and Morgan likened it to the clang of a prison door slamming shut. Her throat tightened. Her hands slicked with sweat as two of the men positioned themselves in front of it as sentries. Morgan eyed the red panic button housed under the ledge of the counter. Never before had she considered pushing it. Now she wondered if it actually worked.

Could I tap the button without them noticing? Would that action bring one of their fingers against the trigger?

"Who is Morgan Adams?"

The boom of the man's voice in the small space caused several people to jump. Morgan's heart slammed against her rib cage. Her lungs seized up in her chest until she couldn't draw breath to answer. Little Bree began to whimper, her chocolate brown eyes wide with fear.

Too much stress can tax her weakened heart into further failure. What do I do? Morgan pulled a single finger to her lips and held Bree's eyes with hers, silently begging for her to be quiet.

If I claim my name, does it mean instant death? Just this morning she'd contemplated ending it all anyway. A bullet to the head was certainly less painful than carbon monoxide poisoning. Was this an acceptable "out" from her pain?

"Morgan Adams!"

The voice thundered through the open space. Most of the people in the unit were visibly shaking. Her own knees felt like jelly melting on a hot sidewalk. Through her peripheral vision, she saw one of her nurses, Izabel, form a pointed finger with her hand at her side and begin to raise it in her direction.

Whatever the outcome, she couldn't let a friend identify her, particularly if it ended in her death. Being responsible for someone else's demise was a life sentence of its own.

She swallowed the coalesced fear in her throat. "I'm Morgan."

Her confession was like calming waters. She heard the sound of Dr. Marshall's voice through the telephone again, begging her for an explanation. The noise of his words receded as she pulled the phone from her ear. Before she laid it in the cradle, she bumped the top end into the panic button, hoping the amount of pressure would be enough to send the signal, yet quiet enough not to draw the gunmen's attention.

With one hand, the lead man motioned to her. "Come around from behind the desk."

He was a few inches taller than she was, probably just shy of six feet, with brown hair. But it was his eyes—cold, dark, gray with just an overcast of green—that drew the strength from her muscles like iron to a magnet. Fierce hatred emanated from the taut muscles ballooned beneath his shirt. She inhaled deeply; the thoughts of *this-isn't-happening* gelled with what was actually occurring, and she clenched her hands to still their shaking.

"Open your fists!" Captain Gray-Eyes ordered.

Morgan splayed them and walked out from behind the nurses' station. "What can I do for you?"

The phone at the counter began to ring.

"Keep walking toward me," he ordered.

Morgan stopped midway between the man and the desk. Though the hostage takers lacked official uniforms, their demeanor screamed seasoned military. She chewed at the inside of her cheek.

For several silent minutes they stood there, each eyeing the other. The timed whoosh as the transport medic delivered breaths to the limp, pale infant on the pram behind the gunmen's presumed leader worked at slowing her own heartbeat. *What is he waiting for? What are his demands?*

It was the flight paramedic clearing his throat that finally broke her gaze.

Drew. How did he get involved with this mess?

"I have a sick baby here," he said. "I really need to get this child into a better place than the middle of this room. My oxygen tank is almost empty."

Morgan knew it was a lie. Any competent flight team member wouldn't run a tank dry from the helipad to the unit. The tank would last several hours.

Helping to save Seth's life bumped Drew up on Morgan's curiosity scale and she learned he had a notable reputation considering he'd been at Sacred Heart such a short time. Questions had been raised by several in the hospital at hiring a man who'd served prison time—even though he'd been exonerated—to work among easy prey. So many people had stepped up to defend him, support his reputation, that it became a public relations goldmine to hire him onto their transport team.

Morgan edged closer to the transport gurney, keeping her eye on Captain Gray-Eyes and his gun. "Can we settle the baby?"

"Not yet." His stare was frigid, determined. "I need everyone to stand behind Ms. Adams. We're going to have a little chat."

The staff moved in slow steps to the center of the room. The phone continued to ring. Gray-Eyes signaled one of his cohorts to answer it. Boots stomped against the faux marble tile as the man approached the desk, picked up the receiver, and slammed it back down.

Silence ensued.

The Captain smiled with relief. "Better. Who has cell phones on them?"

Morgan thought quickly. Even though it was against hospital policy to carry personal phones, she knew several of her coworkers had them tucked into the pocket of their scrubs. "None of them do."

He sneered. "How are you so sure?"

"It's against policy. They'd be written up. I'm not sure what you want to happen here, but we really do need to get this infant settled. I don't think it's your intention for an infant to die here today."

He leveled the weapon at her chest. "I'll state what my intentions are. You don't get to decide that. Not like your father decided for me. Thomas Reeves—that's who we're going to talk about."

Morgan's chest caved a little as her heart sank. *How on earth . . . ?* Now she had to defend her staff for the wrongs of a man she barely knew against a man who threatened her life? What hope did they possibly have?

He stepped closer to Morgan and edged the tip of his rifle into her chest. "But then again, perhaps you should be on my side." He grabbed her arm and scraped the cool metal over her shunt scar. "Did Daddy Dearest offer to give up any body parts for you?"

Her mouth dried. *How could he possibly know that information?*

The sound of sirens drew his gaze briefly to the window. At the turn of his head, Morgan noticed a horseshoe-shaped incision scar on his left scalp. She made a quick decision. *The riskiest move could be the safest.*

Morgan brought her hand down and closed it slowly over the end of the weapon. "If you think holding me hostage will influence a man I didn't know was my father until a few short days ago, you might as well kill me now. Thomas Reeves isn't going to sacrifice anything for me."

The man's eyes widened, his black pupils thinning out the gray-green speckled irises. He shoved the weapon harder into her sternum, causing her to step back to maintain her balance. She held her hand tight.

He cleared his throat. "Dylan, let's see if Ms. Adams is truthful. Go around and empty everyone's pockets. If anyone has a phone, maybe I'll take her up on the offer to be a sacrificial lamb."

Attempting to look as if his statement hadn't fazed her took every ounce of self-control she could muster. She closed her eyes, an unexpected prayer on her tongue. The sound of clothing rustled, a key or two jingling etched fear along her spine.

"Looks like she was telling the truth, Scott. No one has a phone."

Morgan's eyes popped open as relief flooded over her. *The threatening e-mail our nurse manager sent out actually worked? Not possible.*

Morgan leveled her gaze back at the lead gunman.

Scott. Captain Gray-Eyes' name is Scott.

"Now, Scott," she said, "can we get this baby settled? Or will we be standing here all day?"

He motioned the weapon to an empty bedspace. "Hurry up."

"I need Izabel to come with me."

"Fine, everyone else stays right here."

The group huddled together as Morgan helped Drew pull the gurney to the bedside. "Scott," she said, "we're going to need a respiratory therapist in here to manage the ventilators."

He stepped closer in her direction. "That's not going to happen. No one else is going to come in or out of this unit until our demands are met."

She glanced his way over her shoulder. "That's not reasonable. These children require advanced care. Depending on the nursing staff to do this isn't safe for the patients."

He thumbed his nose. "You're going to have to figure it out."

"How long do you think this is going to last?"

He smacked his lips—an annoying dismissal of her question. "Why worry everyone about that right now?"

Drew laid a hand on hers as she worked to unsnap the buckles. "I can do it."

Morgan looked up. "What?"

"The ventilators. They can't be much different than the transport vents, just fancier."

At the cuffs of his flight suit, she could see the kaleidoscope of rich, pigmented colors that had been injected under his skin and tried to remember the design.

Drew disconnected the breathing bag from the tube. Morgan gathered the small bundle into her hands and settled the baby into the middle of the bed. Careful not to dislodge any lines, Drew watched to ensure nothing snagged then rounded to her side of the bed.

"Just bag her for a minute from the tank until I get this thing going."

Morgan reached out and took over providing breathing for the patient while Drew set up the vent. Once completed, he tapped her on the shoulder and she edged back, letting him disconnect the bag and place the baby on the machine. As he worked, Morgan traded out the ECG cords from the transport monitor to the large, PICU monitor that sat above the bedspace.

Izabel's pale green eyes looked at her blankly.

"Can you do an assessment?" Morgan asked.

She nodded and pulled her bright pink stethoscope from her neck. Her hands shook as she listened to breath sounds. She rubbed light fingers over the baby's soft spot. At each bandage site, blood seeped through the gauze. Placing a glove on her hand, Morgan crossed a finger over it.

Still wet.

"How long has this bleeding been happening?" Morgan asked Drew.

"Just as we left the outlying hospital."

"She's in DIC."

"I know."

Morgan turned to their captor. "Scott, I know something must be very concerning in your life to warrant drastic measures like this. To take hostage nurses who are caring for critically ill children. For sure, you are going to get the attention of the news media. Your message will get out." Morgan folded her hands, trying to assume the least aggressive posture. "But I need more people here. I need a doctor to help us care for these children. Do you see all this blood on the baby's dressings?"

He leaned her direction, his eyes dim.

"This little baby is going to bleed to death. Her blood is not clotting the way it should. I need a doctor in here to assess her and write orders for blood products." Morgan glanced at the monitor. "Her blood pressure is very low. She needs special medicine to bring it up."

A monitor behind her began to alarm. Morgan turned, noting the slight drop in another patient's oxygen level.

Seth. She groaned inside.

She turned back to Scott. "I need to go check that patient. What is the plan here? Are you going to give us what we need? A doctor? A respiratory therapist?"

Drew held his hands up. "I'm going to check that young man over there," he said, picking up on Morgan's concern that Seth's oxygen levels were low. If it wasn't corrected soon, his heartbeat would fall as well in protest to its lack of oxygen.

He began to back slowly to the bed.

Morgan stepped between Drew and Scott and locked his eyes with hers. "A dead patient is only going to worsen your hand. Let them see that you are allowing for compassionate care of these kids. It will only help your case."

Drew silenced the alarm behind her. She held Scott's eyes with hers. "Well?"

At first, she saw his mouth relax as he considered her argument, but just at the moment she thought he would acquiesce, something in his eyes changed—hardened.

He began to move away from her. "You're a nurse. Figure it out."

"I can't write doctor's orders. It's outside my scope of practice."

"Come on, Morgan. It's your chance to make Daddy proud. Isn't that what you want?"

She shook her head. "I only care about these children and my staff and making sure they come out of this alive."

"Well, let's just consider any forthcoming deaths collateral damage. Just like we are."

Chapter 27

DETECTIVE NATHAN LONG surveyed the crime scene, his mind going through his obsessive checklist. His missing something would be a defense attorney's biggest gift. It wasn't in his nature to easily allow a police slipup to be the reason someone got a get-out-of-jail-free card.

Nearby, Brett methodically searched through the victim's belongings again. At Nathan's request, of course. He wanted to ensure they had that *one* thing—a single piece of evidence that could prove the truth about what they saw.

It appeared to be suicide.

The body of a well-muscled male, late twenties, lay fully clothed in combat fatigues atop the covers on his bed. The bed was made with military-tightened corners. Dog tags identified the body as Brian Nelson. He appeared to be active duty. An empty bottle of sleeping pills and a half-drunk bottle of water stood on a black nightstand to the soldier's right side. In the living room, Brian's sobbing widow matched the volume of the television, and the two seemed to be competing with one another for who could sound the most distressed.

Watching Brett work brought his partner's other case to Nathan's mind.

"How'd that interview go with Amy?" he asked.

Brett turned to face him. "Very interesting. Not quite sure what to make about what's going on."

"In what way?" Nathan asked.

Brett put on a pair of gloves, straightening them over his fingers. "If I didn't know any better, I'd say I witnessed Zoe give a firsthand account of her murder."

"But you interviewed Amy—the recipient."

"Exactly."

"Zoe's dead."

"Cold in the ground."

"Now, there's what I miss. Your sense of utter compassion."

Brett rubbed his forearm over his forehead. "I'm not kidding about what I said. Amy knew what music was playing on Zoe's headset when she was attacked. How can you account for that?"

"Probably heard it somewhere."

"Listen, I didn't graduate detective school yesterday. Amy's mother swears she doesn't even know who Taylor Swift is."

"Come on . . . even you know who Taylor Swift is, and you're completely out of touch with country music."

"Let's just say that Amy leads a relatively sheltered life."

"Okay, so she knows about the music. Not exactly something to build a murder case on."

"Ah, one thing we agree on. But Amy mentioned something that forced me to go back to the park, several times I might add, to take another look around the crime scene."

"Excellent. Did you find anything?"

"A set of dog tags. Just like Amy described them. Lying just a few feet from where Zoe's body was found."

Nathan paused his searching and stared at Brett. "You're serious? This isn't you just trying to pull my leg and then razz me about it for the whole rest of our lives together?"

Brett pointed a finger at Nathan. "For one, you and I are not married so our partnership's not going to be a 'til-death-do-us-part kind of thing. And two, I am absolutely not joking. Got the name, rank, and serial number. The whole nine yards."

"Did you locate the guy?"

"Not yet. Got a couple of other people on it. Chief Anson's not crazy about the working theory."

Nathan smiled. Not long ago he'd been in the same position.

Brett closed a notebook he'd been perusing. "I went back and talked to your trusty mental health doc, Vanhise. He thinks it could be possible. Says there's documentation that transplant patients have had these experiences."

Nathan had difficulty reasoning it in his mind, but he was always open to theories if they could be proven. Wild goose chases were fine if they could hold up in court and get guilty men into jail. Had there ever been a case of a memory transferred between donor and recipient that led to an actual conviction?

The sound of wood knocking against wood brought Nathan's eyes back to Brett at the dresser. "Find anything?"

Brett shook his head, his brown eyes feigning surprise. "Just the smoking gun."

Nathan frowned. "If only it ever was that easy."

"Sometimes it is that easy. I don't get what has you so perplexed. This is the chipmunk in the forest. Not the zebra."

A reputation was hard to get past, and Nathan's held its own special circumstances. To his department, he was an ace detective. His record for clearing cases could be rivaled by few others. However, he was feeling the pull to leave exacting justice for the deceased in favor of saving the lives of the threatened. Serving with SWAT, even in a limited role, allowed him to revive the negotiator inside and they seemed happy to have an ex-FBI man covering the role. The joy of seeing hostages set free was one of the things Nathan loved most about police work.

With gloved hands, Nathan picked up the calendar from the desk. "Everything is just too perfect."

"If I found you dead, it wouldn't surprise me to find your crime scene in such a pristine state either. Your ghost would probably be tidying up. Maybe he didn't want to leave a mess for his wife to clean."

Nathan neared the body. "See the surgical scar on the left side of his head? The wife says it was a voluntary procedure for research."

"So?" Brett shrugged, standing by the dresser on the other side.

"Since when do recruits do voluntary brain surgery?"

"Nathan, you're not known to be a conspiracy theorist. I, on the other hand, love to entertain a few. It's a chip, of course."

"As in computer chip?"

"Absolutely. You don't think the military would be into something like that? Implanting chips?"

"And what would the purpose of said chip be?"

Brett rubbed his hands together devilishly. "Let me give you just a few morsels off the top of my most genius mind. One, a spy camera. Hard to detect. Soldier doesn't have to be wired. Doesn't have to carry recording equipment to gather intel. Two, a tracking device. Three—"

"All right, I get it. You need to stop listening to that radio program at night. It only adds to my insomnia when you talk about these things. It's why I can't read the book of Revelation."

Brett smiled. "You think outside the box your way. I do it my way."

"It's just that I use sound police theory."

"Wow. You're usually not this feisty until much later in the day."

Nathan ran his hand through his hair. "Let's go over what we know. About a year ago, he had this surgery. Wife doesn't really know what it entailed. His career was on the upswing. He was just promoted."

"Maybe he couldn't take the extra responsibility."

"His wife says it was something he was looking forward to."

Brett pulled the top drawer of the nightstand open. "Okay, I'll agree with you on that. He's got new uniforms hanging in the closet."

Nathan lifted the planner from the desk. "Also, he has appointments set. Nothing appears to be canceled. Why kill yourself now?"

"We do know regardless of what the surgery entailed, the wife states he was having some complications."

Nathan set the planner aside. "Remembering too much. Can that really be a complication? Some women might consider it an improvement to the male condition."

"On that radio program you're so fond of dismembering, I remember some neuro-type doc talking about a person who could never forget anything and how much it plagued her. It's like her brain was never quiet."

Nathan pulled down one of the composition notebooks from the desk. "I wonder if that's why he was keeping these."

Brett turned his direction. "What are they?"

"They remind me of something my grandmother does. She records every single part of her day. What she ate. Who came to visit. Who she got mail from."

"Don't you think that would be more of a test?"

"How so?"

"Well, say you got this surgery and one of the complications was that you began to remember everything. Or, at least in the beginning that's what you thought was happening to you. So to test yourself, you begin to record every little thing you do and then go back and quiz yourself to see if you're actually right."

Nathan thumbed through the pages. "Actually makes sense. Look at you using deductive reasoning."

"The other thing this doc talked about was how every bad decision in the woman's life plagued her. Her mind played this continual loop of memory, and she could see every decision and how it played out in her life. It's like you when you get into overanalyze mode—like now."

"What do you mean?"

"Those moments we all want to forget. The bad decisions we make. For a while, we might sit around and ruminate, but eventually, we do move on and probably don't think of them as much. Sure, one or two might easily come to mind—"

"You allude to Raven Samuals's case."

"Sure. For you as a negotiator, it sidelined you when those people died, but you've worked your way back. For this woman, it's like she's stuck with all these moments. There is no filter."

Nathan put the journal down and ran his thumb over the group of ten. "What you bring up is a good point. Our brain does provide a service to us by filtering out the extra noise and cataloging only the most important things. So, was he just trying to quiet the noise? That's why he killed himself?"

Brett turned back to the body. "I don't know. But what I do know is there isn't anything suspicious. Nothing that would lead me to believe that someone else forced those pills down his throat."

"We'll have to wait for the toxicology screen and autopsy to know for sure. What is the name of the prescribing doctor on those bottles?"

Brett picked one up and a slow whistle escaped his lips. "Cue the *Twilight* music. Dr. Thomas Reeves."

Nathan grabbed his iPad from the desk. "Great. Now I'll be forced to talk to my father-in-law. Actually, why don't you do it, since I have an obvious conflict of interest?"

"Fine. Why is that television so loud?" Brett left the bedroom.

As Nathan finished searching, his pager vibrated.

"Nathan, you better get in here!" Brett called.

"Just a minute!"

He viewed his pager. SWAT was requesting his assistance on scene.

Leaving the bedroom, Nathan turned the corner and saw the grieving widow sitting beside Brett on the couch.

"What's going on?" Nathan asked.

Brett pointed to the television. "They're reporting that three armed men have taken hostages at Sacred Heart. They just showed a photo of the hostage takers. Some grainy image a parent took in the parking lot."

Nathan knew what Brett meant to say. The police wanted control of any images in a volatile situation. How had the media obtained these? Most likely from a citizen and not law enforcement or anyone tied with the hospital.

It was the widow who spoke. "That's one of Brian's friends. He had the surgery, too." She turned and faced Nathan. "That's when all of our trouble started—when he volunteered for that procedure."

Chapter 28

MORGAN STOOD BACK AS Scott pointed his weapon at the lock to the pharmacy door. He fired three consecutive shots, causing small plumes of dust and smoke to fill the hallway. Morgan pushed through the damaged wood and began to scan the meds.

What she hadn't anticipated were the resultant screams of terror from the other side of the PICU main entrance at the sound of the weapon being fired. It was the first moment she'd seen a look of uncertainty cross Scott's eyes.

She turned to face him. "You're going to have to let me call out. They're going to assume you shot someone in here."

"What's the hospital plan for someone being taken hostage?"

"Plan? We rehearse a single armed person flipping out. Not a trio of mercenaries. Isn't that what you are? Trained military?"

His eyes widened at her assessment.

Morgan turned away and scanned the nearest shelf. "We have an alert we rehearse. It puts the hospital in lockdown. We're to get the patients in a safe place. Ask me about a fire, a tornado, a bomb threat, and I'm all over that. You are never expected to be *inside* my unit."

"Seems like poor planning."

"Yeah, well, you can run it by JCAHO on their next visit. Are you going to let me phone the police? Let them know you haven't hurt anybody?"

"Not yet."

Morgan's stomach turned. How would the hospital feel if she stole some Tums and Valium? Would she be able to access the narcotics she needed for her patients? Where was the vial to make the vasopressor drip for Bree? She pulled the dopamine vial from the shelf. One item on her checklist found.

"I need some IV bags. The liter size," Scott said.

The tension in Morgan's chest increased. "What for?"

"To build explosives to rig the doors." He kept the weapon aimed at her and smiled. "Aren't you glad you asked?"

Her hands trembled. His casual, pleasant response was the most disturbing thing he'd said so far. Morgan stepped to the left and found the cache of fluids. Scott stepped in front of her and gathered up six bags in the crook of one arm. With his free hand, he adjusted the weapon. "Let's go to the desk and make that call. Don't say anything I wouldn't say."

She walked back to the nurses' station with the medicine vials clutched in fisted, raised hands. Her sister-in-law was seated at the desk. A Hispanic male, whose name had not yet been mentioned, remained by the door. The other mercenary, *Dylan*, she remembered, lumbered about the room like a bored gorilla looking for food.

Morgan picked up the handset and dialed the operator.

"Sacred Heart Children's Hospital."

"This is Morgan Adams. I'm the charge nurse in the PICU where gunmen are holding people hostage. I need to talk with the police."

There was a scurry of activity on the other side of the phone. Voices muffled through a hand cupped over the receiver.

A deep, male voice took over the line. "Morgan, my name is Lee Watson. I'm commander of the SWAT team. How's everything up there?"

She eyed her captor; a questioning look crossed his face. *How much is he going to allow me to say?*

"I just want you to know that everything's okay up here."

Silence. *Is he contemplating what his next move will be?*

"There have been reports of gunfire," he said.

"I needed to get into our locked pharmacy for medications. They were helping me."

"How many are there?"

Morgan pulled the phone from her ear. "He's asking questions. What do you want me to tell him?"

Scott took a step away from her, his dark eyes like matted, gray paint. "Tell him whatever you like. Just be careful."

Invisible threads wove around her neck and tightened like a noose. Then her defiant streak pushed back. If she was going to die, she might as well go out by helping the others as much as she could. What did she have to live for anyway? A mother who lied to her? A husband whose distance surely spelled divorce? A father—well, which one should she call father and what sort of relationship would they have in the future?

She placed the phone back to her ear.

"Morgan, are you there?"

No time to be polite. "They're going to arm the doors with explosives." The thought of people dying unnecessarily in a heroic rescue attempt was unacceptable. Scott's nonplussed reaction to her statement soured her gut.

"You're not on speaker?"

"No."

The pause told her the answer surprised him.

"Tell me the name of the puppet boy whose nose grew longer when he lied."

Morgan bit into her lip. Surely, this was a test. If she answered incorrectly, he would know for sure his side of the conversation wasn't being listened in on.

"*Sleeping Beauty*. And a few other kids' movies. That would really help with some of the children." *Bree at least.*

Was that a sigh of relief that crossed the line?

"Excellent," Lee Watson said. "How many gunmen are there?"

"It's the one with the three fairy godmothers." She cupped her hand over the receiver to Scott. "Never ask the police for children's movies. Not up on the Disney princesses." He ignored her humor.

Lee's voice in her ear. "Got it. Three men. I'm assuming they are armed. Yes?"

"Correct."

"Have they made threats?"

"Yes."

"Do you know what their demands are?"

She pulled the phone from her ear. "They want to know what you want."

Scott laid the weapon down on the countertop. "Tell him I need to speak to Dr. Thomas Reeves. The one everyone thinks cured post-traumatic stress disorder."

Morgan involuntarily stepped away from the weapon. Definitely an item she never imagined would be at the nurses' station.

Watson's calm voice spoke. "I heard that. Why does he want to speak with Thomas Reeves?"

Her eyebrows rose in a question to Scott. "They want to know why."

"Let's just say he owes us an explanation. Get him here on-site and I'll list my demands."

"Got that, too," Lee said. "Is anyone injured?"

How could she answer that adequately? "There are no new injuries."

"How many children?"

"I have seven patients."

"Staff?"

"Four nurses and one parent. Also a flight team paramedic—it's how they got into the unit."

Scott placed his hand over the gun. Her heart skipped several beats. *Too much information that time?*

"Can any patients be evacuated?"

She eyed the unit. "Three for sure. Four are on ventilators so it would be more difficult."

"Meaning oxygen?"

"Yes."

"And they need power to run?"

"Yes." *Why those two questions?*

"What is it you need up there, Morgan? You are doing a terrific job. I know this is very frightening, but we have lots of people here to help. We're working hard to resolve this peacefully."

She swallowed thick sludge down her throat. It's the same type of speech she gave to parents when things were going south and she didn't want them to panic. Calm them down. Make them feel like someone competent was managing the situation.

"I need a doctor and a respiratory therapist. Or at least phone access to them."

"How about medicine? Food? Water?"

"I have access to the unit's pharmacy. Water is working. There're two vending machines in the staff lounge for food if needed. I have snacks for patients and families in a small refrigerator. It's not ideal, but we'd be okay for a little while."

"How long could you hold out with those current supplies?"

Her throat constricted tighter. He didn't sound hopeful the situation would resolve quickly. If she said how long it could really be, would that give the hostage takers reason to drag out their scenario—whatever that was?

Commander Watson seemed to pick up on her thought process. "Days? You could last days up there?"

"Physically, yes."

"Morgan, I understand. You're in a tough position. Sick children. Worried staff and parents. Does the gunman nearest you have a name?"

"Scott."

"Put him on the phone."

She held the phone out. "He wants to speak with you."

He clicked the speaker button and grabbed her hand to push the handset back. "You're on speaker."

"Scott, I'm Lee. I work with the police."

Silence.

"Morgan?"

"We're here."

"Great. Scott, can you let me in on your plan?"

"Why are you making me repeat what she said? I want to talk to Dr. Thomas Reeves. Get him here and I'll let you in on the rest."

"Okay, we're working on that. Can you give me something in return? Morgan says some of the children could be evacuated. Will you allow her to release the children that can be moved?"

"I'm not ready to do that. We need them here."

"Okay. One, I want to thank you for helping Morgan get access to the pharmacy. That will help her manage the patients. I also want to say thanks for allowing her to contact us. As we work to resolve this issue, can you allow her everything she needs? Will you let a doctor into the unit?"

"Morgan here's been doin' all right. She's been getting the stuff the children need. Ordered blood and everything."

Morgan edged up onto her toes. "Scott, ICU nurses are very smart but we're not doctors. I need one here. I can't manage these patients without one. I don't know everything they need."

He glared at her. "Like I told the police officer, you're doing fine. You don't need anyone else."

"That's not true—" For the first time, the threat of tears made her eyes burn. "Nurses and doctors do different things. Please, don't put me in this position. You're forcing me to operate off my license, and one of these children could be hurt by that. I can't handle the thought of my decision being responsible for a child's death."

His eyes softened. "Because that's already happened, right?"

The room hazed as the blood drained from her head. She gripped the desk for support. *Does he know about Teagan? How could he know that?*

She flinched as he laid a reassuring hand on her shoulder. "I trust you."

His trust in her didn't hold much weight. But did she trust herself? Her own clinical ability? For the last three months, she'd been pushing everyone away to stand on her own.

"Hey, guys," Lee's voice interrupted over the speakerphone.

Morgan was sliding down the slope where Lee didn't want her to go. Her own crisis training had taught her that. Panic and arguing could be the first nail in her coffin. She pressed her thumb and forefinger into her eyes.

"Please, let me at least have access to a doctor over the phone."

"Scott, that seems like a reasonable request on her part."

His fingers coiled around the weapon, tight to the point that the blood was forced from his hands. Why was this so difficult?

"No!"

Morgan jumped. Her heart in her throat. "Please, Scott. One by phone. That's it."

He disconnected the call and glared her way. "You're going to have to do with what you have. Just like we do when we're on a mission."

Morgan took two steps away. "Okay. I understand. I'll make it work."

"Now, you're going to do something for me. Is there someplace we can go that's private?"

Morgan glanced around the unit. Her staff mirrored her concern—more like abject terror. *Why does he want to be alone?* "The staff lounge."

"Great." He signaled to his two cohorts. "Dylan. Jose. Morgan and I are going to take a quick break. You two know what you need to be working on." He tossed the bags of IV solution in their direction. "Be back in a few."

They nodded and went to a more central location. Scott grabbed her arm, his fingers digging into her muscle like talons on scooped prey. "Show me the way."

Her legs felt weak as she began to move. To hasten her, he jammed the weapon between her shoulder blades. She punched the code into the lock and opened the door. The staff lounge TV was on and there was the news feed with the title: *Chaos at Children's.*

"Turn and face me."
She raised her hands and turned slowly.
"We're going to make a little video."

Chapter 29

NATHAN AND BRETT jogged two short blocks to the scene.

The sun bounced bright off the glass, and Nathan wondered how such a beautiful day could hold such darkness. Sacred Heart Children's Hospital sat on a medical campus that housed several other medical facilities. The front entrance was congested with police and the large SWAT command vehicle. The glass doors swooshed as they pulled open, and Nathan partially saluted the officer who was holding vigil at the front door with a hospital employee.

"Where's the command center?" Nathan asked.

"Second floor. Conference Center." He pointed to a bank of glass elevators.

Upon arrival, they were directed to a cavernous boardroom. A team of IT types were setting up additional computers and phones. Brett motioned toward Lee Watson directly across the room, and they headed his direction. A man in a gray, pinstriped suit stood next to him. Lee gave a nod to Nathan when they approached.

"This is Daniel Horton," Lee said by way of introduction. "He's CEO of the hospital." To Horton he said, "This is Nathan Long. He'll be serving as hostage negotiator."

The two shook hands briefly. Nathan said a silent prayer of thanks that Lee had inserted him into the situation so seamlessly. Now he was officially on this case, working in his SWAT capacity, instead of trying to squeeze himself in as a homicide detective.

The CEO pointed to the woman next to him. "This is the nursing supervisor, Kathleen Young. She's our on-site incident commander."

Nathan shook her hand as well. "Nice to meet both of you. Why don't you give me a rundown of what's occurred thus far."

Lee surmised the security guard had been shot to gain access to the roof. What was unknown was how the gunmen would have known a helicopter was landing at that particular time.

"They could be monitoring the dispatch center. Then they'd know when the medical teams were coming and going," Nathan proposed.

Brett shook his head. "That's a lot to bank on. It would mean their plan was pretty fluid. It seems to me, for such high stakes, there's a person in the unit they want control over."

"Has there been any contact?" Nathan asked.

"I just got off the phone with the charge nurse and one of the hostage takers," Lee said.

The nursing supervisor glanced at her clipboard. "Morgan Adams. She's an asset. Good in high stress situations."

Nathan and Brett glanced at one another.

"What is it?" Lee asked.

"Coincidence?" Brett offered.

Nathan shook his head. "I don't think so. I've been taught not to believe in randomness."

"What do the two of you know that you're not telling me?" Lee asked.

Brett turned to Lee and lowered his voice. "We've talked with Dr. Tyler Adams, who is married to Morgan, because his business card was found at the crime scene of a child's murder."

"The case my wife helped you with?" Lee asked.

"Same one. I also think the suspect could possibly be tied to Adams's contract work. Haven't made a solid connection yet. A set of dog tags was also found. Guy could be military."

Nathan leaned against a nearby chair. "We also just came from the scene of an apparent suicide. Military guy, too. Tyler's boss, Dr. Thomas Reeves, wrote his prescriptions and his widow claims one of these men here was involved in the same surgery her husband participated in."

"Any footage of the trio?" Brett asked Lee.

"Some hospital footage. We have the incident on the helipad on security tapes."

"What happened there?"

"They assaulted the medical helicopter as it landed, fired upon it, and injured the flight nurse. She's here but they had to take her to surgery. The pilot was uninjured. At gunpoint, they escorted the flight paramedic with the patient into the unit. Used his badge to get in."

"So the injured security guard gets them the key code for the helipad. The flight crew gets them badged into the unit. And in the unit, they have all hostages they need." Nathan paced a tight circle. "Seems like a lot of work for a simple procedure."

"What do you mean?" Brett asked.

Nathan approached the boardroom table and flopped open several notepads. "For one, couldn't anyone with an ID get them access into the PICU? I assume badge access is not restricted. An employee is going to have unfettered entry. All they had to do was grab anyone walking by with one and they're in. Seems like they did it the hardest way possible—waiting for a helicopter to land."

"Unless they wanted that not to be an option," Lee thought aloud.

Nathan agreed. "That's what I'm afraid of. They don't want to make an escape. Is the helicopter disabled?"

CEO Horton leaned in. "Yes."

Nathan took down a few notes. "Now the helipad is tied up with a lamed aircraft. No room for anything else to land up there."

The nursing supervisor began to shake. "You're saying they don't plan to leave?"

"At least not via the air," Nathan confirmed.

Her voice rose an octave. "But you're making it sound like this is a last-stand type thing."

Why do women have to be so intuitive?

"Let's not make assumptions we can't prove," he said.

Lee settled his hand over the hilt of his weapon. "The issue becomes what this Scott character *really* wants."

"Has he made any demands?" Brett asked.

"Only one—to get Thomas Reeves on-site for a little conversation, but he won't elaborate as to why he wants him here."

The blood scurried from Nathan's face. "What?"

Lee looked his direction, one eye narrowed. "You know him? Evidently he's some well-known physician."

"He's Lilly's father."

Lee raised his eyes to the ceiling. "Great. Your father-in-law? That doesn't leave you in a good position to serve as negotiator."

"I'm not worried about it. We're not close." Nathan rubbed the side of his neck. "Listen, we've got to prioritize here. Lee, what've you done thus far?"

Watson turned back to the CEO. "Fire is working with the building maintenance crew to get a set of structural plans. SWAT teams from Denver, Adams, and Arapahoe County are doing a systematic search and clearing people out. Quick response team is situated down the hall from the PICU."

"You're certain the only present threat is in the pediatric ICU?" Nathan asked.

"Won't know for sure until the search of the building is complete. However, video from the hall confirms them entering the PICU. Bomb squad has a couple of dogs here looking for IEDs, too."

Kathleen continued to take notes. "Is it necessary to put the ER on diversion? We're a regional children's hospital."

Nathan looked at the woman, somewhat surprised she'd thought of the issue versus the CEO. "Absolutely. We don't know the intentions of these men, and we're not going to put anyone else in harm's way. In fact, we need to evacuate."

"Who?" Horton asked.

"Everyone. Patients, staff, and families," Lee stated.

Nathan started to make notes. "Where can patients go?"

"Blue Ridge," Horton said. "We can call and see how many beds they have available for critical patients and those that should be in isolation. A local high school can be used for less sick kids."

"If the ER is closed, can we hold our ECMO babies there? Moving them to another facility would require specialized transport teams," Kathleen said.

Lee looked at Nathan. "It's reasonable. The ER is on the other side of the hospital on the ground floor. Should be safe."

"What's visible from the PICU windows?" Nathan asked.

"Main entrance," Horton said.

Lee adjusted his Kevlar vest. "The ambulance bay is going to be the best bet for evacuation. It's at the rear of the building. Ambulances can load patients who can't travel by bus."

Horton loosened the tie around his neck. "Can you keep them from shooting more people?"

Nathan glanced at the CEO. Daniel Horton's face was almost translucent. He understood the man's horror. Even to Nathan, it felt extreme to discuss clearing a hospital, but they couldn't be certain they could contain the incident to the PICU. They couldn't be certain there weren't planted explosive devices, or other men who were prepared to lend aid to these individuals.

Nathan's mouth dried. He knew he couldn't promise the man no one else would die. Including the children.

"I know all of this seems drastic, and it is. But you need to look at this like your building is on fire and we don't know how the flames are going to spread. The safest thing to do is remove all staff and personnel who don't need to be here and protect those who remain. We don't want to give them any more potential hostages."

Lee nodded in affirmation. "Nathan's right."

The CEO straightened his shoulders. "Has anything like this ever happened in a hospital? A children's hospital?"

Nathan inhaled. "It doesn't matter. We have a situation here we need to control."

The CEO shook his head in resignation. "I'll start making phone calls for two off-site shelters, and bus and ambulance companies. I'll have them line up at the ER entrance."

Kathleen flipped her notebook closed. "I'll call the individual units. Help the nurses make a plan to evacuate their children."

"No one moves until I give the okay. They'll need to be escorted by police," Lee said.

The two walked off to the bank of phones. Lee motioned to Nathan and Brett and they headed to a relatively unpopulated corner of the room.

"You sure you're going to be okay?" Lee asked Nathan.

"Other than I'm working as the negotiator for a hostage situation at a children's hospital?"

"I meant that Dr. Reeves seems to be involved in this."

"Well, we don't know that he is involved. We know the hostage takers have an issue with him."

"I have an appointment set up for today with a military commander," Brett said. "Since there is a connection between my murder suspect and Adams, I think I should keep it. Maybe he knows something about Reeves and his experiments."

"All right, if you think it can help us here, go ahead and go. But be ready to get right back," Nathan said.

As soon as Brett left the room, Lee's radio squawked. "Someone's making a ruckus at the police perimeter." Lee's eyebrows rose slightly. "It's Tyler Adams. Says he has video from one of the assailants."

Chapter 30

NATHAN WATCHED TWO police officers escort Tyler Adams into the board-room. They pulled out a chair and sat him down at the table. Nathan eyed him from a distance. He looked like he'd had a hard night: eyes blood-shot, face pale, hands shaking. He held a cell phone between clenched fingers.

"Do we know how he got the video?" Nathan asked Lee.

"He's saying Morgan sent it to him." Lee's head tilted into his earpiece. "Floors one and two are clear. They're moving up to the third floor."

Nathan approached. "Dr. Adams, I know we've met already. Today, I'm serving as the SWAT negotiator. Can I see what Morgan sent you?"

He nodded, the terror on his face held his voice prisoner. His thumbs quivered over the device while he pulled the footage up on the small screen.

"Who's on the video?" Nathan asked.

"Just Morgan."

He tapped the screen to start playback, and laid the cell flat on the table for others to see.

Morgan was seated at a table, hands open, palms facing down. Curls of fine, blond hair nearly hid the black tubing of her stethoscope as it rested on her chest. Her dark green eyes were fixed in front of her.

A man's voice prompted. "Go ahead, Morgan. Tell them."

The woman paused, swallowed heavily, and brushed her tongue over dry lips. "My name is Morgan Adams. I'm one of the charge nurses for the pediatric ICU. We are being held hostage by three men who are known to Dr. Thomas Reeves." She pressed her hands into the table. "They say they participated in a research experiment conducted by Reeves and are now suffering ill effects. They want to know why."

She folded her hands, pushing one thumb against the other. The gleam from her thumb ring flashed against the lens from the sharp, overhead lights.

"You need to say it, Morgan."

"You can't charge into the unit. The doors are rigged with explosives."

"No, Morgan. Say what you don't want to say."

She momentarily shielded her face with her hands. "They expect a press conference with Dr. Reeves disclosing the experiment and a medical evaluation from an independent party for treatment of their symptoms. If one is not done by 1700, they will begin to shoot hostages."

"Who am I going to start with, Morgan?"

She wiped a single tear from her cheek. "The children . . ."

Nathan's heart sped up, feeding on newly released adrenaline soaring through his veins. He felt lightheaded with a duty-bound obligation to get this fixed before the threat came to fruition.

It was the worst-case scenario.

The shot stilled after Morgan uttered those words, her eyes wide with horror. Nathan's chest felt heavy, like iron chains had wrapped themselves around his lungs and someone was pulling them tighter.

"Do you think they'll do it?" Tyler asked, his face pale.

Nathan waved at the nursing supervisor and she scurried over. In a lowered voice, Nathan posed the question. "What is in that unit they could make a bomb from?"

"You don't think they brought one with them?" Kathleen asked.

"From the surveillance cameras, they don't look loaded down with equipment. Just a few small duffel bags. That's not to say they didn't plant something earlier, but my gut tells me no."

"What sort of chemicals are on the unit?" Lee asked the nursing supervisor.

"Basic things. There would be smaller bottles of rubbing alcohol, hydrogen peroxide, iodine."

Lee cleared his throat. "How many IV bags?"

"Lots. It's an ICU and they have their own satellite pharmacy. Most of the children likely aren't feeding themselves."

"Oxygen tanks? How many?"

"We can check with respiratory therapy to be sure. My guess is one for every bed. If something catastrophic happened to the hospital, each ventilated patient would have to be manually bagged if the wall oxygen stopped working—for whatever reason. Plus, I'm sure they have a couple of extras for patient transport. You always want to have enough."

"How many beds?" Nathan asked.

"It's a twenty-bed unit."

"In this particular situation, having all those supplies is a bad thing," Lee said.

Nathan sighed. "So we know they can accomplish what they say. They could easily build a bomb."

Leaving the group, Nathan rubbed his hand over his face as he walked back to Dr. Adams. He took a chair next to him. "We need to start back a few steps. Why would these men send this video to you?"

"I work for Dr. Reeves."

"Why not send it to him?"

"Maybe they thought I'd be more sympathetic."

Nathan turned back to Lee, who was standing near. "Don't we have a still shot of the three men?"

Lee walked a few paces back and picked up a sheet of paper from the middle of the table.

Nathan slid the photo Tyler's direction. "Do you know them?"

"The middle guy is Scott Clarke. He's likely the leader."

"Why do you say that?" Lee asked.

"He was head of his SEAL unit when he served in the military."

"And the others?" Nathan prompted.

Tyler tapped the photo. "That's Jose . . . Jose something. I can't remember his last name. He and Scott were in the same squad. The third guy with the spiked hair . . . I'm fairly certain that's Dylan Worthy."

Maybe Brett really is on to something.

"Is Scott telling the truth? They were all part of a research experiment?" Nathan asked.

"Scott and Jose, yes. I'm not sure about that third guy, but there are a few subjects I haven't worked with."

"And can you share the particulars of what the study entailed?" Nathan asked.

Tyler looked as if he might collapse onto the table. "I'd have to talk with Dr. Reeves before I say anything."

"Where is Dr. Reeves? Did you try to reach him after you received this?" Lee asked.

"I don't know and I haven't spoken to him. He's upset with me."

"Over what?" Lee pressed.

Tyler pointed a finger into the table. "There are issues with the protocol. We're not sure what is going on. Reeves may not be willing to figure it out."

Lee leaned down. "What are the issues, Dr. Adams? Are these men unstable?"

Nathan frowned at the comment. Didn't they meet crazy criteria already—holding nurses and sick children at gunpoint? He knew what Lee was driving at. There was proving a point, for someone's perceived grievance over an issue, and then there was doing all of those things under an insane, maniacal mind. Maybe even psychosis. Both Lee and Nathan knew what that was like and what it could mean for hostages.

"Are you asking me if they have mental health issues?" Dr. Adams posed, his voice thin and tight.

"That's too narrow. Do these vague problems you refer to have any potential to skew their judgment?" Nathan asked.

"Yes, probably. I can't say for sure."

Lee edged off the table. "Why don't you give us an idea of what to expect."

Tyler inhaled and settled his elbows onto the laminate tabletop as if willing himself to disappear into the furniture. "I could get fired for saying this, but my wife is in there and I'll do whatever I can to save her life. What I can say is they all have had brain surgery."

"All of them?" Lee asked.

"Yes, and some of the patients are having unpleasant side effects."

"Such as?" Nathan prompted.

"Seizures. Hypersensitivity to noise. Some claim their arms and legs have stopped working even though testing shows good nerve conduction. We can't find a reason why they would experience that particular symptom when they don't have evidence of stroke or tumor."

Lee crossed his arms over his chest. "So we have armed men that could seize at any time?"

"That's unknown," Tyler said. "Morgan will know how to handle a seizure if it happens."

"That's going to be real hard for her if they accidentally discharge a weapon in the throes of a convulsion. They injure someone else in the process. Then she'd have two additional victims. And what if she's the one that's injured?"

Nathan held up a hand. "Lee, that's not getting us anywhere." He turned back to Tyler. "What do you think their mental state is? Why have they gone to such extremes?"

"The morale among the participants is low. These men are brave. The toughest. Combat injuries are different in their minds—those are earned. What they are suffering now was inflicted on them—friendly fire, I guess you could say. They want answers for their symptoms. And maybe to protect others from having the same things happen to them."

"And Reeves is unwilling to concede to problems with the protocol?" Nathan asked.

"He's getting pressure from elsewhere. That's all I can say."

"Are you friends with these men?" Nathan asked.

Lee glanced Nathan's way. "We're not sending him in there."

"I didn't say that. I'm just trying to establish why they pulled him into the loop rather than just going for Reeves."

Tyler cleared his throat. "I think we've established Dr. Reeves hasn't been very responsive to their concerns. But what you may not know is that Morgan recently found out that Dr. Reeves is her biological father."

Nathan's stomach cramped. This was the half sister Lilly spoke of? She'd mentioned their meeting, but they'd yet to discuss it in detail. Schedules prevented him from seeing Lilly the last couple days. He reached into his pocket for the foil-wrapped tablets that would ease his discomfort.

"So they're holding his daughter hostage? That's why they're here today. That's why it's that unit," Nathan surmised.

"How long ago did Morgan learn this?" Lee asked.

"Only a few days—just Wednesday."

"How do you think these three men found out?" Nathan asked.

"I know Morgan's mother visited Dr. Reeves on the unit. She disclosed this information."

Lee shifted, placing his black boot on a chair, and leaned forward. "With military types, we should assume the office is bugged. We need to get someone over there to check it out." He nodded at Tyler. "Your residence as well."

Nathan crossed his arms over his chest. "How old is your wife?"

"Twenty-eight."

"Why, after all these years, did your mother-in-law pick this time to divulge the news?" Lee asked.

Tyler locked eyes with Nathan. "Morgan needs a kidney transplant."

"She's on dialysis?" Lee asked.

"Yes."

"When is her next treatment due?" Lee asked.

"Monday."

"And if she doesn't get her treatment?" Nathan followed.

Tyler's eyes darkened. "She'd be okay for a day or two, but the longer she goes without dialysis, the more potential there is for her to—" His voice broke and he couldn't hold Nathan's gaze any longer.

"Die. You were going to say die?" Nathan asked.

Lee motioned for Nathan to join him in the corner. "This is bad, Nathan. What do they do if their prized possession suddenly keels over and they can't use her as currency anymore?"

"I don't know. It just means we need to resolve this thing before anything like that happens."

Lee closed his eyes. "This is going to make the Samuals case look like a cakewalk. SEALs? They're experts at everything. Hiding, booby traps, hand-to-hand combat. Their training is designed to flush out great men— mentally and physically."

One of the battalion officers from the fire department approached their position; his look of concern caused Nathan to pop another antacid. "We're getting reports of smoke in the hallway outside the PICU."

Nathan turned to Lee. "Pull your quick response team back."

Lee nodded. "We need biohazard suits on everyone. We don't know what that substance could be. Hopefully, it's just a smoke canister."

"What could it be if it's not smoke?" Tyler asked.

Lee inhaled before answering. "Nerve gas."

"How do we find out the difference?"

Nathan picked up the phone that went directly to the PICU. "If no one answers the phone, that's going to be bad. Very bad. If it's nerve gas—they'll be dead."

Chapter 31

1200, Saturday, August 11

BRETT PARKED HIS VEHICLE and stayed for a few moments collecting his thoughts.

Just being on a military base made his skin feel like worms were burrowing under it. The black shiny boots, green combat fatigues, and crew cuts of various colors reminded him of the harshness of his father. Not that he was abusive, but there were lines that should never be crossed—and those lines weren't always clear.

Probably where his sarcasm originated from—as a litmus test for determining his father's triggers. Trouble was his nature.

The military never had the same appeal for Brett that it did for his father. He abhorred order, and it still perplexed him how he and Nathan got along so well—especially considering Nathan's OCD-type habits. They reminded him of his father's stringent standards.

Maybe he'd found Daddy in his partner.

Brett shook the thought free. He and his old man had a functional relationship. A visit every ten years sufficed on both ends.

Exiting his vehicle, Brett straightened his clothes and then wanted to slap his own hands for doing so. *How are you supposed to act on one of these bases?* He didn't want to do anything that would raise the ire of the bigwig he was seeing—lest he be even more unwilling to give information.

He referenced the map from the entry gate and double-checked the building. After he entered, he walked up to a short desk hosted by an equally short assistant, in military dress, hair off the collar. She looked at him expectantly.

He extended a hand. She didn't take it.

Okay . . . off to a swimming start.

"I'm Detective Brett Sawyer. I'm here to see Lieutenant Colonel Markel."

"Please, have a seat."

He did.

Nathan would like this place.

Freshly waxed, brown-swirled tile. Wood chairs. Nathan detested sitting on cloth cushions because of what they could absorb and hide. It was surprising Nathan didn't carry a pocket Wood's lamp to verify that what he was sitting on didn't contain any sort of vile substance from another individual.

For Brett, however, the prison-like feel was causing him heat rash, and he thought about taking his tie off and shoving it in his pocket.

He heard the swift steps of heavy boots coming down the hall. Brett stood from his chair as a man emerged from the corridor. Despite himself, Brett couldn't resist giving a salute—though it was half-hearted and full of indecision. He hoped it hadn't come off as a mocking gesture. The man reached for his hand, and his fingers clamped on Brett's like the sticky appendages of a Venus flytrap.

Even the man's pinky has biceps.

Brett tried not to grimace as Lieutenant Colonel Markel comfortably squeezed the bones in his hand to dust. Perhaps that's what he used instead of salt on his food. "Nice to meet you, sir."

"Detective, would you like to come to my office?"

Brett's stomach rolled his insecurity. "Yes, sir." Why hadn't he at least brought a uniformed officer with him? He wanted a chaperone.

Markel's face was taut. Teeth clenched. Sharp blue eyes searched Brett's face for more seconds than he found comfortable. His military cropped dark brown hair echoed the roughness of old acne scars on his face. Before he turned on his heel, Markel set his jaw and tilted his head as if pondering what sort of karate move he could put Brett through to assert his dominance.

Really, the piercing stare, strong facial muscles, and almost shirt-ripping biceps were enough alpha male for Brett.

A warrior in every sense of the word. Body. Mind. Soul.

Brett followed down the hall and felt his feet itch to start marching. What was it about the military? How did the aura of the dress, the ordered feel of the station induce an average citizen into sitting up straighter just by putting feet on their soil?

Markel entered the room first and motioned Brett to sit.

"I appreciate you seeing me today," Brett said as he positioned himself in the chair.

"I'm always willing to help our counterparts on the police force. Lots of places need order to be brought forth." Markel motioned to Brett's tie. He looked down and lined it with the buttons of his shirt.

Great. A mean version of Nathan Long. At least Nathan lets me be me.

Brett cleared his throat. "I understand that Dylan Worthy used to serve under your command."

"Well, not directly under me, of course. But I am aware of the man and his difficulties."

"What were those difficulties?"

Markel steepled his fingers and leaned back into his chair, resting his elbows on the arms. "Mr. Worthy was not an asset to us. We didn't value the same things. He was dishonorably discharged."

"He was a trained SEAL, correct?"

"Yes."

"Well, why was he let go?"

"Conduct unbecoming."

"Which means what? He didn't say the Pledge of Allegiance before breakfast?"

Markel's eyes narrowed and Brett swore the man's laser gaze sizzled a hole right through his chest. He brushed his fingers over his shirt, checking for singed threads.

Markel clasped his hands together. "There were complaints that he acted inappropriately around some of the younger women on base."

"He didn't call them the day after?"

"I wouldn't be privy to that information."

Brett had seen the constellation of signs on Markel's face on previous interviewees. The slightly open lips, tilted head, and widened eyes. A look that begged him to keep probing. He'd disclose the true issue if Brett could find the trigger.

He needed to find out if the dog tags he'd found at the park near Zoe Martin's body belonged to a child murderer. Focus that direction.

"Enlisted women?"

Markel shook his head.

"How young?" Brett prompted.

"Middle to high school aged girls."

Like Zoe? Was that how it started? When the improper touching wasn't enough, he progressed to murdering young girls?

"Why didn't you stop him? Have him face a military court and lock him up, instead of letting him run roughshod over the civilian community?"

"Detective Sawyer, I really don't appreciate your tone. It's unprofessional."

Brett's stomach came up into his throat. Why did these types have such an effect on him? His sassy attitude was usually reserved for coworkers. Those who could understand him and not file a complaint with the public relations officer.

"I apologize, sir. It's just that it would help me considerably if you wouldn't be vague. I have a murdered girl on my hands. A family is grieving."

Markel's shoulders dropped a little. Was he opening the door to the confessional?

"Dylan Worthy was accused of many things. Most couldn't be verified, but there was a well-documented case of improper touching between him and one woman's daughter. From that situation, he was dishonorably discharged."

"And now he's my problem."

"Tell me, Detective. Why do you think Worthy is involved in one of your cases?"

"Gee, I don't know. Because I found his dog tags at my crime scene."

Markel began to drum his fingertips together. "Really?"

"You may think this is the best part of my day, to just randomly interview upstanding military types without cause. But there is a very dangerous man out there, and any insight you offer may help to get him off the streets. Do you have any idea of his whereabouts?"

"I think you need to speak with his wife. Maybe she could help you."

Markel began to type at his keyboard.

Brett cleared his throat. "Had another question for you. Do you know anything about a Dr. Reeves and these brain surgeries he's performing?"

For the briefest moment, Markel's fingers froze. "The military has severed all ties with Dr. Reeves and his research. I can't make any further comment other than that."

When Brett pulled up to Gina Worthy's house, a low whistle escaped his lips. As he climbed out of his car one word came to mind: *McMansion.*

How could she afford a house so ostentatious? Markel didn't believe she and Dylan had divorced, but this monstrosity spoke of newfound money. Brett walked up the Spanish-tiled steps and rang the doorbell. He wondered what those possibilities might be.

Maybe Dylan Worthy had used some contacts with nefarious foes to set up some sort of less-than-legal entrepreneurship. Maybe weapons. Or drugs. Prostitutes? Child slavery?

Brett's shoulders ached while his conspiracy-prone deductive reasoning ran amok.

The door eased open and a homely woman stood in front of him. Freckled. No makeup. Mousy brown hair, washed, but the curls frizzed in the dry Colorado air.

"Can I help you?" Dark shadows under her eyes seemed to suck whatever life remained.

Brett shook his head to clear the explosion of his expectation from the reality before him. "Are you Gina Worthy?"

She inched the door open more. "I am."

"Dylan Worthy's wife?"

"Legally."

Oh. Looks like I just cracked open an encyclopedia.

Brett fished his badge from his back pocket. He flipped it toward her. "I'm Detective Brett Sawyer with Aurora police. I'd like to speak with you about your husband."

What he was used to seeing—either the feigned or truly shocked look when he uttered those words—didn't register on her face. It was like talking to drywall. She merely said, "I thought you'd get here a lot sooner than this." She opened the door wider.

Okay, now. An encyclopedia and a can of worms.

What was immaculate on the outside was a disaster zone on the inside.

House rich. Cash poor.

The home reeked of animal stench. Brett could see kitty-litter trays in two corners of the living room. At least three cats scurried to hide as they walked the short hall. One side of the room held gym equipment that served as the general depository for dirty clothes. Perhaps at one time

Dylan had used it faithfully, but Gina seemed less concerned with physical fitness than her ex-SEAL husband likely was. She motioned to a soiled, obnoxious, floral couch. Brett imagined it had been pilfered from a sidewalk where someone pinned a "Free" sign on it. There were brown patches of dried animal feces stuck to the fibers.

Now I get why Nathan prefers wood or concrete over bacteria-housing foam. I'm gonna have to stop ribbing him about that.

Brett seated himself in the least filthy spot. Placing just one butt cheek against the cushion might make him appear too feminine, he decided, so he settled back fully on the couch. He silently wished for a container of Nathan's hand gel. Maybe he needed to imbibe a little of Markel's alpha male demeanor.

"Mrs. Worthy—"

"Gina, please."

Real cause or imagined, his skin cells screamed to be scratched. A cat leapt onto the cushions between them, and Brett's skeleton nearly jumped free from his body. He clenched his teeth to keep from swearing.

Furry animals were usually not friendly to him—and as if on cue, the cat hissed. Gina scooted the animal off the couch and folded her hands together, her eyes begging him to get to the matter at hand.

He inhaled shallowly and squared his shoulders. "Gina, then. You don't seem surprised to see me."

"You, maybe. But not the police. You don't strike me as the police type."

"Well, you're not the first to say that. I take it as a compliment."

"You're here to learn more about Dylan?"

"You mention that you're not divorced, but your statement leads me to believe that neither are you together."

"Right."

"He's not living here."

"No."

"I just came from talking with Lieutenant Colonel Markel about your husband."

She stilled at those words. "So you know."

Know what?

"Well, he did confirm some of my suspicions," Brett said.

"About the operation and what I did."

Brett's vision clouded a moment. Perhaps the fumes were beginning to overwhelm him. *Operation?*

"Was Dylan involved in these brain surgeries?"

"Yes. But you didn't know that?"

Brett let the silence linger as he thought of what to say.

Gina couldn't take it. "Has Dr. Reeves said what the problem is?"

All the things he should have seen in the room but had missed because the mission he was on was separate from the one Gina expected. The large-screen HDTV set to a news channel, but muted. The picture of Sacred Heart with the banner of *Chaos at Children's* on the screen. Somehow, he had to figure out how all these pieces lined up. Perhaps Gina could provide the missing linchpin.

"Mrs. Worthy. We are going to back up several steps, okay?"

She nodded. Her eyes wide and twitchy.

"When did you and Dylan meet?"

"We were high school sweethearts. I've known him since first grade."

"Married when?"

"Just one year into college. He was focused—always wanted to be in the military. It was his one, solitary goal."

"How was the marriage?"

It was the first moment fear crept across her face. "Dylan is not the man I thought he was."

"Can you be specific?" A smoky gray cat rubbed against her frumpy purple sweatpants.

"Did Markel tell you why he was let go from the military?" Gina asked.

"That he seemed to fancy underage girls."

"Fancy would be an understatement."

"How much of an understatement?" Brett asked.

"A lot."

"So you are aware of actual criminal activity."

"Yes."

"How do you know?"

Gina looked down at her folded hands. "Because he hurt someone in my family."

Brett's gut ached. It's why he did homicide and not sex crimes. There were lots of law breakers. Lots of life takers. But when young kids got hurt, it was easy for him to imagine using lethal force in a not-so-legal way.

"You didn't report it?"

She shook her head, and Brett wanted to ask why. *Could it have been the one moment that would have stopped so many other lives from being damaged?*

"Honestly, Detective, that wasn't the only thing. I wanted more for my life than just to be a warrior's future widow. I was so lonely. He didn't earn enough money. I wanted freedom from that lifestyle. The constant moving. Having to get to know new people every three years. I just wasn't thriving in that environment."

"So you began to look for an out."

"Yes. But something happened that stopped me cold from carrying out what I wanted to do."

"And that was?"

"I got pregnant."

From center mound, the pitch hit him square in the chest. There weren't any sounds in the house of children, only the pitter-patter of multitudes of furry feet scampering about.

"How long ago was that?"

"A couple of years."

"Why did that stop your plans? You were concerned about his affinity for young girls? I would think it would hasten any planning you started. Make it more urgent to break free."

Now there were tears. She raked the cat's fur like it was her last life-line, and the feline scrunched down in desperation. "You would think so, right? Especially after I found out it was a girl."

"So you did fear having a young girl in the house?"

"Yes, absolutely."

"What did you do?"

"I was lost and didn't want to raise a baby on my own. As the child of a single mother, I saw her working three crappy, less-than-minimum-wage jobs. It broke her spirit to do so much and still have trouble keeping me fed and clothed. I didn't want life to be hard. I wanted lots of money in a bank account. I wanted status. Respect. I wanted freedom from a marriage that felt like prison. From motherhood. From what I thought would be a dream life when what I was actually living was hell on earth."

Gina covered her eyes and took a moment to collect herself. Brett pushed his back into the couch and stared at the ceiling. He knew he should offer some type of comfort, but he just wasn't built to be that shoulder to cry on. Eventually, he settled his eyes on the television and watched the headlines scroll across the bottom. Her sobbing eased, but she didn't make any moves to clear the emotional distress from her face.

"Gina, what happened? What was your decision?"

"I got a call that changed my life forever."

"From?"

"Dr. Thomas Reeves."

Okay, now things are getting interesting.

"He said Dylan had volunteered to have this brain surgery that would change the way his memory worked. That he'd be able to remember everything. He had some fancy name for it. Almost like a real life superhero. Said he'd be better than what God created."

"Why was he calling you? Didn't he just need permission from Dylan?"

She gripped the cat so hard, it screeched and leapt from the couch. "He needed something I had."

"What?"

Her hands settled against her stomach. "The graft."

Brett rustled his hands through his hair in a vain attempt to force his mind to connect with what she was saying. "I'm sorry, Gina. I'm not good with science stuff. Almost flunked out of high school."

The maniacal smile that spread across her face crystallized the blood in his veins. The last remnant of life slipped from her eyes, and her pupils dilated as a dark spirit of resignation clawed its way through the gateway straight to her soul.

She pulled a revolver from between the cushions of the couch, gripped it with both hands, and pointed it at her chest.

Brett stood up and held his hands out to her. "No, Gina. This isn't the answer. I want to help you. Help me understand what happened."

Droplets of imprisoned grief dripped off her chin. Gina closed her eyes. If she successfully blocked him out and convinced herself this was the answer, there was little he could do to stop her finger from depressing the trigger.

"Gina, please. Open your eyes and look at me. I want you to tell me what happened. Before you make up your mind, I want you to tell me why you're so sad. Why you think this is the answer."

Her eyes shot open. Still with a hint of resolve but also with a bright flare of anger. Anger was good. He could work with that. The gun wobbled away from her heart.

"Dr. Reeves offered me money. *Lots* of money if she proved a donor match to Dylan."

It was like each of her words inflated a balloon that sat inside his chest. Each utterance filled it with dread.

"But she had to be tested first. So I went in for an amniocentesis. And I *saw* her."

More determination. The gun squared back. Thumb now plumb with the trigger.

Brett whistled to draw her eyes, cursing himself for not paying more attention in crazy-people-wanting-to-off-themselves class. One thing he knew wasn't covered: How the victim's grief and sadness pulled everything of light and help from the room like a ravenous black hole. And how his heart ached at her sadness.

"Gina, I've been where you are. I've done stupid things and I've wanted to kill myself. But I'm here. I'm here for you. I'll do whatever it is you want me to if you'll just put the weapon down."

She rested her head back on the couch and laid the weapon on her lap.

Inwardly, Brett fist-pumped in relief. Movement in the right direction.

"What do you think of someone who sees life and still accepts money for death? What do you think of that person?" Gina asked.

"I know what I see in this job every day is people who are hurting and sometimes they make choices that were the best for them at that time. You were miserable. You wanted out of a bad situation. You saw the money as your ticket to freedom. Many people would have done the same thing. They may not ever admit it, but they would. Dr. Reeves took advantage of your situation. He's the lowlife. Not you."

She smirked at his words. "I aborted my baby so Reeves could use her brain cells. Dylan always wanted a spotlight—to be famous. He wanted the surgery to be something more than he was—which was really just a budding sociopath."

Icy vapors chilled the air. His blood curdled like the time he'd been momentarily locked in the medical examiner's freezer as a sick joke. What had frozen him then was not the subzero temperature his body had been thrust into but the other bodies. The death. The grim reaper counting his collection.

That's what he felt now. Death roving over Gina, whispering in her ear to pick up the gun.

What perplexed him was the one thing he was missing.

Dylan wants glory. To be famous. Touching and killing girls is his sick lifeline. He doesn't want that area of his life exposed. Doesn't want to give it up. Won't give it up.

Brett felt time ticking by too quickly. He kept working the machinations in his mind.

Won't give it up unless he can trade it for his ultimate desire. To be a super-soldier. A science fiction wonder.

But that doesn't work either. He's haunted. Frankenstein's monster is a reality. Humans have begun to use others for body parts, but it's okay when the donor's brain has died. When their humanness has left for the other dimension—or whatever people believe it to be.

Gina Worthy watched him with renewed interest. Curiosity. Waiting to see if he would reach the same conclusion she had.

But what happens to a person when he sacrifices a life that still has humanness, but doesn't give him the payoff he hoped for? When he realizes he has bought a lie? Dylan doesn't become a super soldier. The graft causes problems. He's sick.

Suddenly that odd phrase the widow uttered made sense. Made perfect sense.

That's when all of our trouble started . . .

"Gina, is Dylan one of the hostage takers at the hospital?"

She tilted her head, a look of dismay filling her eyes. "Isn't that why you're here?"

Brett shook his head. The puzzle in his mind had a new picture. His neurons fired crazily at the implications, trying to put the new pieces into place.

She pointed the weapon at him. Both hands firm on the revolver. Instinct caused him to draw his own weapon at her.

"Okay, Gina. This is not the direction to go. Put your weapon down."

"You promised you would do anything for me."

"*If* you put the weapon down. That's what I said."

"Kill me."

"No."

"I can't do it myself."

"Gina, this isn't a game. Put the gun down!"
She pulled the hammer back.
A testy feline jumped from the chair onto her lap.
Brett dove straight at her.

Chapter 32

AT THE OTHER END OF the table, Scott pulled two items from a small duffel bag that he'd hidden in the stairwell. Now he wore a Kevlar vest and added a small handgun to his arsenal. Stuffed envelopes in his back pocket.

Yet, here they still sat.

Making the video had turned into a quest for perfection. From what Morgan could tell, Scott Clarke apparently considered himself a budding filmmaker—in addition to his criminal activities. Take after take, the message he wanted to deliver increased her anxiety each time she uttered the phrase.

How could he deliberately hurt the children?

When she'd sent the video to Tyler, she wanted to die. Though she rehearsed often what her last words to him might have been—left in a note beside her body—she wanted his thoughts of her to be sweet and sorrowful. Realizing that her demise had been at her own hands was something he'd have to learn to live with. It beat the pain of having to live this life without Teagan.

Now, considering the pain watching that video would bring to Tyler broke her. *How could I have seriously thought of putting my husband through so much suffering—willfully breaking his spirit with such a callous act?* Perhaps what they said about suicide was true. It was selfish. Her pain would end, but Tyler's—and her family's—would continue, and intensify.

Could I deliberately hurt him that way?

The clunk of the weapon brought her attention back to the situation at hand. "There's something about you, Morgan. Something I want to know."

She and Scott sat across from one another at the long table with ten chairs. Each headed an end of the table, like a couple who wanted to argue but were fearful of where that disruption might lead. After all, he held a gun and she didn't. His stare became relentless, as if a test of her resolve—for what she didn't know.

There was a way he carried himself. An air of humble superiority that only came from one institution she could think of.

"Are you still in the military?"

He raised an eyebrow at her question, slid his finger through the trigger housing, and pulled the weapon across the table. The sound affected her spine like fingers on a chalkboard.

"Not anymore."

So simple yet so full of implications.

"How can you do this?" she pressed. "A man who served his country. You swore to protect us. Now you're threatening to kill helpless American citizens. What about your oath?"

"Sometimes, if the master is unlawful, action is justified." He turned the weapon so the muzzle faced her. "Wouldn't you agree?"

She slipped one hand over the other. "What is it you expect to happen?"

"I know some things about you."

"Is that supposed to impress me?"

His eyes widened at her tone and he leaned his head to one side. "That you had a baby who died."

"She was murdered, actually."

He nodded, contemplating her statement. "Shaken, right?"

"Yes."

"Like the baby you just admitted."

"Who will probably die, too, if you don't let me back out there to help her."

"That must have been terrible. Losing a baby like that. Murdered, as you say."

Morgan swallowed heavily, her throat tight as she spoke. "The hardest thing ever."

"I know a little about that."

Mentally, she reeled from the statement. "You lost a baby," she confirmed.

He nodded his head slowly. "A boy."

"Is that why you're here? Your son was a patient? From what I understand, my father has never worked in pediatrics. Only with adults."

Scott nodded his head in affirmation—but to which part? His gray-green eyes narrowed at her questions. "My son was never a patient here."

"So this isn't about him?"

"I don't know if I'd say that." The scar on the side of his head gleamed through his hair. "It's about many things."

"Maybe if I knew what those things were, I could help. I want to do what I can to end this matter peacefully."

"I think your father was involved in my son's death."

Morgan gasped. "That's why you're here? For a confession to this crime?"

He twirled the weapon toward himself. Never had she wished for anyone's death other than her own, but this moment qualified.

"Is there something you want to tell me? Are you going to keep me in here forever?"

"I see something in your eyes." He leaned on his elbows, his head lowering like that of an animal that had just sighted prey. "Almost a dare to die."

"Isn't that why you're here? To force my father's hand? And if he doesn't relent—you'll kill me?"

He edged up slightly. "You seem ready to die."

"Shouldn't we all be?"

"There's a difference between being prepared and welcoming it."

"Yet that's what you're doing. Welcoming death. You're not expecting to get out of here alive."

"Why do you say that?"

"Because the cops are never going to allow you to leave. Plus, I saw the envelopes you put in your back pocket. They're letters, right? To give to your family when you're dead. "

Scott Clarke pulled all the way up and leaned back into his chair. "Didn't anyone tell you that mouthing off to a hostage taker is a bad idea?"

Morgan shrugged. "Sometimes it's best not to delay the inevitable."

"Waiting can be a good thing. It makes you reconsider your actions. Pick a different course."

"That's what you want Thomas Reeves to do. Change his mind about something."

"How is he about doing things like that?"

"I wouldn't know. I've never met him."

"You didn't go to him and plead for a kidney?"

Her throat tightened. *So he knows about my mother, too.*

"I've only begged for one thing in my life and it wasn't to him."

He nodded. "Begged God for your child's life," he said. He didn't have to ask. He already knew it was true.

"You got what you wanted. Video of your very persuasive threat. Now, I want to go check on my staff and patients."

He stood and walked to her side of the table. In one swift movement, he clenched her scrub top, yanking her up from the chair.

"Don't assume you can challenge me and get away with it for long."

He grabbed her arm and pulled up the long-sleeved shirt she wore underneath her scrubs to cover up her shunt scar, to keep it from scaring children. He laid the weapon over it; it thumped at the pressure of her pulse.

"Tell me, Morgan Adams. What would happen if I took my knife and cut your shunt wide open?"

She stiffened her muscles to keep her body from shaking. The closeness of his body to hers, the smell of a musky deodorant, his breath hot against her cheek. Morgan turned her head away.

He leaned toward her and whispered in her ear, "What happens?"

She begged her body not to betray her. Ultimately, she didn't want to die with the mask of fear plastered to her face—only strength.

"I'll bleed to death."

He brushed his lips over her ear. She recoiled.

"Something I'll have to remember. SEAL training—discover and exploit your enemy's weakness."

He opened the door and shoved her through it into the hallway. The door just beyond the staff lounge entrance that led to the stairwell was now barricaded with a smaller-size patient crib. She walked quickly around the corner and was shocked to see what her unit had become in the ninety or so minutes that she'd been away.

Blankets and sheets covered all of the windows, held down along the edges with blue painter's tape. Taking out the sunlight made it appear much later in the day. At the main entrance, two empty patient beds were rammed up against the door. On either side were IV bags taped to the frame with cords hanging down. Scott's comrades were now in Kevlar vests as well.

They used IV solution, normally a child's lifesaver, to build bombs.

Morgan's heart sank.

Surveying the room, she saw Jose and Dylan positioned in the middle, standing guard. Lisa was forced to remain at the nurses' station, her face creased with worry. The other nurses were near their patients' beds. Trudy held Bree in her arms as Bree cried.

Morgan saw smoke puff underneath the doorway.

Instinctively, she brought her arm up to cover her nose and mouth and glanced Scott's direction. He seemed nonplussed at her distress. She pulled her hand down and ran toward the door. Heavy footfalls followed in her wake. His hand fisted up her scrub top and whipped her backward. As she pivoted his direction on her heel, his hand came up and the butt of the pistol slammed into her left cheek.

Morgan crumpled to the floor.

Pain seared through the nerves of her face and shot through her brain like hot needles. Her vision dimmed and she blinked several times—wondering if the blow had blinded her with that one swift move.

"Everyone!" his voice boomed.

Morgan's heart thundered in her ears as he kneeled down next to her, his open palm against her chest. Morgan reached up and groped for his face to push him away. Grabbing her hand, he held it firmly to the front of his tactical vest.

"You need to breathe, dear Morgan, or you're going to pass out. I need my trusty charge nurse to stay with me. For now."

She inhaled sharply, the breath fuel to the fiery pain, and black cloudy outlines began to float over her vision like bodiless wraiths. With her other hand, she pressed against her forehead to counteract the hot pokers that bored into her bone.

Scott cleared his throat.

"Morgan thinks she can dictate what happens here today."

With his hand gripping hers, he yanked her from the floor. The room spun like she'd been trapped on a violent merry-go-round and she buckled onto all fours. The red dots that dripped onto the tile finally focused her vision. Reaching up, she felt the thick fluid slide down her cheek.

"What everyone needs to realize," he continued, "is that you can't do anything without my permission. Including beg for your own death." He kneeled beside her and she shrank away from his presence. He clutched her upper arm and pulled her close. "Do we have an understanding, Morgan?"

She nodded and attempted to jerk her arm free. His fingers tightened. "What do you want to do about the smoke?"

The rough outline of a blue flight suit hovered in her peripheral vision, and she could sense Drew's anger as he neared them.

"It's not enough that you've barricaded us in here," Drew said, "but you have to beat up on women, too?"

Scott tossed Morgan back. She pulled up on her knees—blurry figures now solidifying. She stood, a little too quickly, on shaky feet and swayed to maintain the upright position. Drew took two quick steps her direction and wrapped his arm around her waist to support her.

Snot mixed with tears dripped from her nose as blood ran down her chin. "It's fine. Drew, I'm okay." She eased herself down and sat on her heels, determined not to cry. The tilt of the room began to slow. She looked up at Scott. "The children. The smoke could hurt them. We need to put something under the doors to stop it." She covered the wound with the heel of her hand to stop the bleeding.

He nodded. "Well, that's a very good idea. Now, ask me for permission."

She eyed him, her eyes narrowed beams of determination. "Scott, may we put something under the doors to keep the smoke from killing our patients?"

The movement was so sudden she couldn't reach down to prevent his fingers from clasping around her throat. Her pulse raced.

He held, lightly squeezing, black venom in his eyes. "Morgan, I know you want to die. But do you want to take everyone else with you?" His fingers cinched at her throat and her pulse jumped in response. "Ask me nicely."

She placed her hands over his, her vision fuzzy, her blood transferring onto the back of his hands. "Scott, may I please put some wet towels under the doors so that we can keep the smoke out?"

The fire alarm pierced the small space. Those children who were awake covered their ears with trembling hands. Bree's cries were barely audible under the noise. The phone at the nurses' station began to ring.

Scott pointed to Drew. "Would you mind taking care of that wound for Morgan? Looks like she has a phone call."

Drew looked blankly at her. He didn't know where most of their supplies were kept. Another nurse approached her with tentative steps, holding out a washcloth. Scott raised an expectant eyebrow.

Morgan folded her arms over her chest to ease the chill that permeated her bones. "Scott, may I take this washcloth to control the bleeding, and can Lucy help Drew with the towels?"

He nodded. "I see we understand one another."

She took the cloth from Lucy's hands and applied it to the cut. "Can I answer?"

The alarms ceased. Scott acquiesced with a faint tip of his head, and she neared the nurses' station. Lisa stared at her with the wide eyes of a child. Morgan picked up the receiver.

"Morgan?"

One hand held the phone. The other held the washcloth to her cheek. She could hear the man's quickened breath on the other side. His voice was different. Slightly higher in pitch. Concerned.

Troubled.

Like the weight of the world was on his shoulders.

"Yes."

A quick exhalation of relief. "Good to hear your voice. My name's Nathan Long. I'm the negotiator on duty today. We're getting reports of smoke up there."

She eyed Scott, who was a mere two steps from her position. "He wants to know about the smoke."

"Tell them they need to figure it out." Scott walked away.

"Morgan?" the voice in her ear asked.

It was the lean of Drew's shoulder toward Scarlett's crib that caused her skin to prickle with concern. Her response died in her throat. Sometimes, when the soul struggled to edge out of the body, there was a gentle tug of good-bye noticed by body-bound spirits, if they listened. A spiritual summons before the physical body leaked evidence of its inner fire burning out.

The baby's monitor alarmed.

Drew's eyes were pensive and beckoning at the same time. "Morgan . . ." His voice was not panicked, but steely with need for her presence at his side. His boots quick across the tile. Scott turned and aimed his weapon Drew's direction.

Morgan's mind slowed her view of each person's actions.

Scott's finger on the trigger.

Nathan's voice urgent in her ear. "Morgan, what's happening? I need you to answer me so I know you're okay."

Morgan raised her hands up. The phone crashed to the desk and the washcloth to the floor. Her sister-in-law jolted in her chair.

She picked the receiver up and slammed the phone into the cradle. "Scott! Please, the baby. Her heart rate is slowing down. She's dying."

He nodded his approval and lowered the weapon. Morgan scurried around the desk just as the heart rate monitor triple-toned at the deadly rhythm. Izabel pulled the red metal crash cart to the end of the infant's crib and snapped open the lock. From the top drawer, she raked her fingernails at the plastic that covered the medication tray and tore at the small cardboard boxes that housed lifesaving vials of medication. Epinephrine and atropine.

Drew's hands encircled the infant's chest as he began compressions. Morgan pulled the baby off the ventilator and began to manually assist breaths.

Izabel eyed Morgan, holding up the medication like a kindergartner with the right answer.

"It's the epi dose," she said.

Morgan pulled the baby's eyelids up.

Pupils are blown. Just as I feared.

The problem was not really the baby's heart, but her head. The injury from shaking had caused the brain to swell. When the pressure within the skull became too high, structures moved where they were never intended to go. Because of the shearing forces, the edema, the baby's brain stem was being shoved down into her spinal column.

Brain herniation means death.

"Izabel, give that epi and then go into the pharmacy and get me some mannitol and succinylcholine."

"We don't have any orders."

"I'll write verbal orders from Marshall. We're in a little bit of a tight spot here."

Izabel eyed her quizzically. "What do you need the succ—"

"Just do what I tell you!"

The nurse slipped the adrenaline into the IV and followed it with a quick normal saline flush. Hopefully, that would drive the baby's heartbeat higher and they could stop doing compressions. Drew eyed her continuing CPR as they waited for the medication to take effect, but his eyes questioned her intentions.

Mannitol would help with the pressure in the baby's head. Succinylcholine was a paralyzing medication, and the baby was already on a continuous drip of just such an agent.

Drew mouthed. "Why?"

Morgan shrugged and continued to ventilate.

Chapter 33

MORGAN LAID THE INFANT'S pale blue body in the middle of the sheet, leaving the endotracheal tube and lines in place. A quiet dreariness settled over the unit. The three armed men took staggered positions throughout the open space, guns always at the ready but at least pointed toward the floor. To her right, on the bedside table, were two solidifying gel molds of Scarlett's hands.

After Teagan died, similar molds had formed plaster sculptures of her tiny fists. Morgan had expected their arrival at some point during her bereavement leave, but when they finally came to her home, Morgan couldn't contain the grief and joy that spilled from her eyes. Those casts and the small clips of Teagan's hair meant everything. The staff also gave her a book of thoughts on their experiences caring for her family, and she often reviewed it still.

These tokens given to families upon the death of their children were a tradition in the PICU. Fact of life: children died. Families suffered losses like this every day. Memorializing their grief was part of giving some joy back. Knowing that their children had touched the hospital staff helped them in their grief. Having these mementos was a way to remember their short lives and the large impact they'd had. Echoes of a life's imprint on others.

Even though this baby ultimately died at the hands of an abuser, Morgan thought of the woman who was Scarlett's mother. *She's probably out in the front of the hospital right now. Her daughter died, and she was prevented from being here to hold her.*

Morgan wouldn't deny giving these gifts to her.

Thoughts of Tyler filled her mind. *What was it like for him to receive that video of me giving the hostage-takers' demands?* If there was anything she was sure of, it was that he was likely overwrought with the thoughts of her possible death.

What caused her spirit to ache now was how she'd cheated him of affection over the last several months. Losing Teagan, her kidney failure, and the ultimate need for dialysis took away her desire for those marital joys. And sadly, her life hanging in the balance did little to help her want to cling to the world she shared with her husband.

Wouldn't it be better for everyone if I just disappeared? I infuse my grief into every life I know. She'd had enough of it herself.

Morgan gazed at Scarlett's bed and involuntarily superimposed a memory of her own baby over this child's untimely death. She swaddled Scarlett's body in a cloth and trembled badly.

Drew was on the other side of the crib, assisting her. He laid a heavy hand on her forearm and eased it off the cocooned body. He pulled her around the other side and pushed her into a seated position on an empty toddler's bed.

He leaned close to her. "You did everything you could."

Morgan nodded, tears flowing.

"We did everything by the book. They can't hold you responsible for her death."

Her teeth bit into her lip—the irony, salty fluid filled her mouth.

Drew cupped her chin. "Enough of that. One thing at a time."

Morgan nodded. Could she pull it together? So far there hadn't been any sign that someone was coming to save them. No sign that help was present on the floor. A portable TV had been pulled into the center of the unit, and Scott flitted around it like a young moth pondering whether the electric blue light was nirvana or death.

"We need to take care of that cut."

Trudy heard his statement and pulled supplies out of one of the bedside cabinets.

"How bad is it?" Morgan asked.

"How do you feel about stitches without lidocaine?"

"Why don't you just clean it and use butterfly closures?"

"You should have Steri-Strips on the unit somewhere, don't you?"

Izabel nodded. With Scott otherwise occupied, she made slow, steady steps to another cabinet to pull the materials out.

"We need to start feeding people," Drew said as he moistened a cloth at the nearby sink. He dabbed at the dried blood on her face.

Intellectually, she knew what he was doing. It was a common ploy in those who worked with pediatric patients. Talk about the normal. The dull. The everyday stuff to draw attention away from the horrifying thing that was happening to you.

"I know. We can get snacks. Keep people drinking."

Izabel dropped the supplies on the side of the bed. "I can start pulling juice and cheese and crackers out."

"Before the snack, round on the patients. Let's make sure no drips are running out. Patient care needs to continue as normal. Vital signs. Turning. Everything. Team up with Lucy, okay?"

Izabel gave a halfhearted wave and neared Lucy, who stood vigil at Seth's bedside.

Morgan glanced Drew's direction. She picked up the package of Steri-Strips. "You're pretty good at what you do. Staying calm. Making sure things are taken care of. From what I know about paramedics, your type isn't necessarily good at letting others step in and help."

He raised an eyebrow at her. "You think you and I are much different, Ms. Control Freak?"

Morgan tried to separate the thin, plastic sheets so she could open the package. "If I control everything, I can only blame myself when things go wrong. I don't have to worry about someone else letting me down."

"Isn't that lonely? I've found that just surrendering and allowing others to help gives me back more control—particularly if it's the Big Man in Charge." He plied the package from her fingers. "You know my big fingers are not going to be as delicate as they need to be, but you're stuck with them."

"It's all right. It won't hurt any worse than it does now."

She should have kept her lips closed until he was done. Even the gentle probing of his fingers against her cheekbone increased the pain throbbing at her temples.

He reached for more strips. "Ice will help. Some Tylenol for the splitting headache I'm sure you have. I've been clocked a few times in my life and I know it's no fun. Do you think those punches I took improved my mug any?" He paused from dressing her wound and gave her a quick side profile.

She smiled. There was something about Drew. Medical people were known to have a dark sense of humor—particularly when in stressful situations. But his self-deprecating manner was a salve to her sad spirit.

Scott turned up the volume.

What they knew as hostages was only what they saw on the television. Evacuations of the hospital were taking place. They were moving children to a nearby high school gymnasium—at least those who should stay for hospital care. The critical patients who were difficult to move out of the facility were being relocated to the emergency department, which had been closed down to all incoming patients. The campus was closed. All children who could be discharged were being sent home. All surgeries canceled.

There was surreal—and then there was unfathomable. Housed in their little unit, it was hard at times to understand how these three men had altered the course of so many lives. Had anyone else died today because of them?

Suddenly, Scott motioned to his other compatriots. He tilted the portable screen their direction, and Morgan caught sight of the image that had them so enthralled.

Her biological father, Thomas Reeves, appeared before a throng of press. A reporter's mike nearly kissed his lips. The woman edged into his personal space and it looked like he was about to deck her.

With their captors' attention drawn away, Drew patted at the vial of the paralyzing agent in her pocket. He kept his voice low. "Want to tell me what you want to do with that?"

Morgan turned her head toward the blanketed-up windows to shield her voice. "It's not enough to incapacitate all three. Maybe just one. Need to get a needle and syringe to draw it up."

"Cut the head off the snake as they say?"

Morgan nodded. "The others seem to be here to support Scott. That Jose guy is pretty even tempered. The other one, Dylan . . . well, I've got a horrible feeling about him."

"When Scott hit you, Jose was definitely not on board. I saw him almost lunge at Scott to stop him. But I agree about Dylan. During that same moment, it looked like he was next up for an amusement park ride. Pure excitement on his face. It made my skin crawl." Drew motioned with a faint tilt of the head up to the ceiling. "Do you see what I see?"

Morgan glanced around—the three still had their eyes glued to the screen. She ventured a quick look upward. A thin tube protruded from the ceiling.

"SWAT," was all Drew said.

SWAT could see them! They'd snaked a camera through the ceiling and were watching all the drama unfold. But did they have a plan in place?

"How do you think we can do it?" Morgan asked.

Drew placed the last strip in place. "Inject one of them? I don't—"

A sudden slap to the top of the television jolted Morgan's nerves. Quickly, Scott was at their position. He snatched Morgan from the bed. The other two backed up a few steps. He planted her in front of the television.

"What is it with your father?" he screamed, his breath hot against the side of her face. "Does he love anything other than himself?"

Heavy fear spread through her body. Morgan caught the replay. "Whatever these men want, I can't help them. I won't help them."

"Even if it saves the lives of the hostages?"

He pointed a long finger at the camera. "They are responsible for their actions. I can't do anything to change what's already been done. Now please, step aside. Some of us have important work to accomplish today."

Scott turned the television off and grabbed her by the shoulders. "I want you to call him."

"Why?"

"To get him to change his mind."

Morgan took two hands and shoved the middle of Scott's chest, throwing his arms off her body. "I don't have that kind of power over him. I told you, I don't even know him."

His eyes seethed a quiet rage. His fists clenched at his sides. "We're going to have to light a fire under your father."

He stomped toward the crib that held the deceased baby. Morgan scrambled after him and tried to grab the back of his Kevlar vest. He swatted her hand behind him as if to ward off a pesky gnat.

"What are you doing?" Morgan screamed.

He scooped the bundle off the bed. "I'm going to give them a body. Maybe then they'll care a little bit more about what's happening in here."

Morgan grabbed at his arm. "You can't do it. There're lines that should never be crossed."

He shoved her back. "Evidently, you didn't learn that from your father."

With one hand he grabbed the edge of the sheet and unwrapped the body. Morgan scurried around the other side of the crib and clamped her hand down onto his wrist. He pulled his sidearm and aimed it at her chest.

She exhaled slowly to calm her quaking knees. "You told me you lost a child once. How would you like your child's body to be desecrated to prove a point? Imagine how this mother will feel. Are you going to put a bullet into Scarlett and throw her out the door? You don't think they'll be smart enough to tell that the baby had already died?"

He slammed the gun back into its holster and wheeled around.

A thud drew Scott's attention to the front door.

Chapter 34

JOSE FELL NEAR THE DOOR, caught in the throes of a seizure. His automatic weapon banged against the wall as his body flopped against the tile.

Morgan's instinct was to help. She took two steps in the flailing man's direction before Drew crossed in front of her—his face expressed his wish to let nature take its course. She got his unspoken message.

An incapacitated gunman is one less captor for all of us to deal with.

Scott shoved Drew out of the way. "Aren't you going to help him?"

Morgan pointed to the crash cart, and Drew, with slow steps, began to pull it from the crib that held the dead infant.

"Trudy, I need you to get a dose of Ativan out of the Pyxis machine." Morgan neared the flopping body to ease the automatic weapon away. Drew kneeled next to her and gently plucked Jose's sidearm out of its holster. He slid it across the floor.

Scott paced like a rabid dog. "No one else move!" He reached down and picked up Jose's gun and secured it behind his back. "The only people moving are those helping Jose. Does everyone get me?"

To highlight his point, he fired several rounds over their heads. Tufts of ceiling insulation showered over Morgan, Drew, and their patient. Morgan shielded the seizing man's face as pink, cotton candy rained around them. She motioned to Drew. "We need to pull him away from the wall so we have more room to work."

Trudy rolled two vials of Ativan her direction. Morgan opened the third drawer down from the top of the metal cart for a needle and syringe. Drew prepped a line full of saline for the IV.

Scott stormed closer. "What are you doing?"

Drew tightened a blue tourniquet around the thrashing man's arm. The convulsion would make getting the IV in Jose's vein more difficult. Morgan thrust the needle though the gray medication stopper and pulled up the thick, clear fluid. "This is Ativan. It's like Valium. He needs it to stop the seizure."

As Drew leaned over to look at the man's veins, he pulled the vial of succinylcholine out of Morgan's pocket and tucked the medication in his flight suit. Scott missed seeing the maneuver, or didn't understand it enough to know it was a threat to him.

There was a glance between the nurse and the paramedic. Drew's eyes begged her to consider the option of letting this one go. Under normal circumstances she'd never think of intentionally giving medication that would harm an individual, or even possibly kill him. Then again, she also had a rule against administering medicine without a doctor's orders. She'd already broken that rule today. Was the other so hard to overcome? Particularly when it involved someone who had threatened to kill her and her patients?

The problem with succinylcholine is that it also paralyzes the main muscle of respiration—the diaphragm.

If the diaphragm wasn't moving, the patient wasn't breathing, and they'd have to intubate and bag him to save his life. If they didn't, the young man would die of asphyxiation. There was no other conclusion as the result of that action.

Still, here was a chance to hobble the three-man strike force that held them hostage. Maybe a God-given chance. Two were easier to overcome than three.

Can I intentionally risk killing someone?

Drew popped the cover off the IV catheter. "You're going to have to help hold his arm in place."

Morgan slipped the syringe of Ativan into her pocket. She grabbed Jose's mid-forearm, just above his elbow space, and leaned heavily onto the extremity, stabilizing it on the tile floor. Drew punctured the vein on the first stick. Morgan saw the blood flow into the collecting chamber. Drew quickly secured it with tape and connected the bag of normal saline. He stood up holding it.

Morgan looked behind her. "Trudy, get one of the transport monitors."

"Why do you need to do that?" Scott asked, stepping closer.

"To watch his oxygen levels. People react differently to the medication. Some of them stop breathing."

Scott knocked her away from the man's convulsing body. "How do I know you're not going to kill him?"

Morgan eased herself back onto her knees and locked his eyes with hers. "You don't. You absolutely don't know. What I can tell you is that if he seizes long enough, the seizure will kill him."

Morgan reached up and grabbed the small ECG monitor from Trudy's hands, along with ECG patches and a pulse-ox probe that would monitor Jose's oxygen levels. Morgan pulled the young man's shirt up and placed the patches for the leads.

"It's your choice," she said to Scott. "What do you want me to do?"

In the next breath, Scott grabbed Trudy. His arm tight around her throat, his gun pointed at her head. "If he dies, then so does she."

Morgan grabbed the IV line and aimed the blunt needle of the syringe filled with Ativan toward one of the medication hubs. It quivered like a lie detector exposing her intentions. Even if she jabbed herself with it, she wouldn't incur a needle-stick injury.

Like that would be the worst of my problems. First I'd have to live through today. Then I could worry about HIV or hepatitis C infection.

Morgan held her hands up, the syringe balanced between two fingers on the left side. "Just let her go! I'm not giving this med while you're threatening to kill one of my staff."

He dropped his arm from her throat, but as he placed the weapon back and eased away, Trudy flashed into action. She grabbed Jose's gun out of Scott's waistband and pointed it at him.

All the thoughts tumbled from Morgan's mind. *Now what?*

Drew stood up. "All right. Everyone! We just need to calm down. Trudy, that isn't going to solve anything."

Dylan seemed just as stunned as Morgan at first. Then he slowly began to unseat his automatic weapon and leveled its aim their way.

Heat fanned through Morgan's body. "This isn't helping. Trudy, lower that gun. SWAT sees this, and they're storming in. Who knows who will make it out when everybody starts shooting?"

Strangely, Dylan lowered his automatic weapon.

Maybe he doesn't believe an older nurse has the fortitude to fire?

Trudy, however, maintained her position with little cowering. She stood strong and steady.

Half-defused was better than nothing, she decided. Morgan grabbed the IV line and shoved the drug in, opening up the fluids so the flow would flush the medication into the convulsing man's bloodstream.

They waited.

It was so quiet those few seconds. Morgan could almost hear each individual's heartbeat. Each rush of quickened breath. Bree's noisy rasping from her crib. The quiet humming of machines. The random sounds of her work environment could be soothing—almost peaceful.

Jose's muscles went lax and his head lolled to one side. Morgan was not as familiar with adult dosing as she was with pediatric dosing but guessed the double dose would quell the seizure without having to repeat the medication. Her eyes roamed to the monitor. The number that indicated her new patient's number of respirations went to zero, and the other number indicated his oxygen level was sliding the wrong direction.

"Someone grab me an oxygen tank!" Morgan yelled.

"What did you do to him?" Scott yelled, pushing the doors closed to the code cart, nearly trapping her fingers in the metal.

Drew drove him away. "She told you this might happen. If you stop her, he will die."

Morgan jerked the bottom drawer of the code cart and grabbed a bag valve mask device and tore at the wrapping. *Why are these things childproof?*

It finally gave way just as the tinier transport monitor toned an alarm. She shoved the contents around in the drawer until she found an adult-sized mask. She jammed the two together and shoved the mask over Jose's face.

She could deliver breaths, but she still needed the oxygen to get his numbers back up. Izabel rolled a long, green tank her direction.

"Morgan . . . no . . ." Trudy begged.

Her eyes were pinned to her patient's chest when the nurse's admonishment clicked in her mind. Her stomach cramped with nausea. She, too, wanted the same thing. She wanted to let the man die.

Morgan shook her head against the thought but found her hands stopping. The monitor tones loud in her ear. From her peripheral vision, she could see Scott nearly convulsing with rage. His face reddened like a child holding its breath against whatever stimulation he wanted to stop.

"If you let him die, I swear, I will kill you with my bare hands."

Trudy pointed the gun at Morgan. "They're going to kill us and you know it, Morgan. One less of them. I have a gun. Only one left to worry about."

Morgan closed her eyes. So much of her over these last few months wanted death . . . welcomed it like an old friend. It wasn't unheard of for her to skip a dialysis appointment—just as a tap on the grim reaper's door—to see if he was really there.

To see if he would come for her.

Then Tyler's face loomed in her vision. His glacier-blue eyes that sparkled like ice under the sun. His smile. His warm lips against her cheek. And what she could not take was the vision of his sadness in learning that not only did she forfeit her own life, but she'd taken part in the killing of another individual. For him, the circumstances wouldn't matter.

She gritted her teeth and yanked the oxygen tank her direction. Connecting the tubing, she turned the dial until she heard the hissing of oxygen releasing under pressure. She grabbed the breathing device and repositioned the mask on her patient's face, giving several quick breaths.

It wasn't her decision anymore as to whether this man lived or died.

"How can you save him?" Trudy cried.

The weapon lowered an inch.

Scott took the open opportunity and threw the full weight of his body against her.

The gun fired.

Chapter 35

NATHAN'S JAW DROPPED WHEN the bomb squad's robot got stuck in the elevator.

At first he thought the sharp crack he heard was part of the doors repeatedly closing on the pricey piece of equipment, but the more he heard the elevator doors closing, the surer he was that what he actually heard was a gunshot muffled by Wall-E in a trash compactor.

He turned to the bank of monitoring equipment and to the uniformed officer sitting there. "Was that in camera shot? Who fired a weapon?"

"Whatever's going on is out of our view."

Nathan turned to Lee and the fire battalion chief.

"I need two firefighters up there with two SWAT officers. Right now. Full biohazard gear. Figure out what that smoke is. Now we've got weapons discharging and we can't make entry because of the bombs on the doors."

At the sound of Nathan's raised voice, Tyler came out of his chair and charged like a crazed bull. "Enough of all this standing around and analyzing the situation!" Lee laid an affirming hand on his shoulder. He tossed it off. "If you don't get up there, I'm going myself."

Lee rolled his eyes at that. He grabbed Tyler by the arm and shoved him back into a chair.

Nathan put a calming palm up in the air. "Just settle down. Going up there half-cocked is going to put your wife in more danger than she's already in."

"Commander Watson," the Uniform interrupted. "It appears that one of the nurses discharged a weapon. Unsure of which hostage-taker she took it from. It's difficult to tell from the camera's position, but they pulled a metal cart toward the door. None of the patients are in that direction. The only people who've been consistently by the door are two of the hostage takers."

Nathan glanced at Tyler. Allowing him to offer his insight would help diffuse his anger. "Why would they need that?"

"It's the code cart. Something must have happened to one of the men."

Nathan turned back to the officer. "Did they pull it there before or after the gunshot?"

"Before sir. Well before."

"One of them may have become medically incapacitated," Nathan surmised. "One of the staff takes advantage of the situation and grabs one of their weapons?"

Lee folded his arms over his chest. "We can't make assumptions. We need more eyes on the interior. We need to snake in another way." His radio crackled. "They're suiting up. They'll be up there shortly."

"It also looked like a nurse rolled a couple of medication vials across the floor."

"What could it be that Morgan would need that wasn't in the code cart?" Nathan asked.

Tyler shrugged. "You're asking me to guess?"

"Yes. With what you know about the complications these men have been having, what's the most likely adverse reaction that would necessitate medications that weren't in the code cart?"

Tyler sucked in a deep breath and held it. "A seizure. First-line anticonvulsant drugs are benzodiazepines like Valium. They're not kept in a code cart. They have to be locked."

"And the reason for the resuscitation equipment?"

"Because those drugs can stop a patient from breathing. Sometimes the amount required to stop the seizure will knock out the patient's respiratory drive. Devices to assist breathing would be kept in that cart."

"Do you think your wife would intentionally harm someone?" Lee asked.

The look in Tyler's eyes concerned Nathan. They held a wariness to confess the true state of his wife's mind—and how it could hamper or aid their response. "Dr. Adams?" he said.

Tyler sighed. "I don't know what Morgan would do."

The direct phone line from the PICU rang. Nathan took two steps and picked up the call. "This is Nathan." All he heard was heavy breathing. At any other juncture, he would have hung up the phone as the musings of a prank caller. "Are you injured?"

"I need a doctor up here!"

"Scott, are you injured?"

"I am done holding out. I need Thomas Reeves over here now. I want a doctor up here or I will start shooting people. Don't test me on this. I know my life is over, and I really don't care who I take with me."

Nathan's mind whirled. Why the change of heart? Before, he'd been adamant about not letting any additional medical people in the unit.

"Okay, Scott. Let's see what we can get figured out."

Plumes of exhalation came through the phone like bad static. "Jose's not convulsing anymore but now he's not breathing."

"Are the nurses helping him?"

Something slammed against the countertop. "I need someone up here I can trust!"

"Scott, you haven't made that very easy for me. How can I send someone up there when there is an unknown gas in the hallway?"

"It's just a smoke canister. I swear it."

"That's great. Of course we'll need to verify and vent it out. Are there any other devices in the hallway or staircase that we should be aware of?"

"Door and windows. That's it."

Meaning . . . that's the only thing rigged? Something inside Nathan warned him not to push Scott too far in this direction.

"Did someone fire a weapon?"

"Yeah, a stupid nurse grabbed my gun. We've taken care of her."

"Scott, what do you mean by that? Is she still alive?"

"For now. But she will be the first one who gets a bullet to the chest if Thomas Reeves doesn't do as I ask right now. Get me—"

A string of expletives followed and Nathan pulled the phone a few inches away, his ears sharp with pain. At times, it was best to let them yell all they wanted. At least they weren't firing a weapon.

Finally, the mercenary stopped to take a breath.

Nathan put the receiver back. "Scott, if you calm down, I'm going to see how we can come to a compromise. Can you hold tight for a few minutes? Let me discuss your needs with some of my colleagues and I'll call you back."

"Just hurry."

Nathan set the phone back on its cradle. What was the wisest choice at this juncture? Tensions inside that small space were mounting.

Tyler gently nudged Lee away and took a step closer to Nathan, the look on his face one of quiet contrition.

"Send me in. I'll willingly go. I'll sign whatever waiver you need me to sign. I know two of these men. I can try to help talk some reason into Scott."

Nathan shook his head. "No, absolutely not."

He wasn't about to give them another hostage. Another positional murder victim.

Lee placed his hands on his hips. "It may not be a bad idea," he said.

Nathan reeled his head back. "Is this not against every SWAT directive known to man? We are not going to give them more hostages!"

Lee pulled Nathan to the side. "I'm not saying we do it for free. Let's get something out of it. Have them release the children."

"How are we going to do that? Some of them are on ventilators. We would need additional medical personnel up there to help get them down to the ER. Do we even have enough beds left in the ER?"

"Okay, how about those children who can be moved? I think only four are on ventilators. Get the mother out of there. Maybe the nurses."

"Can Morgan and Tyler care for those remaining four kids? That puts them in a very tight spot. Will they have enough hands for an emergency? I'm not going to short them that."

"Okay, the children who can be moved. The parent. And the soldier who dropped from whatever happened."

Nathan shook his head again. "Tyler's not an unbiased participant. That complicates the situation exponentially. It's his wife in there. You don't think he's going to function mostly on her behalf?"

"What's the problem with that?" Lee asked.

"It adds another unknown. What do we expect him to do when the gun is to her head? He's going to act rationally? The actuality of gunfire set him on edge."

"That's because he didn't know if she was safe. Adams knows these guys and their issues. He's a doc who can also help care for the patients. For me, the benefits outweigh the risks."

Nathan approached Tyler, who had taken a seat back at the conference table. "Dr. Adams, if I send you in there, you have to do as we say and not act like some maverick trying to rescue everyone. Help care for the children. But mostly, try to talk some sense into this Scott Clarke character."

"I will."

"Don't try to physically disarm him. Try to get him to give up his weapons voluntarily."

"Got it."

"Absolutely no heroics. That's what I've got these guys for."

"Right."

Something about his ready answers made Nathan more uneasy.

Lee's head tilted toward his earpiece. "Nathan, it is confirmed. Just smoke at the entrance of the unit. Found the canister. They're going to start venting the hall."

Finally, something favorable.

"Lee, we need to start a rotation," he said. "I want eyes on that door and the back stairwell. Every thirty minutes, trade out bodies. I want the men at their sharpest. Let's get a few small cameras for Tyler here to set up on the unit for us."

Nathan placed the call to the PICU. It rang and rang, unanswered.

Someone pick up this phone!

Finally, a click and then the audible heave of someone's rapid breathing on the other side.

"Morgan?"

"She's busy. Did you reach the great and powerful Dr. Reeves?"

"Scott." Nathan inhaled to calm the adrenaline that thickened the muscles in his throat. "I'd like to work a compromise with you. Dr. Reeves is having some difficulty getting to the scene, but I have one of his colleagues here, Dr. Adams."

Nathan waited. The man's breathing paused. Nathan hoped it was in positive contemplation of this proposal.

"Tyler is here?"

"Yes, and he'd like to come in and offer a hand. Talk with you about some of the things that are going on. See if he can offer some answers. Have a one-on-one conversation."

Nathan watched the seconds pass on his watch.

Come on, work with me on this one.

"Fine. Send him in."

"Scott, that's great. Thanks for being willing to let him come in and help. But as an act of good faith, I need you to do something for me in return. Can you put Morgan on the line? Put me on speaker?"

There was static on the other side as a hasty hand was placed over the receiver. Nathan heard muffled yelling. He took a chair at the table and prayed silently.

Lord, you know Colorado cannot take another incident like this. I need to bring everyone out alive. Show me that you are there. Show me that you can help. I can't do this again on my own. They're just children. Very sick children.

"I'm here, Nathan."

Hearing Morgan's voice brought a wave of relief washing over Nathan.

"Morgan," he said. "It's good to hear your voice. Listen, Scott has agreed to allow Dr. Adams to come in and help—"

"No, you can't do that!"

What? The protest came from Morgan. Nathan started to fume. *Why is the hostage not helping me?* "Our goal is to resolve this peacefully. This will be a step in the right direction."

"I'm asking you not to do this. Don't allow Tyler to come in here. I can handle things on my own."

What is going on here?

"Morgan, Scott has agreed to this. In return, I'm asking him to release the children who aren't ventilated, the parent, and any extra nursing staff you can do without." He glanced back at Tyler. Lee seemed to be briefing him as he fitted him in a flak vest.

A hard smack echoed through the phone line. A faint whimper. Then Scott's voice. "I decide what happens in this unit."

Had Scott hit Morgan?

"Okay, Scott," Nathan said. "What's your decision?"

"Tyler comes in. Then we'll release everyone who can walk or be carried out."

Nathan's gut churned. He'd just allowed someone to become a hostage. Something he never imagined doing. "It looks like you have yourself a physician."

Chapter 36

MORGAN HAD TO PHYSICALLY pull Lisa up off her chair to get her near the door.

She scratched at her, spittle hitting her face as she screamed. "How could you do this? I'm not leaving Seth. I'm not leaving my son."

Morgan let go of her arms, and Lisa backpedaled and fell onto her butt, sliding a few inches back on the tile. Her mouth gaped. Morgan sighed, and scanned the unit.

Drew was at the door near Jose. He'd been forced to intubate him and now he was pinned there trying to keep one of their hostage takers alive. Scott paced at the center of the unit. Trudy, Izabel, and Lucy were vying to be let out, but Morgan couldn't let everybody go and still care for the remaining ventilated patients adequately enough. She didn't know how long the situation would last, and if she didn't provide at least basic nursing care, the patients would suffer complications.

Dylan worked at the door, removing the IV bag bombs to allow traffic through them again. Drew was pointing to his patient and the transport gurney he'd brought Scarlett in on. Scott stomped his direction and scooped down to pick up his friend's limp body. Drew motioned for Dylan to give Jose breaths so he could grab the transport monitor.

Why in the world did Tyler agree to this?

In her heart, she knew it was to save her. He still worried she'd be reckless with her own life.

Maybe he's right. A hostage taker's bullet is an easy out. More sympathetic than straight-up suicide.

Scott eased Jose onto the transport pram. Perhaps they weren't on opposite ends of the spectrum after all. What had caused the death of his infant son? Something niggled in her mind. She needed to figure out exactly what had happened.

Morgan took a knee to the floor, and forced her mind to focus on the tantrum happening in front of her. She took a breath quick in her chest, felt the fire of adrenaline funneling her thoughts. She spoke in a low, determined voice. "Lisa, do you realize what's going on here? I need you to cooperate with me."

"I don't trust you."

"I know."

"I don't trust you to take care of Seth."

Morgan dropped down to both knees. "I know you don't. And I know if I said I would take care of him just like I took care of Teagan, that wouldn't help any."

"It won't. You don't remember it, do you?"

"What, Lisa? What is it that you want me to remember? Why is it that you keep punishing me for Teagan's death?"

Lisa slapped at her chest. "Because you knew! In your heart you really knew what was happening to Teagan. You didn't listen to yourself. You didn't listen to what your own experience was telling you."

Morgan's face paled and she slumped all the way to the floor. "What are you talking about?"

"Weeks before that day, you came to me concerned about some bruising on her face. You said a baby that young should never have bruising there."

"But there was a plausible explanation."

"As much as you talk about denial, you're living it every day. You wiped it from your own memory because your pride won't allow you to believe that it was really your inaction that took Teagan's life!"

"I do blame myself!"

"Guilt is not the same as confession. Think about that. And now you want me to leave my baby in your hands? I just watched another infant die because you couldn't save her."

Morgan buried her head under her arms. Nothing made sense anymore. Was her confidence in her ability really arrogance that blinded her to the truth? She wasn't a good nurse. She'd ultimately failed her own daughter by not acting on what her gut had told her. She was failing as a wife and her marriage was ending. Lisa had every right to distrust her. In the end, she'd fail Seth, too.

Likely, everything she'd ever known was going to be gone. She'd lose her license for operating outside her scope of practice. She'd be fired for the same. Tyler would leave her and she'd deserve it for pushing him away. Then she could do as she planned. Leave this vile, dreaded earth and find the place where Teagan had gone.

Would it be so wrong to hasten all this to its conclusion? She gathered herself up off the floor and stared at her sister-in-law.

"Lisa, you are leaving. I need you to carry Bree." She looked to the rest of her staff. "I need one nurse to stay and help me care for the patients. Tyler will help when he's here. We'll have three patients too unstable to move safely. Who will stay with me?"

"I'll stay," Drew volunteered. "I know I'm not a nurse, but I'll record vital signs and do the vents. You can worry about care and medications."

Three critically ill patients. Typically, two per nurse was the maximum limit. But if no one else volunteered, how could she expect any of them to stay and possibly die?

"Thank you, Drew. Is the door clear?"

Dylan nodded and eased the door open a hair. "Looks like they're ready. I can see a man in scrubs out there."

The phone rang. Scott nodded his permission for Morgan to answer.

Nathan's calm voice in her ear. "Morgan?"

"I'm here."

"What's the plan?"

"The nurses are leaving. Drew and I are staying. There are three patients that can't be easily moved. Plus, the parent is leaving."

"Okay, that's great. You ready for this?"

"Yes."

"Everyone who leaves will need to have hands raised up unless they are carrying a patient."

"Got it."

"Let's get them lined up. Nurses, patients, and parent out first."

"Okay."

"Then we'll put Tyler in."

Morgan hung up the phone and grabbed Lisa, pulling her to Bree's crib. She unplugged the IV pumps and wrapped the cords around the pole. Reaching down, she lifted the small toddler in her arms, positioning her in the crook of one arm, and grabbed the IV pole with her free hand. "You'll have to hold her like this. She can't go without the pump."

Lisa reached for the girl. At first, Bree snaked her arms around Morgan's neck, and it immediately brought thoughts of how it would have felt to have Teagan do the same. Morgan hugged tightly.

"Sweet girl," she said, "this is Lisa. She's a super-nice lady." Morgan eased the child back. "She's going to take you to your mommy, who I know is very worried about you."

Lisa grabbed the girl, and Bree latched herself to her in the same fashion. Lisa took hold of the pump. "Morgan . . ."

"It's all right. I'll take care of Seth. I swear it. I'll give up my life for his if I have to."

Lisa began to cry as she held on to the young girl. "I'm sorry."

"For what?"

"Are we ready?" Scott yelled.

Lisa jumped and bit into her lip. "That Teagan died. I'm sorry that you're sick. Please, I can't bear the thought of Seth dying."

"I know that—"

"I know you did save Seth's life and I'm thankful for it."

With those words, she edged around Morgan to the front door, the squeak of the wheels the only sound in the silence.

The whole exchange seemed surreal. Each nurse carried a patient who could be moved, with the exception of Trudy, who carried Scarlett's tiny body. Perhaps, after firing that gun, she felt unworthy to carry an innocent out of the danger. Her once vibrant eyes were now dull with sadness and regret.

A moment later Tyler came through the door. He was dressed in his blue scrubs, with a black flak vest over his chest. His blue eyes were dark with intensity of a promise fulfilled, yet shadowed by the odds not being entirely in his favor. He walked with determination toward her, but Scott stepped between them.

"Are we going to have a heartfelt reunion?"

Tyler crossed his arms over his chest. "I'd like to assess the patients and figure out what their current treatment plan is."

"Dr. Adams—you're not here to discuss things with me? To see if you can change my mind?"

"Of course. That is one of the reasons I'm here. But the better shape these remaining children are in, the better your leverage will be, don't you think?"

Scott tapped his weapon against his other hand. A moment of thought turned into an overt threat. "What I don't understand is your boss, Dr. Reeves. How holding children hostage doesn't seem to be a motivating factor for him. Can you explain that to me?"

"Dr. Reeves and I haven't been on the same page for a while. I can't speak to his motivations or lack thereof."

"Well, I think it's time to force his hand a little bit."

Scott drew another weapon. This one had a heavy black tube on the end.

A silencer.

Morgan's heart rate tripled in her chest. Without the noise, SWAT would have a hard time discerning that tensions inside the unit were escalating. Would they come in?

Dylan increased the volume on the television.

The movement to cover up the noise caused Morgan's knees to slump. She leaned against Seth's bed for support. From the corner of her eye she saw Dylan reach for his cell phone.

To record.

This is going to be bad. Very bad.

"Relationships are a funny thing, aren't they?" Scott asked, a distant, withdrawn look suffocating what little light remained in his eyes. A dark spirit took residence there.

Both Morgan and Tyler stood stock still. Tyler's blue eyes grabbed hers. He mouthed, "It's okay." Followed by "I love you."

Morgan tightened her hands into fists.

Scott continued. "The two of you have had a hard time. They say the death of a child usually kills a marriage, yet here you are." Scott paced toward Morgan and pulled her against his body. "Choices are even funnier."

"What is it you want from us?" Tyler asked.

He wielded the gun Tyler's direction. "From Reeves, I want the truth. I want to know why I have visions of my son's death playing in my mind like a relentless recorder. I wasn't there the day he died. Why do I see it?"

Tyler kept his hands low, nonthreatening. "I'm sorry, Scott. I didn't realize you had children."

Scott's chest heaved against Morgan's back. "That's just the thing. Some say he wasn't alive. But I feel the fire of his life burn through my veins. I dream of limbs splitting from bodies and crazy, open-mouthed water screams. I want the truth of what you think happened to me. I want everyone to know it." He settled the steel against Morgan's temple. "Does this motivate you any?"

The blood drained from Tyler's face. He took a step in their direction. Morgan's heart raced and she shook her head quickly against any further movement. He settled back on his heels.

"I'm not entirely sure what's going on, Scott," he said. "Dr. Reeves shut down my access to the data."

"Then we'll need to convince him to release it." Scott waved his gun in the direction of Seth's bedspace. "You two are related to this young man, correct?"

Morgan's stomach flipped violently inside her abdomen. What once had been the joyful feeling of Teagan growing inside her now was doom at something sinister brewing. She swallowed the saliva that funneled into her mouth.

Tyler nodded his head, his lips tight.

"Your nephew? Evidently there is some discord in the family. For a while I wasn't sure of their relationship. Morgan tried to protect your sister by not mentioning it."

Tyler's teeth clenched so tight, his muscles quivered at the side of his face. "Morgan saved Seth's life. My sister doesn't have an issue with her."

Scott waved the weapon like a finger tsking a young child. "That's not the vibe I got at all." Scott wrapped his arms around Morgan's chest. "My, my, my—your heart is just racing like a rabbit. Since Dr. Reeves isn't taking me seriously, I'm going to offer Morgan a choice to force his hand. Who will die right here, right now, Morgan? Your husband or your nephew?"

Morgan closed her eyes against the humming vibration that scrambled her thoughts. Darkness enveloped her, and for a moment she could pretend she wasn't being asked to be someone's proxy executioner. Even if it wasn't her finger that put the weight against the trigger, her words would be the catalyst to put the events into place.

His lips drew close to her ear. "And you can't pick yourself. That's not an option."

Against her will, her mind began to weigh through the cost of the decision. She settled her hand against her stomach to suppress the stabbing pain. Regardless of the promise she'd made to Lisa, in a sense, Seth's death wouldn't hurt him. He was paralyzed and sedated, suspended in a requiem of opiate-induced euphoria. Unbeknownst to him, he'd simply be thrust into heaven in an instant, none the wiser of the choice Morgan had made.

Tyler, however, would know. He'd feel the full realization of her betrayal. More painful than the bullet piercing his skin and rupturing whatever vital organ Scott thought would cause the quickest demise, Tyler would comprehend her betrayal. When she had said "till death do us part," she hadn't meant by her own words.

The iron ball and chain that people often referred to as the wife in a marriage would be her, pulling Tyler six feet under.

In her heart, she couldn't do it. She couldn't be responsible for another mother's pain. She wouldn't curse another woman with her same fate. With the overwhelming sadness. With the wanton desire to slip from the bounds of this physical body.

"Morgan!"

She jumped and opened her eyes. "I can't do what you're asking me to do!"

"If you don't choose, I'll kill them both."

Tyler pulled at the Velcro that held the flak jacket in place, not in surrender to Scott's weapon but relinquishing his life to hers. "There's only one choice, Morgan. I don't hold you responsible. It's okay. I love you. I'll always be with you."

The moan from her lips sounded like an animal. She hadn't realized any human could make such a painful noise from sheer emotional distress.

"I can get each of them in two seconds, Morgan. Two seconds for you to say which name. One . . ."

She tried to run Tyler's direction. Scott grabbed the back of her scrub top and held her steady. "Morgan—"

And as the words fell from her lips, she wanted the world to swallow her into its belly where caverns of fire burned.

It surprised her how quickly Scott could fire with such accuracy.

The next thing that surprised her was how silent the weapon was, yet how destructive a power it rendered. She gaped in horror as blood flowed freely from Tyler's chest.

As her husband crumpled to the ground, Dylan walked over, grinning. He took a picture.

Chapter 37

LILLY REEVES GRIPPED THE nearest counter when she saw the news scroll about the hostage situation at Sacred Heart. Watching Morgan's tape on the same station caused the food in her stomach to curdle. Over the last few hours, she'd been involved in opening up beds in her own hospital to take in pediatric patients evacuated from Sacred Heart. Those who shouldn't be exposed to other people's germs came here; the rest were housed at a high school gymnasium.

There's a reason I didn't go into pediatric oncology.

Now, she was in a sea of bald-headed, mask-faced frenzy as she worked with the adult oncology nurses to place patients in their unit. Why did she ever volunteer to train as an incident commander? Natural disasters were one thing, but man-made were quite another. How had the possibility escaped her that Morgan could be involved? That the demands to release the hostages centered on her father?

The very thing the hostage takers wanted from Thomas Reeves, he would never willingly give up. Even if it led to another death in her family.

After the majority of the pediatric patients were settled, still with their nurses caring for them in their new home, she relinquished her duties to another ER attending. She didn't bother to clean up before heading straight for her father's medical complex.

Nothing like seeing your estranged father two days in a row.

Lilly found the door to his office cracked open. The medical unit seemed deserted. Only one nurse sat at the nurses' station, one patient's chart open beside her. She motioned her okay for Lilly to enter.

Reeves's normally organized office was a sea of open charts, notes, and one notebook. She recognized the notebook as one similar to what Tyler Adams had been scrawling in during her last visit. His hair was disheveled. An empty brandy bottle perched next to him on the desk. A new glass container sat at the ready, with glass flames adorning the bottom of the bottle and the lid. The reddish cognac was reminiscent of true fire—the epitome of the state of her father's current life.

Enclosed in a glass bubble and going up in flames.

At the sound of the door swinging wide, he reached for it momentarily, his fingers lingering over the glass.

His eyes took in her arrival. He raced his hands over his cheeks, then crossed his arms over his chest. "What are you doing here?" he said. "Come to see my demise firsthand?"

Lilly leaned against the doorframe. His raised hackles at her presence weren't a surprise at all. Fingers of doubt burrowed into her chest, leaving tingling tunnels of apprehension for her heart to cave into. Her stomach knotted as she thought of what to say.

He stole the moment from her, like so many other things.

"I didn't get tested, yet." He swept his arm at the door, his voice booming across the space. "You can sign me off and out of your life. I'm done hoping you'll forgive me so we can try to have a relationship."

So many things she wanted to say would have lit and burned whatever thread still held them together. It was her nature to push back, particularly when she had every reason in the world to cut this man off from her life. The pressure in her chest intensified as waves of heat tempted her tongue to light a fuse to words that would undo the very tentative steps each had taken toward the other.

Sticks and stones may break my bones but words will never hurt me.

A lie.

For once, she held them back.

She swallowed hard. "That's not why I'm here."

"Then why?" Reeves faced her squarely, chest heaving like a bull's, daring her to raise the red cape.

Why had she come? At the forefront of her mind was, of course, to save her sister's life. But considering their history, did she really expect him to have a change of heart?

She inhaled and held her breath, exhaling the words to diffuse the tension. "I came to help you."

"Why?"

"To save Morgan's life."

Start with the easiest, least controversial answer.

"I don't know if that's going to happen."

"To me, it looks like you're trying to do as they ask."

He sighed and surveyed the tornado-strewn paperwork around his desk. He slumped into his chair. "I am."

Lilly pushed away from the doorframe and entered the room, easing the door closed behind her. "How can I help?"

"I guess I'd better first explain the protocol to you."

She sat on the chair in front of his desk as he pushed a blank piece of paper toward her and began to draw. "We took doctored fetal neural cells and transplanted them into soldiers' brains."

"Why?" Lilly asked.

"To enhance their memory. To give them superior autobiographical memory to be exact."

"How would you classify that exactly?"

"A very minute percentage of the population has some extraordinary memory capabilities. Photographic memory might be the simplest form." A whimsical lightness spread over his face. "Imagine being able to recall events from each day of your life like a video camera. Not just those significant moments that mark our lives, but *all* the data. The weather, who we visited with, the faces of those people who touch us for only a moment in passing but impact us in infinite ways." He took a deep breath and reached for her across the desk. "Imagine being able to see the threads of our decisions like a road map and how they got us to where we are today."

Lilly raised her head slightly as she contemplated what her father was saying. *Is this experiment of his really a grasp at redeeming his life? Has Thomas Reeves developed a scientific protocol as a way to analyze and repair his mistakes?*

His voice drew her back. "The military applications are extraordinary. Just the multitude of maps, reports, data on targets, it's amazing. Having to carry computers just adds to a soldier's load—and it's a potential source of secrets leaking out if they get into enemy hands. It's really not practical. But if you could supercharge someone's memory so that analyzing and memorizing these battle plans, this minutia of how to capture the enemy, is built in, you'd have—"

"A real life Captain America."

"Exactly."

"Worth a lot of money."

"Of course."

"And fame . . ." Lilly let the rest of the phrase drop. It was the first she'd seen him look defeated. As if all he hoped to accomplish was disintegrating around him. "So what went wrong?"

He flopped the notebook in front of her. "I think my associate was on to something. I just can't figure out what it is."

Lilly pulled the notebook closer. It was a list of patients and what appeared to be their adverse reactions to the graft. Seizures. Development of cranial masses that on biopsy turned out to be the grafted cells—sometimes they even wandered from their original place of implantation. Nightmares. Hypersensitivity.

"With the exception of the seizures and tumors, their symptoms are reminiscent of classic post-traumatic stress disorder. That's your field of expertise."

"I know. I can see that, but the majority of these men hadn't seen battle."

"How do you explain it?"

Reeves flipped the notebook forward several more pages. "This is another list Tyler was making. A significant percentage of the men began to exhibit truly bizarre symptoms."

"Such as?"

"Well, nonuse of limbs."

"That shouldn't be so surprising. They had brain surgery. A stroke is the most likely explanation."

Reeves shuddered. "But there wasn't any medical evidence to back it up. Nothing on CT or MRI scans. Intact nerve impulses. There wasn't any clear medical reason for them to—" He stopped, smoothing his palms over his face. "To act as if these limbs were amputated."

"Stroke patients can act like that though. After a while, they'll just ignore the extremity that doesn't work anymore."

He shook his head, grabbed the full bottle of cognac and lifted the glass stopper.

Lilly reached forward and eased the bottle away. "Not until we think through this. Come up with an answer."

A tremor took hold of Reeves. *Is he going through withdrawal?* Regardless of Lilly's personal feelings toward her father, she ached to see him unraveling in front of her.

"What is it you're not telling me?" Lilly asked.

He reached to the floor beside him and picked up another notebook. Sleek and black. He opened the front cover and began to leaf through the pages. "This is a list of the conditions of the donor specimens and who got their cells."

Reeves plopped it open in front of her and then grabbed Tyler's notebook. "In the donor notebook, the graft was denoted by a tracing number. Dr. Adams's patient notebook had the graft number paired with the patient. That's what Tyler had been matching up. Read to me what he wrote."

"Patient Brad Winters exhibits intermittent nonuse of left arm. Medical testing revealed absence of any sign of stroke. EMG and nerve conduction testing don't reveal any evidence as to why the patient claims he doesn't have an arm anymore."

Reeves tapped the other notebook. "Now look at the condition of the donor."

"During retrieval of the neural graft, donor specimen delivered"—dread filled Lilly's chest—"without left arm . . ." Lilly raised her head, her body felt weak, tired. Was Thomas Reeves thinking what she was thinking?

Reeves raked his fingers through his beard. "What makes us human, Lilly? What marks our distinction from every other biological creature on the planet?"

This was certainly traveling down an unexpected road.

If she spoke about God to an atheist, about his weaving evidence of his existence into human DNA, surely Reeves would just laugh. He'd view her beliefs as the musings of a tortured soul gone astray looking for anything—scientifically provable or not—to make sense of what happened to her.

"Why don't you tell me what you think," Lilly offered, folding her hands to quell their trembling.

"I would say *memory*. Awareness of self. The ability to process pain and know what it means."

"Okay."

He rustled through the papers. "What is this? You use it every day."

"The Glasgow Coma Scale?"

He tapped the scale again. "Yes, the neuro part."

"What about it?"

"Patients score higher the more aware of self they are. A patient who can obey commands?"

"Gets the highest score."

"And what's the next highest level?"

"Localizing pain."

"Which means?"

"They reach across their midline to remove a painful stimulus."

"Which means pain receptors have to be intact, an awareness of self, the instinct for self preservation."

"Okay . . ."

Reeves yanked the bottle of liquor back his direction and then sloppily poured it into his tumbler. He motioned her direction. Lilly waved him off.

She wanted to stop him. "What is it you're not telling me?"

"They're fused," he gulped the liquor fast.

"What's fused?"

"Their memories."

"Whose?"

"The donors' and recipients' memories! It's the only explanation as to why a grown man would have any knowledge of an amputation that took place in a donor not yet born."

Chapter 38

MORGAN RACED THE short distance to Tyler.

"Go ahead and try, Morgan. See if you can save him." Scott walked around Tyler's fallen body and met Dylan in the middle of the room.

Dark liquid bloomed through his thin blue scrubs from the left side of his chest.

"Drew! Bring the crash cart. Now!"

She could hear the roar of the wheels over the tile, the metal drawers clanging against one another as he hurried from the other side of the unit. From her pocket, Morgan grabbed her trauma shears and cut up the middle of his shirt, pushing each side away to expose his torso. The wound gaped open, a mocking hole of hellish destruction as Tyler's life poured out. Morgan used the palms of both hands, one over the other, to stem the rush of blood.

She felt a small shudder race up her arms. She couldn't tell if it came from Tyler exhaling his last breath or from her sheer panic at the thought that her husband had died right in front of her.

As Morgan leaned heavily into the wound, Tyler opened his eyes and grabbed her hand to shove it off, his face wild with confusion. Drew began to toss needed items onto the floor from the cart. Morgan slammed her knees down on Tyler's arm to keep him from rolling away from her and further injuring himself.

Relief washed over her. *Movement is good. Movement means life.*

"Tyler. Stop! Look at me."

He slammed his head several times against the tile, his eyes bunched tight against the pain. "Get off me!" He began to buck against her and she wondered if he truly realized what had happened. Patients in severe pain couldn't think clearly.

Drew wrapped a tourniquet tight around his arm.

Keeping pressure on the wound, Morgan bent down and set her cheek against his. The lightness in her chest that he was alive brought untold joy. A sensation she hadn't felt since before Teagan's death. That effervescent giddiness that all could still be right with the world. His cheek was cool and doughy against hers. "Tyler . . . shh . . . listen to me. You've been shot. Drew and I are helping you."

He rolled over and threw her off.

Another reason to work with kids. They're so much easier to drop-tackle.

She scrambled back. The floor was becoming a horrific finger painting of Tyler's blood as he attempted to get up. She and Drew both pushed down the good shoulder.

"Tyler!" Morgan yelled. Finally, he opened his eyes to hers. She smiled. Something he likely hadn't seen in months. She eased her palm back down onto the wound. "Please, look at me." His dilated pupils engaged hers. "Hold still. Drew's going to put a line in."

He reached up with his right, bloodied hand and grabbed the side of her face. "Morgan . . ." Her name faint, distant.

She shook her head. His eyes were wide, glassy, the red veins even lightened, almost gray, as the blood leaked from his body.

Tyler barely registered the needle in his arm. Drew grabbed for the bag of IV fluids and tore at more packages to get tubing.

A moan escaped from Tyler's lips. He licked at the drying skin. "I'm . . ."

She wanted to clamp her palm over his mouth. Drew connected the fluids and ran to an open bedspace, snatching an IV pole to free his hands. As he grabbed that, he also unclamped a patient monitor from the wall and set it on the floor next to Tyler.

Tears coursed down her cheeks. She squinted against them. How could it be that God would allow her husband to die here—in the same place she'd lost Teagan?

"I won't let you say it," she whispered.

His eyes grew heavy, and his hand slipped from her face. He jolted, his eyes opened, locking on hers again. "I love you."

"Then stay with me."

His hand slid to the floor. Morgan kept pressing against his wound. She leaned her head onto her bloodied hands. She felt her soul awkwardly tearing in half.

She'd begged God over and over to save her little girl, to save Teagan's life. And she still died. Now she didn't trust God to do anything on her behalf. But in that moment, it was all she could think to do.

Jesus, please save Tyler. You can't do this to me again! If you do and there is hell, I will gladly go there, because I can't imagine loving a God who would do this to me twice. Whatever it is you want from me—surrender? I give up. I give in. Just please, not Tyler, not here, not now.

Drew grabbed her shoulder and shook it. "Morgan, I need you. Tyler needs you. We have to think through this."

Morgan lifted her head. It was true. There was never any time in the PICU for tears. At least not in the moment of crisis.

She swiped her hands over her cheeks and glanced around the room. She wanted to be aware of where the hostage takers had gone. Scott and Dylan were both by the door, looking at the death photo on Dylan's phone.

"Morgan! I need your help!" Drew's voice sounded so far away. "I don't know where everything is."

The warmness of Tyler's blood still leaking from under her palms somehow was the catalyst that kicked her clinical mind back into gear.

"Right," she said. "Right. Let's get a pressure dressing on this."

Drew ripped open several packages and began to layer the 4x4s into a big stack. Morgan lifted her hand as Drew slipped the pile into place. From the code cart, Morgan grabbed thick, elastic tape and layered it over the gauze. Groping again through the drawers, she pulled out an oxygen mask. "Under the bed over there, grab the oxygen tank."

Drew scurried across the tile and slid the heavy, green metal tank along the floor toward her. She handed him the tubing for the tank and slipped the mask over Tyler's face. The rush of oxygen as it fed into the tubing was the only sound in the space for that moment. Like the faint hint of air escaping a balloon as it slowly shriveled up and died.

Morgan pointed to the monitor. Drew flipped it on as she pulled ECG patches and a pulse ox probe from the second drawer. She could see Tyler's breath misting inside the mask at a quickened pace.

Drew took the packages from her, and Morgan pulled her stethoscope from her neck and placed the ends in her ears.

Listening to heart tones wasn't generally the strength of any nurse. But she knew what normal sounded like, and if the classic lub-dub of his heart pounding and pushing blood through his body sounded like it was at the other end of a tunnel, it meant blood could be collecting around his heart.

His heart tones easily discerned—though fast.

Breath sounds were clear and equal.

Did the bullet miss his vital structures? Morgan felt hope, unbidden, seeping into her fractured soul.

Drew pulled the I-stat off the top of the cart and handed it to her. "Let's see where his crit is at." He unwrapped a syringe and placed a needle. Morgan readied the machine to run. Then he drew blood from a vein lower than his IV site.

The machine was like having a lab in the PICU, where immediate test results could save lives—information like how well the patient was breathing and what his blood counts were. That's what she and Drew needed to know fast. How much blood had Tyler lost?

Drew handed her the syringe of blood. She injected the flat cartridge with it and snapped it into place.

Now, two minutes to wait.

For the first time, Morgan stole a glance at the monitor. Each colored line represented one of Tyler's vital functions. The sharp, mountained complexes for his heart rhythm. That clipped along at 140. *Fast.* That meant his heart was pumping faster so his red cells could unload more oxygen. It also meant there were less of them to do the job, as many of their compatriots had flooded out on the tile she now kneeled on.

Same with his respiratory rate. Fast—to load up the remaining oxygen deliverers faster.

Oxygen level. Low but still normal.

The machine toned. She glanced at the numbers.

What Tyler, her husband and her patient, had clinically told her was just confirmed by her hand-held lab test.

Drew looked down at her. "He needs blood."

"How bad?" she asked.

"Bad."

The explosion was so loud, the pulse wave so powerful that Morgan felt like the floor was about to open up and take Tyler, her, and Drew all the way to the first floor.

Morgan's ears rang. She could see Drew was trying to speak to her, motioning to the back of the unit, to the hall where the staff lounge was.

Dust and debris billowed from there.

Morgan looked back at Drew. His eyes were wide with fright, which intensified her own angst.

This man, who survived years in prison, looks like a scared rabbit ready to run.

Evidently the back exit wasn't an option anymore.

Tyler's monitor alarmed. His oxygen levels were plummeting.

Chapter 39

THE EXPLOSION SHOOK the boardroom.

Nathan gripped a chair to steady himself as his stomach sank at the implication. Even with the floor vibrating under his feet, he tore across the room to the only camera they had inside the unit.

"What in heaven's name was that!" the CEO cried from the other side of the room. Police radios squawked. Lee was close on Nathan's heels as they neared the monitor.

The picture was smoky but the interior of the room was intact.

"Lee—"

Nathan stopped. Lee Watson was speaking into his radio, checking with his officers on-site.

"It's the back stairwell," he said after a moment. "But everyone is accounted for. No injured officers."

Nathan slapped his hand against the top of the monitor. "But we don't know about the hostages. What's happened to them?"

Out of nowhere, Brett Sawyer plowed through the group of people and grabbed Nathan by the shoulder.

Nathan threw his hand off. "What's with you?"

"We've got problems," Brett said.

"I know that! A bomb just went off."

Lee motioned that he was calling the unit. Nathan nodded his head, doubtful that Scott would pick up. Would Morgan be allowed to answer?

Could she answer?

There was a plan in play, and Nathan needed to figure it out. Posthaste. Ten minutes ago.

"Remember the heart transplant girl? The dog tags?"

Nathan looked at him incredulously. "Brett, I don't have time for your murder case right now. I just had an IED explode in a children's hospital!"

Brett grabbed both of his shoulders. "I know one of the hostage takers. I know why he's here today. I think it will help you."

"You've got two minutes. SWAT's getting ready to go in. I'm not standing back this time. Not like I did before. I'm not waiting."

"Okay, two minutes and then you're off to wrestle with your demons. I get it." Brett angled Nathan toward a chair.

Nathan noticed the blood on his shirt. He pointed his finger at the stain. "What's that from?"

"Gina Worthy."

"You shot someone?"

"No. I try to limit my use of deadly force to truly violent criminals. Not for suicidal, depressed women. I tackled her when she aimed a gun at me. Accidentally broke her nose. One cat may not make it. Can't be sure at this point." Brett pressed on Nathan's shoulders. "Listen to me, partner. Please. Sit down."

Nathan's fist curled under a surge of fire. He wanted to connect it with Brett's face.

I'm not a two-year-old that needs a time-out.

Brett pulled his jacket over the red, crusty patch.

"Gina Worthy's husband killed Zoe Martin, I'm sure of it. Dylan Worthy's dog tags were found at the scene of Zoe's murder. He was dishonorably discharged from the military because he had a thing for teenage girls."

"That's awesome. Now I have something more emergent."

Brett angled down. "You don't get it. Dylan Worthy is one of your hostage takers."

Nathan fumed. "I know that! We can add your murder to his arrest warrant."

"Dylan is hungry for fame. It's why he did Reeves's experiment. To become greater than any other man. But the entire protocol is being kept quiet, so his abilities aren't public knowledge. Well, turns out that situation doesn't fulfill the psychopath's greatest need. Bad side is Dylan's hunger for girls, but Dylan doesn't want that to become known because that's what keeps him alive. So he has to have something big that will make him more famous than the hero the military won't let him be. But he doesn't want to go down with a needle in his arm either."

Nathan saw the cards falling into place. "He wants a hero's death."

"Exactly. And if he dies for a cause, it may not matter to the public what his other ills were . . . like murder. That's your main problem. He wants to die. He served his country. Wasn't enough. He got lots of money through nefarious means. Burned through all of it. That wasn't enough. Then he found out Reeves was using relatives for these graft donations."

"What do you mean?"

"Matches. Reeves paid Dylan's wife to terminate her pregnancy. That's where he got the neural cells for the transplant."

Nathan struggled to understand. Was his father-in-law that callous to use unborn babies for parts? "On all of them? All of the soldiers?"

"I don't know for sure. It seemed that Reeves made that choice late in the protocol because they were having trouble with rejection. But now, imagine it's an infant that would have been *your* child stuck in *your* head. Problem is, I don't think Reeves was very forthright with the families about that little caveat. Where's Tyler Adams? Can't you ask him?"

Nathan's chest felt heavy. "He's in the PICU."

"You gave them Reeves's little minion? What—"

"I got people out. I got children out. That's what I was thinking. Lee was in agreement."

Brett stood and ruffled his hands through his hair. "Regardless, Dylan Worthy wants this to be his blaze of glory, going to his death in protest of Thomas Reeves's wicked science."

Nathan nodded slowly. *If that's Dylan's motivation, then what is Scott's?*

The noise in the room suddenly intensified. Nathan saw a photograph from a tabloid newscast flash on one of the TV screens. He came up out of his seat like a bullet.

Tyler Adams was on the floor in the PICU. Sticky redness on the left side of his chest.

Shot? Is he alive?

When Nathan turned, Lee was a few inches behind him.

"How did we not hear that shot?" Nathan yelled.

"Silencer. More importantly, why did they do it? That's what we need to figure out. They're not stupid. They know this is going to bring us in on their heads."

Nathan furiously drummed his fingers on top of the monitor. The boardroom was in chaos. This was not the vision any CEO of a children's hospital wanted to deal with. The tranquil image of this institution as a place of healing just blew up like the IED. Closing his eyes, Nathan thought through all the possibilities.

Why now? Why Adams?

"It's to force Reeves's hand," he said out loud.

"Why not pick the daughter?" Lee asked, instinctively picking up the train of thought.

"Because Scott's probably figured out by now that Reeves and Morgan aren't close. Otherwise, Reeves would have done something to save her life. I take it you couldn't get Morgan on the line?"

"No answer."

The sharp shrill of the phone silenced the room. Nathan picked it up. "This is Nathan."

"I need blood." Morgan's voice—tightened on the verge of hysteria.

"Is Tyler alive?"

"How did you know?"

"It seems our hostage takers sent a photo to a tabloid reporter who didn't have any qualms about posting it. They released the photo on television. Was he shot?"

"Yes. I need blood. Two units of O negative packed cells from the blood bank."

Nathan snapped his finger to the CEO, who hurried toward him. The nursing supervisor followed. He cupped his palm over the receiver. "Whatever you have to do, get her what she's asked for. I need it done in the next two minutes. SWAT can get it up there."

"No." The supervisor shook her head. "There's a tube system. The blood bank can send it that way."

"Good, get it done." Nathan uncupped his hand from the phone. "Morgan, we're getting those to you. What was the explosion? Do you know?"

"The stairwell. It's not passable."

"Is Scott there with you?"

"No, he and Dylan are by the door."

"Does he see you on the phone?"

"He gave permission for me to call for the blood."

"Why did he shoot Tyler?"

"To buy Reeves's confession."

Morgan's words confirmed Nathan's suspicions. But Scott hadn't fatally wounded Tyler. *Why not?* That was an unknown. Nathan's mind worked furiously to sort out known variables.

Dylan Worthy may have a death wish, but maybe Scott Clarke still wants to live.

That meant there was room to bargain.

Chapter 40

Dr. Thomas Reeves grasped Lilly's hand as she worked to adjust the tie around his neck. What he deserved at her hands was a noose. What she was giving him was a lifeline. At his touch, her piercing blue eyes gazed into his, question and promise unrealized.

"Why?" he said.

Lilly rested her palm against his chest for a brief moment, then busied herself with picking off invisible particles of lint. "Why what?"

"Why are you still here?"

"You asked me to go with you."

His heart ached. Would knowing the truth ease this pain he'd carried? His mind pled his mouth to speak the words. "Why did you actually come in the first place? Was it really just for Morgan?"

So much in Reeves admired the woman Lilly had grown into—and grieved in the same breath at how little he'd had to do with it. His distance. His abandonment. His hope for a moment like this, now realized, but given in the worst instant of his life. Why did there have to be both joy and sorrow in this day?

"I know, and yet I don't know." She turned to the desk and handed him a cup of coffee. "Double strength."

He took the cup from her hands. The warmth begged off the chill of what his mind pleaded against him doing, teetering on a fence of indecision. "I really do want to know."

She motioned to the wing chairs that faced one another. Each of them took a seat. "How long do you think I should hold on to the bitterness?"

He sipped slowly, mulling over her words. "The same length of time that the inflictor of such pain merits."

"But for you, that would be a lifetime."

He set the cup on his knee. "I think I deserve that. Every word. I wasn't a father to you."

"But it poisons me more than it ever hurt you. That's the problem."

He shook his head. "I don't get what you mean."

Lilly sighed. "My anger with you stops me from having joy in my life. It affects me every day, but honestly, it's probably not something you think much about. I dwell on anger. It just creates overwhelming sadness."

"And how did you come to this realization?"

"Nathan, for one. We've been talking a lot about forgiveness. I want him to forgive himself for what happened all those years ago when John Samuals killed his own family members. It just taints everything he does—the constant ruminating about how he failed. That's what he thinks, despite what the facts in evidence show. Why he carries his misdeeds in his pocket everywhere he goes. Neither one of us knew where to turn, so we started to read a lot about it."

"And this led to some epiphany? You're reading the Bible?" His question was sincere.

"Epiphany—maybe not. There aren't hallelujah choruses of angels singing. It's easy and hard and compelling. So many layers."

"I'm glad it's working for you."

"It didn't play out very well yesterday, I'm afraid." Lilly looked at him and placed her hand over his. "Nathan would talk a lot to me about forgiving you. He never suggested I'd get over it—more like I'd come to a place where I could feel lightness in my soul."

"Nathan's a good man." A man Reeves wished he'd been for her. "I'm glad you two are together."

Lilly smiled at his words. Even at her age and with the distance between them, she still craved his approval. She pulled her hand away. "Morgan is who changed my mind."

"She spoke to you about forgiveness?"

"Not at all." Lilly turned her eyes out the window. "She's in that dark place. That well of bitterness that's so comforting, yet a prison all the same. She blames herself for her daughter's death. Can't get past it."

His heart stalled, just briefly, a sudden realization that Lilly was speaking about his deceased granddaughter.

He cleared his throat. "And that changed your mind? Her grief?"

"In a way. I saw the effect it was having on her. On her marriage." Lilly smoothed her palms over her legs. "Something happened to me to change the way I think about a lot of things. About how I want my family to be. About what kind of relationships I want to have."

"I know—your rape. I still grieve what happened to you."

"No, not that. Something different."

"What?"

"I'm going to have to delay getting tested myself—to see if I'm a match for Morgan."

"Why? Lilly—"

"Because I'm pregnant."

Reeves's mouth drifted open. "Does Nathan—"

"Know?" Lilly softly smiled. "We have a date night set for this weekend. I'm going to tell him then."

"I'm the first."

"You're the first."

She'd trusted him with this incredible news. Felt safe enough with him to disclose it. A sharp pang pierced deep inside of him as though a raw, ragged wound had begun to heal.

"I want a healthy family for this baby." She folded her hands as if to pray . . . almost pleading. She searched his eyes. "I want the baby to know you. You're the only one who really knows about my mother and can share her in a way I can't."

Here it was. A chance for him to change everything. Instead of destroying life, he could invest his time in other children. And Lilly trusted him with his grandchild.

His throat was tight as he spoke. "I will. I promise. I will respect her memory in that way. I'll tell the baby all about her."

Lilly smiled. "Good."

There was so much that he'd missed while pursuing work, pursuing destruction over his family. There was no going back to that life. Not after today.

"I know it's not easy. I know this is just a start. I'll do whatever you want. Counseling—"

Lilly put her hands up. Full stop. "I appreciate the thought. But let's get you through the next half hour first. It's almost time. Are you ready?"

"No."

Chapter 41

TYLER WATCHED MORGAN disconnect the unit of blood while Drew checked his blood counts on the small I-stat machine.

"I think one pint did it," Drew announced.

Morgan turned off the pump. "How are you feeling?"

"Not as bad as you might think."

She smiled faintly and then walked over to Seth's bed, getting another set of vital signs.

Tyler's whole left chest ached but he was relieved to have sensation and strength into his left arm. He'd been spared from nerve damage. Worse than the pain of the injury was the mask of agony Morgan wore on her face over her decision of choosing him instead of Seth. It echoed his remembrance of her in the moment when they were told Teagan was brain dead.

Drew put a firm hand over his. "You hangin' in there?"

Tyler pulled the blanket up, watching Scott and Dylan hover like vultures. "How can I make her understand that it's okay?"

"Man, I don't know." He exhaled slowly. "Seems like the two of you have . . . how do I say this in a nice way . . . issues."

Heaviness settled over Tyler. "We lost a baby. It's been hard."

"I bet that's one of the toughest things a couple can live through. Do you have faith?"

Tyler adjusted in the bed. "I did once. It's been hard to find that peace again."

"Maybe you're just holding on when you should be letting go."

Funny, I said those same words to Morgan. Am I holding on to her too tight? Suffocating her from working through her grief in a healthy way?

"I'm afraid that if I let go . . . she'll die."

"Weird thing about God is he wants everything we have. Our time.

Our money. Everything turned over to him. I've seen parents struggle with this about their kids. Thinking about giving their lives over to God—not controlling every aspect of the decisions they make haunts them. A parent's work is to protect their children. So it seems counterintuitive to let go and let God deal with them directly. But, overall, it's a trust issue. Do you trust God to do what's best on Morgan's behalf? I'm not saying be reckless. If you think she's going to harm herself, God would want you to step in. But in the absence of that, he may want you to step back so he can do his work, too."

Morgan returned to his bedside. "You need to be resting. I didn't take Drew to be such a chatterbox."

Did she overhear the conversation?

"We need to think of a plan," Drew said.

"I agree . . ." Tyler coughed briefly.

"No, we wait," Morgan said.

"If we're not proactive, all that's going to happen is that we get shot in the melee," Drew said.

"You don't trust SWAT very much," Morgan said.

"No, I trust them. I don't trust the hostage takers."

"Do you still have the med in your pocket?" Morgan asked Drew.

"What med?" Tyler asked.

"A paralyzing agent," Drew said.

Tyler shook his head. "No, you two are crazy. How are you going to get close enough to inject it? Unarmed, I might add."

Morgan glanced at the two remaining hostage takers. They were turned away from her. She held her hand out. "Give it to me."

"I don't know." Drew rubbed his face with his hands. "I don't feel right about that."

"I'll have a better chance to inject it. Now that Tyler is injured, who do you think they'll grab next?" Tyler moved to sit up. Morgan eased him back. "Hurry."

He pulled a syringe from his flight suit. "I drew the med up."

She grabbed it and tucked it into her pocket.

"Morgan, it's not a good idea." Tyler's voice had grown soft. Weaker. "Drew."

"I'll check his blood pressure again."

"I wish you two would stop poking me."

Scott grabbed the television and rolled it in their direction.

"My sweet Morgan. Ready to see your long-lost father on television?" Scott smiled maliciously. "If he doesn't confess what's really happening to me and everyone, the next time I shoot, it will be to kill."

Chapter 42

Dr. Thomas Reeves slid his fingers down the metal handle of the podium. He adjusted the microphone toward his mouth and felt his heart thump at the base of his throat.

When he'd built this conference room at NeuroGenics, he'd imagined this moment would be one of pure scientific joy. Something akin to accepting the Nobel Prize for Physiology and Medicine. Definitely not something like this.

The sea of reporters hazed in front of him. He leaned his chin into his shoulder to compose his thoughts. He turned back to the pages of his prepared statement, but they shook like leaves in a wind tunnel until he laid his palms over them, leaving moist handprints. He heard Lilly's heels against the plank floor behind him, but he waved her back to her seat.

When he glanced again at the faces, they were a melded mass of vampire bats waiting for the night sky to be born—to hunt.

Just as the sun was setting now on so many things.

He cleared his throat and tapped the mike. Shoulders straightened and pens poised.

"My name is Dr. Thomas Reeves. I'm CEO and president of Neuro-Genics, as well as the lead researcher."

"Dr. Reeves!" a voice yelled from the back.

He held his hand up. "Please, I'll take questions at the end, but I would like to get through my statement without interruption."

His tongue was thick and dry. When he looked back at Lilly, she gave him a reassuring nod. A reminder that he was trading the privileged life he knew for one he didn't understand much. Did Lilly really mean it? Would she allow him to know his grandchild? He both dreaded and welcomed the opportunity. Being responsible for someone other than just himself was terrifying.

Being vulnerable is terrifying.

One of his knees gave as he turned back around. He clutched the podium tighter to steady himself.

"The human mind has always been a fascination for me," he intoned. "I wanted to help heal those who suffered under the weight of brutal traumatic experiences. My desire was to aid them in leading productive lives again. To lessen the remembering of these experiences and the power it was having over their lives, which is how the drug MemoryEase was born."

He inhaled deeply.

"The process of how we form memories—a living, breathing record of our lives—became an obsession. What our brains choose to retain still leaves much that is lost."

He couldn't help but glance back at Lilly. As she wiped her tears away, he felt a physical pain flash through him and his spirit broke. This is what he had caused. All of it. He wasn't a healer . . . more like a sanctioned executioner. He pressed his fingers against his eyes to keep his emotions in check. Saving lives was now paramount.

He rested his hands over his notes. "From this, I learned of a woman who had superior autobiographical memory. She could remember precise details of each of her days from the age of eight. Very explicit details. What was also unique was the emotional attachment she had to her life-changing experiences. Many of us remember these like old movies—rarely are significant emotions attached to them—unless it's been a truly horrifying or life-changing event."

He cleared his throat to keep it from wavering. "I wanted what she had."

This time, he couldn't bear to turn around.

"So I began to research how memories were formed and how I could improve on the biological and structural nature of our brains as the scientific community understands them."

Here it came. Compared to what was next, everything prior to this had been easy to say.

"Fetal grafts have been used in research before. They've been looked at as a mechanism to improve the memory of Alzheimer's patients and used as a way to foster the release of dopamine into the brains of those suffering from Parkinson's disease.

"What I did—without getting into too much scientific minutia—was harvest neural grafts, doctor them with a chemical, and graft them into the brains of men who were part of private security forces fighting overseas."

A voice shouted at him from the front row. "Weren't these men at one time serving in the military?"

"How old were these fetuses, Dr. Reeves?" another woman interrupted.

Reeves's throat began to swell. Grainy ultrasound pictures filled his mind. The ones from his relentless nightmares when he'd helped harvest donor tissue.

"I'm sure my research protocol will be fodder for all those on both sides of this debate, but for the sake of the lives currently being held hostage at Sacred Heart Children's Hospital, please allow me to finish."

The room fell silent once more.

"The volunteers began to suffer side effects. Seizures. Stroke-like symptoms. I thought maybe it was a biological response of the participant's body rejecting the graft, so we began to look for closer donor matches."

Reeves felt bile percolate in his gut. *Would I have been so cavalier that even Lilly's baby would have been considered for donation? And if not, why would that be different?*

He turned his focus back to the crowd. "In two cases, I used neural grafts from the volunteer's progeny. Children they'd helped to conceive."

All Reeves could focus on were the accusatory, stunned glares, like a sea of disembodied marbles. He blinked.

"These research volunteers are two of the three men holding my daughter hostage right now. Scott Clarke and Dylan Worthy."

There was a low murmur building among the reporters.

Reeves sensed his control of the press conference slipping. He wanted to disappear. If lightning could just strike him from the earth. The noise level of the room hummed in his ears. Hands shot into the air, but he ignored them.

"Detailed records were kept of the condition of the donor at the time of the graft retrieval."

He closed his eyes and shook his head.

"What is happening to each of these men is a reflection of his donor's condition at time of death."

Reeves skimmed his hands over his face. "In Mr. Clarke's case, after the graft had been placed, the traumatic event the donor suffered—the loss of a limb—became real to him, and he experienced nonuse of that limb."

A strange silence settled over the throng.

"Let me ask all of you here today, what is it that makes us human? What is it that differentiates us from animals—even intelligent ones. Is it awareness of self? Is it the ability to comprehend and understand pain? Is it self-preservation? Is it the ability to form and recall memories?"

Reeves sipped from a glass of water under the podium. It did little to quench his thirst.

"I was asked once to assist in obtaining a neural graft. What I saw in those sonogram images was a *baby* trying to protect itself. Others will ostensibly have another opinion. But what has been ingrained in me as a scientist is to deduce the most logical reasoning, even if it points to something that is contrary to my belief.

"When the graft was implanted, somehow the recipient exhibited a subconscious manifestation of what the donor experienced. How else could that occur if this traumatic experience wasn't transferred between the two?

"Based on these findings, I am terminating this research protocol. I can only hope those whom I have injured will forgive me."

People were coming up out of their seats. Reeves looked directly into the red glare of the camera that broadcast his confession to millions.

"Scott, I used your son in your procedure. I paid your wife a very large sum of money to accomplish this goal. I am sorry you were unaware of her desire to participate as a way to retaliate against you. I wanted to make you a man like no other on this earth."

Reeves swallowed hard.

"What I can say now is that I deserve society's condemnation for my acts. For those who think my work was within the bounds of ethical research, I only ask you to offer an alternate explanation for the data before you decide my theory is not plausible.

"Memory is a sense of self. Sense of self is humanness. And what I learned is that these things are present in utero. And because of that, I can't continue this work.

"Some will be ready to commit me to the closest psychiatric unit for my understanding of what's happened in this experiment. That's fine. But this is why I think Mr. Clarke and Mr. Worthy have taken my own daughter hostage. Because they recognize that I killed their children, and they want to exact revenge on my daughter."

Reeves placed his hands together. The lights caused sweat to pool at his lower back. He began to shake.

"Scott, Dylan, asking forgiveness is foreign to me, and I know it will likely sound hollow to you, but I do ask your forgiveness. I know I can't bring back the life of your children. But I beg that you spare the life of my daughter and those others you are holding captive."

The wave of screamed questions hit Reeves full force.

Chapter 43

For several seconds, Scott Clarke just stood motionless, staring at the television.

The cacophony of reporters screaming questions at Reeves stalled him for several minutes. Dylan seemed unsatisfied with the news, restless, the muscles in his arms bunching as he gripped his weapon and paced a tight circle between the doors and the shrouded bay of windows.

It was brief, but Morgan saw a black shadow of resolution cross over Scott's face. He thumped the top of the television with a clenched fist and stormed her direction. Morgan backed up a few steps, but there was no exit. He was upon her in seconds, his fingers once again gathering up her scrub top. This was different. She knew this look. She knew what it meant. It was the look she saw in her own mirror every morning.

He no longer wants to live.

And so he didn't care what happened from that point.

"I thought if I knew it would be better, but it isn't," he seethed.

Morgan held her hands up, exuding as much submissive calm as she could. "Scott, we have both lost babies. I understand your grief."

"You don't live with it," he shouted. Particles of acrid spit dotted her face. His breath was as fetid as the death he was about to deliver.

To all of them.

Unless Morgan could change something about the trajectory of the moment as it had been given to her. She didn't care about her safety. But others were counting on her—of all people—to do everything she could to get them out of it alive.

"Explain to me," she said.

He jabbed his index finger into his temple. "In here. Nightmares. Visions of torture. Is it true what your father says? That's what I'm remembering? His murder?"

"The only way for you to know for sure is to get out of this alive." Morgan swallowed hard. She reached to hold his hand. He edged it away. "Scott, you're an American soldier. Murdering your fellow citizens goes against everything you hold honorable."

He twisted her top and pulled her close. "You don't get it. I don't think that way anymore. Not after what's been done to me"—he spat the last words out—"for love of country."

Scott holstered his sidearm and then drew what looked like a hunting knife. He shoved Morgan back, slid his hand down her arm, pushed up her long sleeve, and then clamped onto her wrist like a vise. He set the cold blade against the skin over her dialysis shunt. The knife ticked like a metronome at her increased heartbeat.

Tyler came up out of the bed. Yanking the IV line free from his arm, he stumbled in her direction. Her heart broke to see him struggle. To see what those words from her lips had wrought on his life.

All choices have consequences.

"Scott, please," he yelled. "You can't do this to her. If you cut open that shunt, she'll die in a matter of minutes. None of us will be able to save her."

The soldier drew the sharp metal edge away from her arm and pointed it at Tyler. "This is something that I want you to live with. Seeing her life bleed from her."

He set the blade again and looked at her—not with a killer's hatred but with a shared spirit of commiseration. "Don't you want this, Morgan? Isn't this what you really want? To leave this earth and find your daughter—wherever it is she might be? Heaven? Another dimension?"

It is what I—

Tyler's voice interrupted her silent confession.

"Morgan, you have to fight. I know you don't think you can do that anymore, but I'm not leaving you. I know you think there is no reparation for choosing me over Seth. But I forgive you. I don't blame you. I know there's love in your heart for me and what we can still have together."

She shook her head against his words. The question of life was always an interesting one. When did it start? When did it end? These questions were thin chalked lines on a blackboard—easily smudged by whoever held the eraser.

But her inaction, her denial had led to Teagan's death. For this she should be punished.

Tyler edged closer. "Morgan! Don't leave me alone. I can't do it. You blame yourself for not seeing what happened to our baby. I am just as responsible. I'm a doctor, too. I work with kids every day. I should have seen, and known the signs of abuse. And I didn't. I didn't want to see it. I'm the guilty one."

Her chest burned as she held her breath. A hard life? An easy death? Tears coursed down her cheeks. Wouldn't it be fitting to die in the same place her daughter had been set free?

"Morgan, I am begging you to hold on to our life. Don't give him permission. You have to fight."

She clenched her teeth as she eased her free hand into her pocket and edged the cap off the needle.

"Morgan," Scott sang to her as he pressed the blade harder into her skin.

She opened her eyes and settled them on his. It was the first time she'd seen a difference between them. His gray, hardened eyes still surrendered to death.

She felt in her own eyes a tiny ember of life trying to light under the oxygen-fueled breath of Tyler's love.

Clutching the syringe in her hand, she said. "Go ahead and do it."

Scott concentrated on drawing the blade across her arm.

She chose then to act.

Morgan pulled the syringe from her pocket and sank the needle into his thigh. She squeezed the plunger with all her might.

He was quick and batted the needle away in one swift move . . . but the change in his position altered the direction of his knife.

Blood from her shunt pulsed from her arm in a thin, fine spray.

"Morgan!" Tyler yelled.

She looked at the small slice and was surprised at how quickly she bled. She clasped her hand over her arm and held it tightly. A tingly sensation washed over her, and her mind settled on the resolve that it was okay to die.

Scott eyed her like a wild-eyed wounded hunter. He rubbed his hand against the injection site. "What did you do?"

"It's a paralyzing drug," Morgan answered.

He wobbled down onto his knees. His hand gripped his chest. He reached for his sidearm again but didn't have the strength to lift it from the holster.

Dylan advanced to their position. "Whatever you gave him—fix it right now. If he dies, you die." He pointed the weapon right at Drew's chest.

"I need Morgan to help me. Let me dress that cut and we'll give Scott the antidote."

Morgan knew Drew was lying. There was no reversal agent for succinylcholine.

He waved his weapon. "Go, fast."

Drew pulled packages from the cart to place a pressure dressing on her cut. Tyler had short stepped back to lean against the bed.

Scott slumped to the floor. Drew hurried to her and slapped several 4x4s over the wound, then wrapped it tight with an elasticized dressing that would stick to itself.

"Hurry," Morgan said.

"I don't want to," Drew replied, wrapping the bandage tighter. A small dot of red was already showing through the gauze.

"You have to."

"Not after what he's done to us." Drew began to add more layers to the dressing.

"He'll stop breathing."

"I know."

"It's murder."

"Call it what you want."

Without warning, Morgan's world blew up.

It took her a scattered moment to register that a SWAT team had blown a gaping hole in the wall behind the nurses' station. Six SWAT officers were inside the unit in seconds.

Dylan didn't hesitate. He rushed to Morgan and yanked her away from Drew. Then he pulled her against his chest, abandoning the larger automatic weapon and drawing his sidearm instead. He dug the muzzle into her ribs.

"I prefer choking the life out of people but in Scott's honor, I think bleeding to death is a good way to go."

He tore the dressing off of her arm.

Chapter 44

1635, Saturday, August 11

NATHAN WAS POSITIONED behind Lee and his shield.

Lee held a pistol to the other side of the barrier, aimed at the hostage taker. Dylan Worthy hid behind Morgan like a coward. The kill shot was directly behind her head.

"Where's Scott?" Nathan called.

The man shook his gel spiked blond points. "He's the one lying on the ground."

Sweat dripped down Nathan's neck.

Not again. This is not going to happen again.

Dylan repositioned his sidearm, moving it from Morgan's rib cage to her head. "I'm picking up where Scott left off."

Pressure squeezed at Nathan's heart, and each breath spread chills through his chest.

"Dylan, correct?" Nathan said.

He edged out a little from behind Morgan. The corner of one lip curled up. Outright disdain. Nathan assumed he had the right target. The right information. Which meant the situation was volatile.

How do you give a serial murderer a hero's death—and not lose innocent lives?

What concerned Nathan even more was the misting puff of blood that spewed from Morgan's arm with each rapid heartbeat and formed a small pool of red on the floor that grew larger each second.

"Let's say we start with something easy," Nathan said. "This is between you and me. Let everyone who can walk leave right now."

"Fine."

A faint wash of relief eased through Nathan, immediately replaced by a seed of doubt. *That was easy. Too easy, really.* Nathan turned his head.

Drew. Good to see you're still alive.

But his friend hadn't budged.

"Drew," Nathan said. "Please."

Drew placed prayerful hands to his lips. "Nathan, you don't have much time. She's bleeding because her dialysis shunt's been nicked. It's like an artery. She'll bleed out if you don't end this soon."

"Okay, Drew. I got it. Now move. Out. Out. Out." The drips of Morgan's blood were her sand in the hourglass. "Dr. Adams, you too."

He shook his head defiantly. "I'm not leaving her."

The muscles of Lee's shoulder tensed under Nathan's hand. The placement kept him aware of his position in relation to his protection. They didn't need any more variables inserted into this scenario. "Tyler—"

"It's not an option."

Nathan eased farther from Lee, partially to be a target to Dylan's weapon. "What is it that you want? Spell it out for me."

Why did Dylan tuck himself and Morgan into the corner?

"Fame."

An explosion shattered the windows next to Morgan and Dylan.

The shock wave knocked the entire SWAT team off their feet. Nathan's ears were left with a horrifying ring. Shards of glass and shredded blankets blew out from the open space. The wind whistled in with the vengeance of a beast unleashed. Dust and debris felt like a sandblaster against Nathan's face.

His stomach catapulted—from fear or explosive force, he couldn't be sure at that moment. He scrambled to stand up. Quickly, he eyed each of his team members to be sure everyone else was still alive.

They, too, worked quickly to get back up.

Dylan began to step Morgan back to the jagged hole in the wall. Nathan fully exposed himself.

"Nathan," Lee warned. "Get back behind me."

"Do you have a shot?"

Lee shook his head. Nathan glanced at the other SWAT members. Their eyes told him they didn't have any shots either.

Nathan held his hands up.

"Dylan, this isn't the answer. You won't be viewed as a hero by pulling an innocent woman from a seven-story window. You'll be viewed as a coward. We can give you what you want. Fame. Glory. A soldier's burial. But you have to let her go."

Nathan expected Morgan's eyes to be wild with fear at her impending crisis. But they were soft. Resigned. She was calm. She didn't offer the man any resistance. There wasn't anything she was going to do to prevent what she apparently wished for in her heart.

"Sometimes dying for a cause is good, but being famous for being bad lasts longer. Everybody remembers Jesse James, right? They'll remember me for Zoe Martin and all the others."

Another step back. Two steps from the edge. From the corner of his eye, Nathan saw Tyler begin to move toward his wife. Nathan held a palm up to his movement and nudged Lee to step forward. Closer.

Morgan shook uncontrollably.

Finally, engagement. But what does it mean? Fear? Shock? Both?

"Dylan, I'm not going to let you do it," Nathan said.

"How will you stop me?" A challenge.

Another step back. The wind blew at Morgan's hair and the blond locks momentarily washed over Dylan's eyes.

Tyler lunged.

And Nathan followed.

Then Dylan pulled Morgan out the window.

Tyler snatched onto a piece of Morgan's body. Nathan sprang into the air. He grabbed onto both of Tyler's legs. The weight of bodies falling out of the window pulled them surprisingly fast toward a peacefully soft, clouded blue sky.

Nathan's body felt like a woodworker's plane going over rough timber as he was dragged through the remnants of the explosion. Glass bit into his skin. The smell of burned gunpowder smothered each breath. He dug his toes into the floor in an attempt to slow his body's progression.

Tyler dropped out the window.

In Nathan's mind flashed the thought of what it would feel like to fall to the concrete, his bones and muscles crushing against each other into one bloodied heap.

Then he thought of Lilly having to bear witness to another death.

She might not recover from that.

He hoped against hope that Lee would catch him. Soon.

Chapter 45

1640, Saturday, August 11

MORGAN'S STOMACH WAS IN her throat. Her brain had trouble deciphering the dizzying images that loomed in front of her. Dylan held on to her bloodied arm with one hand, and Tyler held on to her ankle with both his hands.

A scream burst through the air—surely the last reserve of air and strength she had left—as Dylan began to shake and pull. Sharp pains shot down her arm into her hand as muscle and ligaments tore. Dylan worked to anchor his legs against the side of the building to further yank his weight against hers in hopes of sending her plummeting to her death.

And still she didn't know which she preferred. Life or death. *Teagan or Tyler?* That really was the choice to make. Her dead baby or her living husband.

She screamed again as Dylan pulled—hard—and all that held her shoulder in one place stretched and ripped more. She brought up her free hand and clasped it tight over the joint in a futile attempt to fight against the dislocation happening in her shoulder.

"Morgan!"

Tyler's voice. Distant. The wind took his words and scattered them like dead leaves.

"Morgan Adams, you do not give up!"

His fingers around her ankle began to shake. She heard more glass breaking beneath her.

"Morgan . . ." Dylan's voice now. "Isn't it a nice day to die?"

She dug her fingers into the skin of her shoulder. Her blood ran over Dylan's hand and droplets fell onto this face. He licked at them with satisfaction. "Just let it all go."

The heel of her shoe came off. Her sock slid up her ankle the wrong direction—an undressing with her life on the line.

She heard the pop of a weapon firing, and registered a look of horror crossing Dylan's face as red bloomed on his forehead. His hand slipped off hers. No sound, not even a scream, escaped his lips as he fell toward the ground. His body bounced once on the concrete walkway then stopped. Twisted and bent like a marionette with its strings cut, he no longer held any vestige of this life.

From the window below, two additional SWAT members appeared and looked up at her. They tried to grab for her hands.

Just out of reach.

Her shoe came off. She watched it sail downward, landing near Dylan's crumpled body.

Her sock inched farther off her leg.

"Morgan Renee Adams! You grab onto me."

She closed both her eyes and let her arms relax into the soft breeze. What she'd wanted for three months was seconds away. To leave this life. To leave all the death and grief behind. And just be free.

"Morgan!"

Tyler's screams pierced her solitude. His fingers around her ankle shook uncontrollably.

He would drop her. If she didn't do something to help save herself.

"You have to fight!"

She opened her eyes and looked below. Her body dangled against the side of the building. Her head pounded with the rush of blood in her ears. More SWAT faces below her. Two had climbed out the window in harnesses, trying to figure out a way up. Morgan teased her fingers out to the other man's outstretched hands. Inches. Merely inches from the protective grasp of the police officer.

He looked up at her. "Morgan. It's okay. I'm going to catch you."

Was there a way to avoid his grasp? Was death still an option? Was it what she truly wanted?

"Tell Tyler to let you go."

There was something about those brown eyes that spoke truth into her heart. It's what Tyler had been trying to say on the night he'd thought she'd claimed her own life.

Surrender everything.

Let go and be saved. Stop trying to control everything. Pride goes before the fall.

Was it really so simple?

Had she been hoping for death or clinging to life with everything in her?

She just hadn't realized which battle she was fighting.

Her skin ripped against Tyler's, and she dropped another inch. She wiggled her fingers again.

"Morgan!" Tyler screamed.

"Tyler, let me go!"

"No! I'm not letting you die."

"It's okay. You can't see him, but he's here."

Morgan heard Nathan's voice as he argued with Tyler. She wiggled her hands again. Both outstretched. A faint brush of skin cells against skin cells.

So close.

"Tyler! I want to be with you. I want to live."

And she felt his fingers release her.

Chapter 46

MORGAN NEVER THOUGHT A hospital bed could be so comfortable. Even the soft whir of the dialysis machine was a welcome relief, though having a temporary catheter placed in her groin was clearly not joyous. The shunt in her arm had been permanently damaged. The dialysis nurse eyed her with a warning. She snuggled into the starched pillowcase and stared at the silver-haired man who'd always been beside her but never got enough credit. She gazed into the softness of his blue eyes and tried to move her arm toward him, momentarily forgetting that her forearm was in a bulky dressing, and the same shoulder was encased in a sling. Sharp pain ceased further movement.

He eased his fingers to his lips. "You need to be still."

A rush of emotions overwhelmed her. A messy mix of regret, sadness, joy all spun together in her tears. "Daddy, I'm sorry."

He clasped her remaining hand between both of his. "Morgan, there's nothing—"

Her chest caved under his forgiveness. "I was so spiteful to Mom."

"You were hurt. I understand it. I'm just glad you weren't taken from me so that I could make you understand." He exhaled heavily. "I know you're not mine in the biological sense, but you are my daughter. The single most important relationship we can have is not bound by blood but by adoption. By the acceptance of a free gift." He wiped her tears from her cheeks, the pads of his fingers rough like a cat's tongue. "I want you to find that again. The joy of your faith."

She smiled at the memory of so many moments like this laced through her childhood.

"I know, Daddy."

"You've stopped with the death wish?"

"Yes."

Doubt flooded his eyes.

She grabbed his hand. "I promise."

There was a soft knock at the door, and then the small crack widened. Lilly and Thomas Reeves walked into the room. Lilly held a vase overflowing with white, light pink, and pale lavender roses.

"You are looking much better," Lilly said, crossing the room and setting the flowers on her bedside table.

Morgan's father stood and crossed the room to Dr. Reeves. He held out his hand, both in greeting and in peace offering.

"Nice to meet you, Dr. Reeves."

"You, too. She's got to have a strong spirit to survive what happened. You and her mother must be very proud."

"We are, absolutely." He returned to Morgan's side and gave her a light kiss on the forehead. "I'm going to find a cup of coffee."

She nodded her head. Lilly took the seat where her father had been. Thomas Reeves stood on the other side of the bed. "You look better than the press photo of you dangling upside down outside a building."

"Well, you can only go up after you've been pulled out a window."

He smiled. "Yes, I guess that's true."

"What's happened since your announcement?"

Reeves rocked back and forth on his feet. "I'm closing down NeuroGenics. A lot of people don't know what to think. They want to be angry about what I did, but they can't be angry if they continue to fight for unfettered abortions. Honestly, people are confused."

He looked away, appearing to study the faux Monet that was affixed to the opposite wall.

"In the end, I think much will stay the same. People are very good about justifying a position regardless of evidence. For me, it isn't about changing someone else's mind or demanding new legislation. It was ultimately what I deduced the evidence to be."

"What will you do?" Morgan asked.

"I don't know. That's the question, isn't it? I thought I'd be broke, but many offers are pouring in. Maybe I need to retire and take care of two girls in whose place I substituted my career as a relationship. It seems I have a—"

"Dad, let me tell her."

Morgan turned to Lilly. "Tell me what?"

Lilly caressed her fingers over her arm. "I'm going to keep my promise and get tested to see if I can donate a kidney but it will have to wait."

Morgan's heart thumped in her chest.

"Nathan and I are pregnant. I couldn't have a surgery like that until well after delivery."

Morgan pressed her fingers against her tear ducts in a feeble attempt to hide her disappointment. "Lilly, that's wonderful. What a blessing. Does Nathan know?"

Lilly's eyes met hers. "Of course he knows. I told him right after he didn't die half falling out that window."

"I know . . . that was my fault."

Lilly shook her head against the words. "It's his job and I know it. I thought his being a negotiator would keep him out of harm's way, but I also knew he'd do everything in his power not to let another innocent life be lost again. It's a risk I understand."

"I'm really happy for you two. I know you've been through a lot."

"I hope this pregnancy doesn't cause you to feel like you have to stay at arm's length."

"Lilly—"

"It would break my heart to no end—"

"I promise. I really do. I want to be part of this little one's life."

"Good, because there's something else I want to ask you." Lilly clutched her hand and pulled it to her chest. "I'd like to use Teagan as the middle name. Boy or girl. Would it be all right?"

Morgan eased her hand away from Lilly's and pulled tissue from a nearby box. Without doubt, her heart swelled with the genuineness of her sister's offer. But there was something about giving up her daughter's name. Of hearing it in another context, attached to another child. Almost as if she would lose claim to Teagan's memories being her own.

"Lilly, I just . . . "

"I get it." Lilly sat back and tried to hide her disappointment. "It's okay. I just wanted to ask."

Morgan leaned her head back onto her pillow. This was her issue. Always holding on too tightly. Trying to control too much. Teagan wasn't just hers to own. Her life had touched others—even an aunt's who had never met her. She turned her face toward Lilly.

"No, I'd be honored. Honestly I would."

Lilly softly clapped. "I know that I should have waited to ask until you were all better, but ER doctors are very impatient creatures."

Thomas Reeves cleared his throat. "I shouldn't interrupt all this sisterly affection but I know we're not the only ones waiting to see you. I'll get tested as well but it may not be necessary."

Morgan looked in Reeves's direction. Her pulse increased.

All he could do was shake his head. "Tyler's outside and will explain everything."

A soft rap at the door. "I'm not waiting any longer." Muffled and joyful.

Tyler rolled through the door in his wheelchair. The bullet had missed his vital structures. Even missing nerves, so eventually, once the pain of the injury healed, he'd be able to operate again. In her heart, she chose to believe Scott had intentionally placed the bullet there. Able to make his point but not take a life.

What Morgan wasn't expecting was the tall, gorgeous African American woman who pushed her husband through the door. She tried to sit up in bed, but Tyler motioned her to ease back.

"Morgan, this is Ayan." Tyler looked back at his chaperone. "Did I pronounce that right?"

She smirked and then patted his shoulder. "Good try," she said. "But it's not like *Ian*. It's a long *a* sound. Ay-an."

Tyler laughed. "Right. I'll do better. I swear." He placed his hand on Morgan's leg. "Months ago, when I found out I wasn't a match, I was just heartsick. I don't want to see you have this kind of life either."

All of it was becoming too much. Morgan felt it in her chest, the sense of wanting to flee real life again. Why did it have to be so hard to reach out for help?

"Right after you chose to start hemodialysis, I started looking into some alternatives like paired donor exchange programs."

"You did? Without ever saying a word?" Morgan said.

"Well, I'm not a match for you. And Ayan . . ." Tyler gave a sheepish grin.

"You got it right this time."

"Excellent," he continued. "Ayan is not a match for her husband, who also needs a kidney."

"So no one gets what they need?" Lilly asked.

Tyler shook his head. "No, everyone gets what they need. Ayan is a match for you, and I'm one for her husband. She's agreed to donate one of her kidneys to you, and I'll do the same for her husband."

Morgan wanted to crawl out of the bed and embrace the woman with all her might.

Ayan smiled warmly. "Once you and your husband are well enough for surgery, we'll get you off this machine."

Chapter 47

MORGAN NEARLY DIED OF happiness when she saw Seth walk through the door of her hospital room. His eyes were bright. The quirky lopsided smile he always wore when he was nervous started shining the minute he stepped inside.

Walking a few paces in front of his mother, he neared her bedside, leaned over, and hugged her so tight she could barely breathe.

Lisa stepped forward to pull him back. "Seth, you'll crush her. She just got a new kidney a few days ago. Give her some space."

He stepped back and patted his chest. "I got my own shocker now because of that weird heart rhythm they found."

Morgan smiled. "I heard that."

"It does freak me out a little bit to think about having a defibrillator in my chest. But I'd rather have that than be put on ice like Han Solo again."

"Yes, that's probably something to consider," Morgan said. "You look awesome. Do you remember much?"

He glanced back at his mother. She nodded her head with approval. Conflict roiled in his eyes as he faced Morgan again. "I saw someone. I need to talk to you about it."

"What do you mean?" Morgan asked.

It looked like he wanted to curl up and die more than he wanted to share what was on his mind.

"Mom?"

"All right, I'll let the two of you chat." Lisa gave him an awkward side hug and stepped from the room.

Morgan looked at Seth questioningly, surprised Lisa would agree to leave the two of them alone. But then, she guessed her sister-in-law shared her choice where Seth's life was concerned. Lisa had been much softer with her after the hostage situation ended.

"Seth, really, what is it?" Morgan asked, searching his eyes.

He pulled up a chair and sat down. "Do kids ever talk with you about dying. What happens after . . . if they come back?"

"You mean a near-death experience?"

"Right. Seeing Jesus and angels and stuff like that."

Morgan exhaled through loose lips. "Not really. But once they're better, they don't stay very long in the ICU. I don't get to find out what happens after they leave."

Seth clutched his hands together. "Aunt Morgan, I'm only asking you this because you're a nurse and you almost died with all that blood loss. Did you see anything?"

Morgan ached with his distress. "Seth, I never died. I was just really sick. My heart never stopped like yours did."

"I saw you."

"When?"

"At the ball park."

"Yes, Tyler and I were there."

He shook his head. "No, I *saw* you trying to save me. I was floating above you looking down. I saw Mom crying."

Seth turned away from her and Morgan reached for his hand. "It's okay, Seth. I'm sure you're still trying to process what happened to you."

"After that was everything weird you hear about. The tunnel. The bright light." He shifted uneasily. "There was someone waiting for me." There was a look in his eyes Morgan had never experienced before. Sadness and joy. He whispered, "Teagan."

Morgan felt a rush of air flood her lungs. "What?"

"Aunt Morgan, I promise it's true. I'm not making it up. She was there. An older girl, but I knew with everything in me that it was her."

Morgan began to shake.

Seth reached for her water. "Oh, man. Please, I don't know what to do when girls cry."

She laughed as she took the water from him. "It's okay, Seth. These are happy tears."

He looked at her, his eyes boring into her spirit. "Teagan's okay. She's so happy. She's waiting for you, but she said there are more kids for you to take care of."

Morgan nodded through her tears. "Thank you, Seth. Thanks for telling me."

"If it's okay—don't tell my mom. I'll tell her, I promise. I'm just not ready yet. She still tears up half the time when she looks at me."

"Okay, as long as you promise me you will someday."

He crossed his heart. "Promise."

"Soon." Morgan tweaked his nose like she used to when he was a few years younger.

"I know." He swatted her hand away. "You know I'm too old for that. Always was."

"I know."

Chapter 48

One Year Later

MORGAN PULLED THE FRAMED picture away from her chest, placed it on the stack of pink tissue paper, and folded the thin sheets over Teagan's image. The knock at the door caused her to quickly brush the tears from her cheeks.

Perhaps it's better this way. Like ripping off a Band-Aid.

She set the wrapped photo in the box and put the flaps in place.

"It's open!" she called.

Nathan eased inside with baby Samantha Teagan Long in his arms. A happy, healthy four-month-old with Lilly's black hair but Nathan's softer blue eyes. "Need help up here? Sam is offering her assistance." He took her hand and waved it. The infant cooed.

"Well, she's a little late. I just finished with the last box." Morgan grabbed a roll of tape and began to secure the top. "Where is everyone?"

"Tyler and Lilly left to grab some food. I offered to stay back and keep track of this little one. Plus, I wanted to talk to you."

Getting to know Nathan over the last year had been a true blessing, but there was always something that unnerved Morgan about him. His ability to get to the heart of any matter in mere seconds. That gazing stare but helpful face. It was no wonder people found it so easy to open up to him. What could he want to discuss?

Because all the gunmen died during the siege, there weren't any trials to suffer through. Dylan Worthy had been positively linked in more ways than one to Zoe Martin's murder and police were looking at several other cases.

Of course, dead hostage takers didn't mean her suffering ended. There was the personal work of dealing with the darkness of Teagan's death and recapturing those things she loved about Tyler. Of making Tyler and her family believe that she was fully back with them.

"About what?" she said.

"Why are you and Tyler going to India?" he asked.

Morgan smoothed her hand over the taped box and wrote Lilly's name across the top. "Lilly said she'd keep these safe for me."

Nathan swayed Sam in his arms, watching her eyes grow heavy. "I thought ICU nurses were good at answering a direct question."

She smiled and held her hands out. He eased the baby into her arms and Morgan snuggled her close. It was hard not to think about Teagan being just this size when she died. Even the soft lilac scent of Sam's lotion had been what she'd used for her own baby. Was it a sisterly thing?

"Sometimes the hardest places to go are the easiest places to find forgiveness," Morgan said.

"You're not running away?"

"Maybe. Probably. But the need is so great, and they never have enough medical people. Kids there will die if they don't get these heart surgeries."

He leaned against the wall. "I know you've had trouble forgiving yourself for Teagan's death. I understand how it is—holding the weight of that responsibility, feeling the need to repay for losing someone's life under your watch."

"But you saved me. You saved all of us that day."

"Just as you will save many children." From his pocket, Nathan pulled an envelope. "I have a favor to ask."

Sam sighed from her peaceful state. "Come back?"

Nathan smiled. "Yes, I definitely want you to come back and live close to us at some point. Lilly won't say it, but she's sick you'll be so far away. She hasn't really had family, and now she wants to hold on too tightly I think."

"This little one will keep her busy."

Nathan shifted his weight. It might have been the first time Morgan had seen him unnerved.

"Many years ago, I created this list." Nathan tapped the envelope against his other hand. "I call it my unforgivables. Ways I've let people down. Ways people died because of decisions I'd made. You probably keep something like this, too. Maybe it's not physical like mine—maybe just an image. I think we're alike in this way. Holding on to our mistakes."

Morgan clutched the baby tighter.

"When I helped to save you and the others I finally felt like I was ready to let go of this list. But I need it far away so I'm not tempted to look at it again. I'm asking you because I know you understand it. I'm asking you because, through your work, I know you'll get to the same place. When you reach India, will you burn this for me?"

Morgan's hand shook as she took the envelope from him. In her agreement, Morgan knew forgiving herself *was* possible.

It's built into everyone.

About the Author

Jordyn Redwood has served patients and their families for twenty years and currently works as a pediatric ER nurse. As a self-proclaimed medical nerd and trauma junkie, she was drawn to the controlled chaotic environments of critical care and emergency nursing. Her love of teaching developed early and she was among the youngest CPR instructors for the American Red Cross at the age of seventeen. Since then, she has continued to teach advanced resuscitation classes to participants ranging from first responders to MDs.

Her discovery that she also had a fondness for answering medical questions for authors led to the creation of Redwood's Medical Edge at http://jordynredwood.com. This blog is devoted to helping contemporary and historical authors write medically accurate fiction.

Jordyn lives in Colorado with her husband, two daughters, and one crazy hound dog. In her spare time she also enjoys reading her favorite authors, quilting, and cross-stitching. Jordyn loves to hear from her readers and can be contacted at jredwood1@gmail.com.

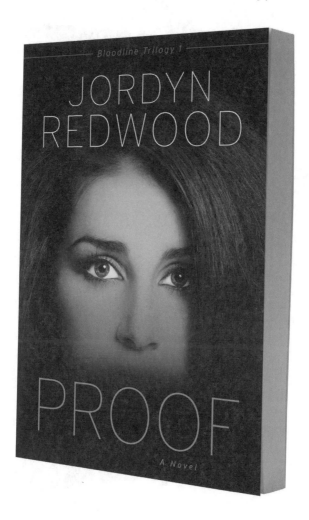

Dr. Lilly Reeves is a young, accomplished ER physician with her whole life ahead of her. But that life instantly changes when she becomes the fifth victim of a serial rapist. Believing it's the only way to recover her reputation and secure peace for herself, Lilly sets out to find—and punish—her assailant. Sporting a mysterious tattoo and unusually colored eyes, the rapist should be easy to identify. He even leaves what police would consider solid evidence. But when Lilly believes she has found him, DNA testing clears him as a suspect. How can she prove he is guilty if science says he is not?

ISBN: 978-0-8254-4238-4

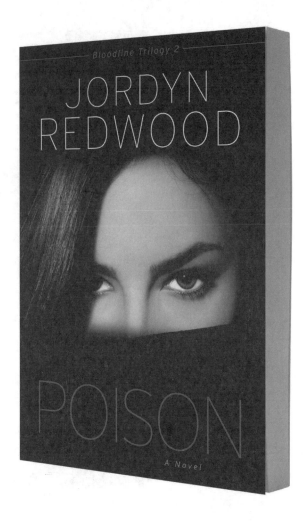

Five years ago, Keelyn Blake's stepfather took her family hostage, raving about Lucent, a being who forced him to commit unspeakable acts. But when Lee Watson—the best of the FBI's hostage negotiators—failed to overcome her father's delusions, she and her half-sister, Raven, were the only two to make it out alive. Now Lucent is back, and he's no hallucination—he is a very real person with dangerous plans. When he kidnaps Raven's daughter, Keelyn and Lee must work together to save what family she has left. But when others who were involved in that fateful day start dying, some by mysterious circumstances, Keelyn wonders if she and Lee can emerge unscathed a second time.

ISBN: 978-0-8254-4212-4